C000040521

Deception in Siena

Frank Curtiss

Frank Curtiss

An Intellect Publishing Book

www.IntellectPublishing.com

Copyright 2021 Frank Curtis

ISBN: 978-1-954693-19-7

First Edition: July 2021
F-7 HB

All rights reserved. No part of this book may be reproduced in any form or by any electronic, mechanical, or other means now known or hereafter invented, including photocopying or recording, or stored in any information storage or retrieval systems without the express written permission of the publisher, except for newspaper, magazine, or other reviewers who wish to quote brief passages in connection with a review. Please respect Author's Rights.

Inquiries to: info@IntellectPublishing.com

Contact the Author:

Frank Curtiss
11744 158th Ave. NE
Redmond, WA 98052
C: 425-269-3909

Email: curtissliterary@gmail.com
www.frankcurtiss.com
www.deceptioninsiena.com

Dedication

This book is dedicated to Rhonda Curtiss, my inspiration, and wife of forty-eight years.

Frank Curtiss

Deception in Siena

Frank Curtiss

Chapter One

Wednesday

Shut up legs! Antonio thought, as he pounded his way up the long grade, his legs screaming at him—his lungs and heart pushing their limits. *I should think of something more original.* His road bike at home in Seattle had a decal on the top tube which said just that, "Shut up legs". Among cyclists it is a well-known quote from Jens Voigt, the famous German cyclist, now retired.

Pace yourself, Antonio. Just spin. He backed off a little, knowing his heart rate was higher than he liked. He could always tell. His fingers and toes started to feel numb. *No need for a heart attack.* He loved cycling, but when the hills were this long … this steep, he asked himself why. He knew the answer. *The pain pushes back the pain.*

I'll never catch Giulia, he thought. *She's way younger and lighter than I am.* His cousin's slender figure and ponytail bobbed back and forth as she climbed the hill ahead of him. On these narrow, hilly roads of Chianti she was like a rabbit. Of course, she'd been riding them since she was a child with her father and brothers.

Giulia was one of many good cyclists in her family. Her brother Leonardo, twelve years older, had ridden several times in the Giro de Italia—and other pro races—even once in the Tour de France. Their father, Nicolo, was also an accomplished rider. He rode nearly every Wednesday morning, weather permitting. His plan to be with them this morning got squashed by a last-minute phone call. A body found in Siena, the third murder victim in a week.

Nicolo was Antonio's uncle. He was the youngest of four siblings—more than twenty years younger than Antonio's mother, Elena. Though nearly sixty, the competitive fire in his belly still burned. Nobody in this family gave in easily to the ravages of aging.

As Antonio struggled up the hill, he heard a high-pitched roar. A motorcycle screamed by on his left—seemed like inches away. *What the ... scared the crap out of me!* His stomach flipped and he could feel a knot develop in his neck and shoulders as his muscles tensed. He rotated his head and neck, instructing himself to relax and regulate his breathing. *Just spin,* he told his aching legs again, calling on the last of his reserves. He noticed the smell of exhaust and caught a glint of the morning sun on shiny metal as the motorcycle raced away toward the curve beyond Giulia. *Looks like a Ducati,* he thought. *God, I envy him right now—all that power beneath him.*

The rider was clad in full black-leather riding gear. Antonio watched him maneuver the curve. It seemed like the Ducati was almost lying on its side, handlebars nearly touching the ground. He always marveled at how Italians—who never seemed in a hurry to eat, govern, or provide services of any kind—morphed into different creatures when you put them on wheels. He thought of the memorial wall in the Duomo of Siena, with a dozen or more motorcycle helmets on it. His gut wrenched the first time he saw it.

*****

When Antonio and Giulia started out from the house that morning, they turned south on the road which came south from Castellina. They rode casually for about two kilometers and parked their bikes in front of the trattoria, located above the two-lane road, across from the tiny hamlet of Fonterutoli. Antonio desperately needed coffee to fuel his ride. He was still feeling the effects of jet lag.

The trattoria opened early for breakfast and espresso. The aroma of coffee pulled them inside. As the espresso machine made that welcome vibrato sound, he thought about the ride ahead—a nearly fifty-kilometer loop—about thirty miles—through this part of Tuscany. This distance was easy for him. It was the climbing he wasn't looking forward to. He'd never been a great hill climber.

Stop whining, he chided himself. *You'll be fine.* But he had his doubts. It didn't help that he hadn't slept well last night after celebrating his arrival with aunts, uncles and cousins. He was regretting his overindulgence of food and wine. *How does one stop when it just keeps coming?*

They took their coffee outside to enjoy the beautiful late summer morning—straight espresso for Giulia, and a triple latte for him. Antonio cheered himself with the thought that the weather was perfect for cycling. With autumn a few days away, the air was crisp, but the sun was warm on his skin. Every now and then, a puffy white cumulus cloud skittered in front of the sun and a chill would bring goose bumps to his skin.

He had only taken a couple of sips of his coffee when Giulia asked the question he always dreaded, "How are you doing, Zio Tonio?" She added, "And don't just tell me fine." She called him uncle even though they were cousins. Deference to his age, he supposed.

He felt a grimace come and go and stared at the gel-padded gloves still on his hands. "Better than last time you saw me." The hesitation that followed felt awkward. He never knew how to answer this question, not since terror had struck his life three years ago.

"There are no easy days," he continued, glancing up at her briefly and attempting a smile. "But riding with my cousin on a day like today helps." He meant that, though he knew it sounded trite when he said it. "I know you miss them too."

Giulia wore her heart on her sleeve. Her eyes told the story. He thought about how close she had been to his wife, Randi, and daughter Christina. Christina was like a big sister to her.

While growing up, Antonio spent a month in Tuscany with his family every summer. Later, while his own kids were young, he and Randi brought them here every other year to visit their aunts, uncles, and cousins.

Giulia, with her parents, Zio Nicolo and Zia Sofia, had also come to visit them in Seattle.

Christina was a precocious seven-year-old when Giulia was born. A year later they finally met. Christina fell in love with Giulia the moment she saw her. She cherished having someone to be a big sister to. The two would disappear for hours. As they got older, Christina taught Giulia how to put on makeup and about American teen pop culture and music. Giulia taught Christina a love of Italian pop. They would dance for hours, often on top of the bed. The memory made him smile.

Giulia's eyes had a faraway look, focused on some distant time and place.

"What are you thinking about?"

"That spring my mom took me to visit Christina in Paris." The moisture in her eyes caught a glint of the sun. "The best week of my life. Christina took me to her music school. We climbed the Eiffel Tower, went to the Louvre, all the things I'd ever dreamed of."

She met his gaze. "It all came crashing down that night you called from Nice. Now it seems like only a dream."

*****

Antonio was grateful to be riding such a well-made bike. The De Rosa was one of several owned by Leonardo from his pro days. He now worked as a rep for the company, which allowed him to travel throughout Europe. The light-weight carbon fiber frame was the same size as

Antonio's, but this bike was more responsive, and outfitted with higher quality gears and disk brakes. He didn't want to think about how much it cost.

They crested the hill. *Thank God,* he thought. He pedaled hard for a few seconds, then stopped pedaling and tucked his torso low as they came into a long downhill descent. His breathing and heart rate came back down to earth and he caught up to Giulia in her bright-red jersey. She had never allowed herself to get very far ahead, though he knew she could have. She flashed a smile at him. "Nice of you to join me, Zio Tonio."

That smile—God, she reminds me of Christina. He thought how they both had an inner and outer beauty, and enthusiasm about life. And they were both creative spirits. Christina had been a music student, a phenomenal violinist—Giulia an art student in Firenze. She chose to bail on her classes this week to be with her favorite uncle.

"So, how's art school?" he asked, as he pulled beside her, looking behind to make sure no cars were approaching.

She laughed. "Silly question, Zio. What do you think? Studying art in Firenze—the city with the richest art history in the world?"

"Yeah. I can imagine." The city Americans call Florence was once the epicenter of the Renaissance—where it all began—its very heartbeat. He had been there many times.

"I love being near enough to come home for weekends when I want," she said, "but far enough away to be out from under the watchful eyes of Raphe and Leonardo."

Her sly smile made him laugh. Raphe was Giulia's nickname for her oldest brother, Raphael. The two brothers, named for the artists, not the Teenage Mutant Ninja Turtles, were overprotective to the nth degree. Giulia had been born later in life, a happy surprise when Sofia was in her early forties. It had been hard for her to have a boyfriend, or even be friends with a boy, with her brothers around.

The road leveled out, then went into a series of gently rolling hills. Antonio dropped in behind Giulia again. It's remarkable how much energy one can save by drafting. Typically, he would stay within a wheel's length for maximum benefit. But that would require too much mental focus. He gave himself some extra distance. He wanted to drink in the landscape he had missed so much—the undulating hills, vineyards, clumps of forest and olive groves, golden wheat fields, and the occasional field of sunflowers. He believed there was no better way to see a place than on a bicycle. Crowning some of the hilltops stood old-world castles and tiny villages, many of them wineries now. In some of the vineyards, he saw clusters of men and women harvesting grapes. At times, he could see the historic city of Siena to the south—pristinely perched—a golden tiara in the morning light.

He suddenly realized that he felt at peace. *When was the last time I felt this way?* He wondered. *Better enjoy it while I can.* He was so tired of grieving. He longed for the happiness he used to take for granted.

Being on a bike always helped. The wind in his face, the sense of freedom, the endorphins released by a strenuous workout. Cycling made him feel younger than he was. Combined with the serenity of the Tuscan countryside, and riding with Giulia, he found joy. Joy which had been so elusive, ever since the night he lost Randi and Christina.

*****

Coming over a rise, Antonio caught his first glimpse of Castellina, one of three main villages of Chianti. *What a welcome sight,* he thought. *Only about five kilometers to go — more downhill than up.* He knew he would make it now. They passed a green Ape, one of those single-seat, three-wheeled vehicles used for transport. The back of it was filled with overflowing baskets of grapes.

They rode single file as the two-lane road neared the edge of town. Giulia put her right hand down, palm toward him, indicating she was slowing. They coasted to a relaxed pace, watching for cars turning on and off the road into the heart of the village, which lay on their left. Antonio took a long, cool sip of energy drink. He was placing the bottle back in its holder when he glanced to their right and saw the Ducati sitting just off the road. It looked like the Scrambler model. *What a beautiful bike,* he thought. *I wonder why he's just sitting there with his helmet on?*

As they passed, the rider pulled out his cell phone and began to type. He supposed that gave him his answer. Antonio could not see the face behind the tinted visor, but he had a strange feeling—the feeling that those eyes were following them as they rode past.

On the slight downhill grade leaving town, Antonio felt fresh energy enter his legs. He shifted and hit it hard, quickening his cadence rapidly. He shot past Giulia with a grin. "See you at home!" he shouted. She accelerated quickly but he'd caught her off guard; and he was a faster descender, having the extra pounds to carry him downhill. Before long he was several bike lengths ahead of her. *Enjoy the glory while you can, Antonio*, he chuckled to himself, knowing she was sure to catch him on the next climb.

He pedaled hard as the road leveled, went over a short rise, then into another shallow descent. He still had his lead. He did another quick burst of pedaling, then stopped and tucked his body forward for aerodynamics. *She's just toying with me, waiting to pounce on the next hill.*

More than a kilometer past town, the black Ducati came over the rise and into view behind them. Antonio moved right, as he always did when a vehicle approached from behind. He waited for the Ducati to blow past him again. It didn't. It slowed and stayed on his tail. *What's he doing? Why isn't he passing?* He got an uneasy feeling in his gut—that feeling most detectives—or ex-detective in his case—are familiar with. *Something's not right!*

Chapter Two

Wednesday evening

Antonio awoke, disoriented. *Where am I?* His brain felt twisted, contorted. The room was dim, lit only by the digital read-outs of the medical equipment located near his head. He smelled that all-too-familiar antiseptic smell and realized he was in a hospital bed. He glanced out the window. It was dark. *Why am I here?* His head throbbed and his body hurt like hell all over.

He began to test his limbs and neck, moving them one by one. Everything seemed to move okay. When he twisted his torso though, he felt a searing pain in his left ribcage. He let out a groan. It caught the attention of Leonardo, who was dozing in the chair next to his bed.

"You're awake, Antonio. Thank God!"

"What's going on? I remember a ..."

"You've been unconscious most of the day. You have a concussion. Not too serious they say. You probably would have woken sooner, but they gave you some serious doses of pain meds and sedatives. You also have some badly bruised ribs and nasty scrapes and contusions. Thankfully, nothing is broken."

"What hospital is this? Is Giulia okay?"

A shadow of concern fell over Leonardo's face. "We're very worried, Antonio. She's much worse off than you ..." Antonio heard the crack in his voice. He kept silent until Leonardo, typically so cheerful, was ready to go on.

"She's in a coma. We can only guess what happened. When you crashed, it appears she swerved to miss you. She lost control ... went off the road, hit a rock and was thrown, hitting her head. She broke two ribs. Punctured a lung. She has a serious concussion and swelling on the brain. She's fighting for her life, Antonio."

"I want to see her!" Antonio sat up quickly. A bad move. A wave of pain, dizziness, and nausea hit him. He lay back and let it pass.

"Take it easy, Antonio! Most of the family is with her. We took turns, one of us here with you so you wouldn't wake up alone. This is the Santa Maria alle Scotte, the university hospital in Siena."

Antonio was familiar with the place.

"What happened on the road, Antonio? What caused you to crash?"

"What? You don't know? We ..." It dawned on him—Leonardo did not know it was an intentional act, surely meant to bring harm. But why?

"Go grab your father, Leonardo. He needs to hear this."

*****

While Leonardo was away, Antonio tried to clear the fog from his mind. The images were jumbled, like a film-strip someone cut up and spliced back together wrong. He was groggy, feeling the effects of the meds. *Damn it, I bet they gave me opioids. C'mon, Antonio. Think! Don't let the drugs mess with your head.*

A few minutes later, Nicolo entered the room with Leonardo and his older brother, Raphael. Raphe was in his early thirties, two years older than Leonardo. He had been a competitive soccer player and now coached a regional team. He was the serious and intense one. Nicolo was still wearing the dark blue suit he had on this morning when he left the house. He had loosened his tie. His grave expression scared Antonio.

"Nicolo. I'm so sorry for what happened to Giulia. I should have protected her."

"What? What are you saying? What happened out there?" His tone showed concern, not accusation.

"This was no accident, Zio! Someone tried to hurt us. Or maybe even kill us."

"What the hell! What did they do?" Raphael blurted.

Antonio told the story as clearly as his foggy mind would allow. "We were run off the road by a Ducati motorcycle, or at least I was. Giulia was behind me. Wait. To be more accurate, the Ducati tried to run me into an oncoming car, an Alfa Romeo."

Raphael clenched and unclenched his fists. He began to say something but Nicolo held up his hand. Raphael glared at him, his face red. Nicolo stuck to his tried-and-true interview methods, even in the midst of his own distraught state. You'll always get more from a witness if you keep your mouth shut, especially when they pause. Questions can come later.

Antonio continued, trying not to ramble. He told them of their first encounter with the Ducati, and how he had seen it by the road in Castellina. He paused to catch his breath and take a long drink of water. His mouth felt like the Mojave.

"We were more than a kilometer beyond Castellina when the Ducati showed up behind me. I moved right. He slowed and stayed right behind me. I knew something was wrong. We were on a slight downhill grade, so we were doing close to fifty kilometers per hour. Giulia was behind me. The Ducati squeezed in between us and just stayed on my rear wheel.

"After a minute or so he began to move up along on my right side, his front wheel just inches from my rear. I pulled left and he moved up alongside me and started moving toward me, edging me toward the center line. I hit the brakes but he seemed to anticipate it, staying right with me. Then suddenly he swerved left, nudging me into the oncoming lane. We were coming into a slight right bend in the road. That's when I saw the red Alfa 'Giulia' coming around the curve."

19

The irony of the name hit him as he said it, and the brothers looked at one another. Leonardo's scowl now appeared to match Raphael's. Nicolo's brow was furrowed but he somehow kept cool, his thirty-something years as a detective in Siena serving him well.

"It happened so quickly. The car was coming right at me. I had no place to go. I hit the brakes hard and jerked right. The Ducati started to move away. The sudden stop sent me flying over the handlebars. I think I glanced off the mirror on the side of the Alfa and hit the pavement in an awkward tumble. I just missed a head-on collision. That's the last thing I remember before waking up here."

Nicolo leapt out of his chair. "I need to make a call. You guys ask your questions," he said, looking at his sons. "I'm calling the magistrate. We need investigators on this right away."

Antonio tried to sit up again. This time was better. He threw off his bed linens and saw his left knee and lower leg bandaged. Blood was seeping through. He had sizeable bruises on his legs, and both forearms were bandaged.

*****

"Help me up, guys. I want to see Giulia."

"I don't think you should do that yet, Antonio," Raphe cautioned. "You're pretty beat up."

"Take me now!" The firmness in his voice surprised him. He felt as if he was outside his body listening to himself. "Stay by me so I can hold on to your shoulders."

Antonio looked at the monitor by the bed. Surprisingly, his heartbeat and blood pressure were only slightly elevated. He yanked the attachments off his chest and unwrapped the tape on his arm. He pulled out the intravenous needle, which he guessed to be the pain meds. "Damned if that's going back in," he growled.

The world spun when he stood up. He almost blacked out, but after a few moments he felt lucid. The two brothers each took a side, not well balanced because of Raphael's height advantage. They walked slowly. The pain was excruciating but Antonio kept moving. They led him down the hall towards the elevator. The cold on his rear end reminded him that all he was wearing was a hospital gown, open in the back. *Great!* he thought, *the whole world can see my ass.*

A petite, dark-haired nurse showed up and began to scold them vociferously, "Where the hell do you think you're going? You can't leave!" She planted her feet like a linebacker. "I won't allow it!" She spoke in Italian. Antonio understood every word. He spoke the language well after all the time he'd spent here growing up.

She's a tough little cookie, he thought, but refused to yield. "I'm not leaving. We are going to see my niece in ICU."

"You can't do that either!"

"Watch me." They brushed past her. She hurried away in search of the doctor. They made it to the elevator and pushed the button for the fourth floor, ICU. When the elevator door opened, they spotted an unattended wheelchair in the corridor. They appropriated it, setting Antonio down like breakable porcelain.

They made their way to Giulia's room, where Antonio quickly saw there were more people than any hospital rules would allow. Sofia sat on the edge of the bed, holding Giulia's limp hand—her mascara damp and smeared. Nicolo's older sisters, aunts Chiara and Frankie, stood behind her. Chiara's three grown daughters were huddled at the end of the bed.

The mood in the room lifted when they saw him. "Antonio!" his cousin Angelica cried out. She was Chiara's eldest and closest in age to Antonio—free spirited, artistic, flirtatious. Growing up, he'd always had a crush on her. She married a judge from Perugia, a serious man. He never saw the fit.

They surrounded him. Though overjoyed to see him, their concern was evident—for Giulia mostly—but they reserved a little for him. He knew he looked like crap. Zia Sofia rose and gave him the gentlest touch and kiss on the cheek.

He rolled next to the bed and took Giulia's hand. He thought he felt a twitch. *Does she know it's me?* Sorrow nearly pushed him over the cliff's edge. The pain of it far exceeded what his body was feeling. Guilt washed over him, and that all-too-familiar feeling of helplessness. "I'm so sorry, Giulia. I should have seen it coming … I should have protected you."

He was no stranger to these feelings. Memories came roaring back of the terrorist attack in Nice, the summer of 2016. Then his mind travelled further back in time—to the autumn prior to that—when a series of terror attacks shook Paris to its core. He and Randi worried themselves sick, not knowing if Christina was okay. Phone lines were jammed. It took hours to get through. He'd nearly gone crazy, not being there to protect his little girl. He and Randi wanted her to come home right away. She talked them out of it.

He made a resolution that day: *If I'm ever present when a terrorist attack occurs, I won't run ... won't hide. I'll face it ... do whatever it takes to protect the people I love.*

But when that fateful night in Nice occurred, he'd been helpless to protect Randi and Christina. He was still battling the guilt, and the guilt nearly always won. His friends and family did everything they could to convince him that his thinking was wrong—that his guilt was unfounded. Part of him knew they were right. But he had a conviction deep in his core. As a husband, a father, and now a cousin, it was his job to protect. Serve and protect— his job for twenty years. But when the time came, he'd been unable to protect the people he loved most dearly. And now he'd failed that task once again.

*****

Giulia's doctor entered the room and scowled at the number of people there. Doctor Michele Giordano was a family friend, so he had bent the rules, but now he put his foot down. "Okay, you guys, time to clear this place out. Two people can stay. It's unlikely we'll see any change in Giulia's condition tonight. The rest of you can wait in the waiting room or go home. I'd suggest the latter. This is going to be a long road."

"Except for you, of course." He looked hard at Antonio. "If you don't get back to your room in a hurry, I may not be able to protect you from nurse Isabella."

Antonio caught a glint of humor in his eyes.

In the hallway, his aunts and cousins bid him goodnight. Chiara's daughters were heading back to their own homes and families in Tuscany and Umbria. Aunts Chiara and Frankie planned to stay on to help Nicolo and Sofia.

Nicolo stepped out of the elevator, his eyes looking for an explanation of why Antonio was here. The boys raised their hands as though to say, "Don't look at us." He glared at them anyway.

Chapter Three

Thursday morning

Antonio awoke with the morning sun streaming in the east window. His head still throbbed. His body hurt everywhere, including places he didn't remember from last night.

He had slept fitfully—the memory of the accident haunting his dreams and half-awake moments. The pain meds and sleeping aid messed with his sense of time and made him tense. He wanted to grow claws and climb a tree.

He thought back to last night. The brothers brought him back to his room, past the glaring nurse Isabella. Before he could go to sleep, they picked his fuzzy brain for every last detail. Leonardo seemed to have regained some composure. Raphael, not so much. Yet it was Raphael who asked the most pertinent questions. *The kid should be a detective*, Antonio thought. But he could see the dark thoughts they were thinking. Their overbearing, overprotective, big-brother inclinations were in overdrive. Nobody messed with their little sister. The desire for revenge was in their eyes. He understood. He was having those feelings, but he fought them off. He knew they would cloud his mind and judgment. He wanted a clear head.

Nicolo had joined them ten minutes later, looking haggard and full of despair. When the others left, Doctor Giordano broke the news to him and Sofia. Giulia's prognosis was not good. He didn't know if she would survive, and if she did, whether the damage to her brain would allow any quality of life. Antonio didn't think he could stand another loss like that.

The last thing he remembered before falling asleep was pleading with God for Giulia. He wondered if he had any faith remaining. And he wondered if God listened to men who were angry at him. He awoke this morning to the same questions.

*****

For Nicolo, things with the magistrate went exactly as anticipated. The magistrate decided to involve the Carabinieri. The reasons were obvious. Nicolo was too close to be objective. Any evidence he came up with could easily be challenged in court.

Before the investigators arrived, Nicolo asked Antonio how well he understood the various law enforcement agencies in Italy.

"Some. Refresh me."

"Alright. Here's your Italian civics lesson. There are three national law enforcement agencies in Italy: the Polizia di Stato, the Carabinieri, and the Guardia di Finanza. The latter two are military forces but fall under different ministries. The GDF is under the Ministry of Economy and Finances. They're responsible for smuggling, drug trade, and financial crimes such as money laundering, which means they get heavily involved with mafia activities. The Carabinieri fall under the Ministry of Defense. Though military, they primarily carry out domestic policing duties—a national gendarmerie so to speak. They also have responsibility for policing the military and participate in military missions abroad."

Antonio nodded, "I thought the Polizia were the national gendarmerie?"

"I know it seems like a confusing mess. It is sometimes. There's overlap between the jurisdiction of the Polizia di Stato and Carabinieri. It often creates a tug-of-war. The Carabinieri operate more in rural areas. The Polizia handle the larger cities, like Roma, and Milano. Siena has offices for both."

"You're right. Sounds like a mess. Probably not any worse than ours, though, with our local police, state troopers, FBI, DEA, ATF. Sometimes it works well. Sometimes horribly."

"Same here. With both in Siena, I could have requested either," Nicolo continued. "The Carabinieri get a bad rap, often the butt of jokes. Probably deserved in some places. But I highly respect their people here. We've worked together many times. I asked the magistrate if they could handle this. I asked for two in particular. I was shocked when she gave me what I wanted." He paused and gave a weary half-smile. "We'll be working with Marcello Bianchi, a Carabinieri colonel, and Major Gabriella Ferrara. They've both been in Siena a decade or longer. Unusually long postings for Carabinieri. They know this city as well as I do."

Antonio questioned Nicolo's motives, wondering if his relationship with them would allow him to stick his nose in where it didn't belong. Probably so.

Nicolo continued, "The majority of the Carabinieri come from the south. Most people believe it's because it is less affluent. May be true for some, but many have told me it's because they've seen the horrible influence the mob has on life there. They want to fight back. But they're not allowed to serve in their home regions until they have at least eight years of service."

"What about Bianchi and Ferrara?"

"Marcello comes from up north, born and raised near Verona; Gabriella comes from Molise."

Tiny Molise was Italy's most remote region, located on the Adriatic Sea, east of Roma and the Appenines. Antonio had always wanted to go there. The idea of a region with so few tourists appealed to him.

*****

Marcello Bianchi and Gabriella Ferrara arrived late morning. Nicolo introduced them, then disappeared. Gabriella asked Antonio if he was okay being on a first name basis. He nodded. *With a smile like hers, who could say no?*

Antonio guessed Gabriella was in her mid-forties. She had a classic southern Italian look, dark hair, and olive skin. Her high cheekbones reminded him of Sophia Loren. She wore her long hair in a ponytail, not a single loose strand. Her black Carabinieri uniform was expertly tailored to show off her slender waist.

Marcello was a little older, probably early fifties, close to Antonio's own age. He was tall, slender, a handsome man, with ruddy skin. His close-cut beard and the hair on his temples were turning grey. His eyes were like an eagle's: sharp, focused, intelligent, not bothered by much. Instead of a uniform, he wore a charcoal-grey double-breasted suit. It was expensive. He wasn't unfriendly but didn't smile much.

Marcello excused himself to make some phone calls. Gabriella began, in excellent English, with just a hint of an accent. She told him what they had accomplished so far.

"As soon as the magistrate called Marcello, he called Nicolo. We wanted you to rest." She paused and her smile lit up her eyes. "Marcello called the local gendarmes from Castellina — the first responders. We met them at the scene this morning to learn what they found. Everything fit what Nicolo told us. Now we need to hear it from you. Start at the beginning, *per favore* — everything you can remember."

Her dark-brown eyes locked on his as he told the story. *Disarming,* he thought. She only interrupted him once for clarification. His mind was running on two tracks: telling the story as succinctly as possible, while at the same time trying to read her. He had already discovered the opposing sides of her personality. She was smart and articulate, with a toughness about her, tempered by gentleness and compassion. Something told him life had taught her some hard lessons.

Marcello returned in time to break the spell. Antonio was just explaining what had happened after they passed through Castellina. When he finished the story, he lay his head back on the pillow, closed his eyes, and took a deep breath.

Gabriella gave him a moment. "Would you like a break before we continue? I have some questions."

"No. I'm fine. Just whacked out from pain meds and lousy sleep."

"I understand. But we'd like to dig out every detail so we can get started."

"Of course."

"Did either man look familiar? The motorcycle rider or driver of the Alfa Romeo?"

"No. The Ducati rider's helmet had a dark visor. I never saw his face. And I did not get much of a look at whoever was driving the Alfa—it came too fast. It had tinted windows and the man was wearing a ball cap and sunglasses. He might have been wearing a roll-neck collar, or scarf—something pulled up over the lower part of his face. He looked Mediterranean, probably Italian—dark hair. Maybe thirty or forty. I'm far from certain of that."

"Heavy, thin?"

"Slender, I think."

"What about the Ducati rider? Any other identifying characteristics? Size, weight, unique clothing?"

Antonio tried to capture the picture in his mind. "Also on the slender side. Probably medium height. He was wearing full black-leather riding gear. I didn't see any logos." He considered how many times he'd been the one asking the questions, and how frustrating it was when the answers were so sketchy. "Sorry, that's all I've got."

"That's okay. You have my contact info if you remember anything else."

"Of course." He glanced at the business cards they'd given him.

"Antonio," she looked at Marcello, for reasons unknown, "do you have any enemies in Italy that you are aware of?"

"I haven't spent much time here in recent years. I've never crossed anyone, to my knowledge."

"Any American enemies who might have followed you here … or might have Italian connections?"

"I've had no threats, no vendettas I'm aware of. Nicolo probably told you that I used to be a detective in Newport Beach, in Southern California. I was on the force twenty years … retired nine years ago after an injury and moved to Seattle. Even if there was an old vendetta — say someone who got out of prison — they probably would have lost track of me. Besides, why would they follow me all the way over here? Highly unlikely."

Marcello joined the conversation for the first time. "Nicolo pulled me aside after my call. He thinks they might have mistaken you for him. Do you think it's possible? You guys are similar in size and you look enough alike."

Sudden clarity caused his body to jerk forward. *Of course! Why didn't it occur to me?* He blamed the opioid drugs.

Gabriella waited patiently for him to speak.

"Can't believe it didn't occur to me. It's the only thing that makes sense. Nicolo was supposed to be riding with us. I was wearing one of his jerseys and helmet. I bring my own riding shorts, shoes, cycling glasses. Everything else I borrow from him or Leonardo."

Cogs were turning in his brain. "Do you really think we look enough alike, that they would confuse me for him?"

"With a helmet and cycling glasses. Yes. I do. It doesn't sound like they saw you up close. There's not that much of an age difference. You're probably a few pounds heavier, but you guys could pass as brothers. I'm curious, by the way. Your last name—Cortese? I know your mother is Italian, but Nicolo said your father was American. Is he of Italian heritage?"

"Very little, and not really Italian. He was killed eighteen years ago in his final weeks as a detective. His grandfather, Emilio Cortese, emigrated from Corsica. Came through Ellis Island before World War I, just in time to get drafted and shipped back to France. You probably know that many Corsican families have Italian surnames. When he came home from the war, he married a Danish woman. Don't ask me how that happened."

"Nicolo said you own a pizzeria?" Marcello added.

"Yes. My second career."

"I'd love to hear more," Gabriella interrupted, giving Marcello a look, "but let's get back on task. I can see you're beginning to fade. What about Giulia? Do you think they were trying to harm her?"

"I doubt it. She was collateral damage." *What a crude reference.* "Remember, we were kind of racing at that point. She was trying to catch me. What I don't understand is why she didn't fall back when she saw what was going on." He paused to consider this. "The key question as I see it is who would want to kill or injure Nicolo? And why? And how would they have known to expect him on that road at that time?"

"Good questions," Gabriella answered. "Ones I've been asking myself. If our supposition is true, and it's plausible, whoever planned this attack expected Nicolo on that road. So, it was someone close to him, or they found out from someone who was."

Marcello and Gabriella asked a few more questions. Did Antonio see license plates? How did he know the model of the car and motorcycle? Anything else unusual or suspicious?

Gabriella pulled out her cell phone and pulled up images of an Alfa Romeo "Giulia" and a Ducati "Scrambler". She showed them to Antonio for confirmation.

"I'm certain on the Alfa. Ninety percent on the Ducati," he said. "A few months ago, I visited a Ducati showroom. I'm not an impulsive guy. But I almost bought one."

Gabriella reminded him again, "You were a detective, Antonio. You know the tiniest detail matters. If anything else comes to mind—anything—make sure we know about it."

As they headed for the door, Gabriella turned and smiled at him. "*Ciao, ciao*! Get well quickly."

As he watched them walk out the door, he had a feeling that his life had just changed.

Chapter Four

Thursday afternoon

After Marcello and Gabriella left, Antonio summoned enough strength to go to Giulia's room again. He made it without help this time. The nurses had given him a walker to use, encouraging him to walk around the second-floor corridor where his room was located. He didn't need it. His dizziness was gone. But he used it as cover to make his way to the elevator, unseen by nurse Isabella—who was back on duty—keeping an eagle eye on him.

In Giulia's room he found an exhausted Nicolo, Sofia—her eyes still red—and Aunt Chiara. The color had returned to Chiara's cheeks. She'd gone back to Nicolo and Sofia's house for a few hours' sleep. She and Aunt Frankie would take turns sitting with Sofia, who refused to leave her daughter's side. There had been no change in Giulia's condition.

Nicolo pulled Antonio outside the room. They discussed the theory that the attackers were really after Nicolo. They were in total agreement. No other scenario made sense. The questions loomed: who and why? Who wanted to harm him, and expected him to be on the road that morning?

As they kicked these questions about, Nicolo got a call from Marcello. Antonio could tell it was something big. He overheard the words "prison escape".

Nicolo hung up. His arms hung limp and his eyes went dull. "We have our suspect. Two days ago, the day before the road incident, a local mob boss, Sandro Pucci, escaped prison. I put him there six months ago. He threatened revenge. I'll tell you more later." Nicolo turned and left without saying another word.

*****

Antonio managed to nap for an hour. Mid-afternoon they wheeled him off for an MRI to confirm there was no brain trauma beyond what the initial tests indicated. Afterwards, he made his way back to Giulia's room. There was no longer any need to sneak past the nurses. He was doing well enough. Entering the room, he was surprised to find Gabriella. She was alone with Giulia, holding her hand. Her eyes were wet. She looked at him with an embarrassed smile, pulled out a tissue and daubed them carefully.

"I sent the girls out for some coffee," she said softly. "They looked exhausted."

He took a seat beside her, considering her thoughtfulness.

"This case is personal to me, Antonio. If Marcello knew how much, he'd probably pull me off. I suspect that's why Nicolo asked for us." She nodded her head toward Giulia, "I know her well. She and my daughter were close friends. I coached their soccer team." She turned to Antonio, "You came to a game once, with Sofia, and your wife and daughter. Do you remember?"

Antonio nodded, wondering about her use of the word *were*. "I do. That was you coaching?"

"Yes. I remember how Giulia lit up when she saw your daughter. She played one of her best games ever."

Antonio stared at Giulia's colorless face. "Doesn't surprise me. Giulia and Christina were like sisters. Giulia is like another daughter to me."

Gabriella looked at him. "I've heard about your loss, Antonio. I'm so sorry. I hope you are finding peace." She paused, glancing away. He watched a faraway look, a shadow, fall over her.

"I know your pain." She locked her eyes on his. "My daughter, Liliana, died of leukemia four years ago. She was only fifteen. Her father, my husband Renato, was killed on a peacekeeping mission to Albania when she was a baby." Antonio wanted to say something but bit his lip. "We had hoped to have another child. But he was gone too soon." Her eyes reflected the conflict within, a measure of peace, with an underlayment of sadness.

How could she find any peace, with her husband and only child gone? At least he still had his son, Jonathan, who was married to wonderful Leah. She was expecting twins in a few months.

"Must be lonely," he said.

"Spoken from personal experience, I'm guessing." Silence fell again as she turned her eyes back toward Giulia. "I have my girls. My dogs," she clarified, "and my nieces and nephews. Most are teens now, or older. But my youngest niece, Serena—she's eleven—so amazing. We're very close. She was born late in life, like I was, and Giulia." She stared at her still form. "And like Giulia ... and me ...," she laughed, "she has *very* overprotective big brothers."

Antonio chuckled. Even Gabriella knew how Raphael and Leonardo were with Giulia.

*****

Gabriella kissed him on the cheek and left. Antonio sat with Giulia a while longer, thinking about the things she shared with him. *What a remarkable woman.*

His own guilt and sadness were driving him toward rage. He didn't know what to do with it. The peace he had felt on their ride was long gone now. *Will I ever find it again?* he asked. It had been so elusive in recent years. Whenever it showed up, he would try to grasp it, grip it tightly, but it would slip through his fingers, like sand in an hourglass. He had become accustomed to this place of tension: anger and forgiveness, peace and turmoil. *Why is life so cruel at times*, he asked himself, *and so wonderful at times?*

Sofia and Chiara returned. He sat with them for a while, trying to be strong, to be someone they could lean on. But after a while the exhaustion and pain caught up with him. He headed back to his room before they caught sight of the cracks in his rusted armor.

Chapter Five

Thursday evening

Antonio was exhausted, but sleep would not come. His mind roiled with anxious thoughts, like soiled laundry tossed about in a washing machine. *Damned opioids,* he thought, knowing it was more than that. He took a few deep breaths and tried to collect himself. Looking for something positive to dwell on, he turned his mind back to the events of the past few days, now mostly a blur.

He flew into Pisa on Monday, traveling with his favorite aunt, Francesca. Everyone called her Frankie. She made the long, grueling flight go quickly, talking his ear off for hours. She loved to tell stories, stitching together one after the other of growing up in Tuscany, and her years in California. But his favorites were the humorous tales about his mother, her older sister, Elena. She finally wore herself out and he was able to grab some sleep.

Frankie had come to Seattle for Elena's 80th birthday party. Though approaching seventy herself, Frankie brimmed with life. She and Pasquale, her husband of forty-something years, owned a charming little hotel, precariously perched on a hillside overlooking the sea in

Positano, on the Amalfi Coast. She fit the role perfectly. Like all the sisters, she looked younger than she was, and still beautiful. She wore her silver-white hair in a wavy hairdo, and dressed in colorful, beach-style clothing. Her fingernails and toenails were painted the color of the sea on a bright, sunny day. She was planning to stay the week with the family in Tuscany before taking the train south.

Their plane descended through scattered morning clouds into Pisa's Galileo Galilei International Airport. From there, they collected their luggage and took the crowded express train to the bustling Firenze station. There they were greeted with hugs and kisses by Nicolo and Sofia.

Antonio could hardly believe he was in Tuscany again. Nicolo bypassed the main highway and drove them south on the winding country roads. He and Antonio hardly got a word in as the girls shared all the latest. Before he knew it, they were pulling onto the familiar gravel country road where Sofia and Nicolo's home was located, not far from the tiny hamlet of Fonterutoli in Chianti. The house was beautifully situated on the brow of a hill, with a view to the south and east that seemed to go on forever.

Seeing the house brought a flood of memories. He'd always thought of it as his second home. It was five years since he was here last. He tried to understand why he waited so long. The home had belonged to his grandparents. He felt a pang of guilt for not having returned for their memorial services. He hadn't been ready to face another loss. The house would feel very different without their presence.

Nonno Tommaso and Nonna Valentina had bought the run-down farmhouse after the war, but it was a half-century older than that. It was here Antonio spent weeks each summer while growing up. He thought about how he, Randi, and Christina were planning to come here following their visit to Nice three summers ago. He stuffed that memory away for now.

His mother, Elena, was born and spent her earliest years in Panzano, not far north of here. She was the only sibling born before the war, before her father Tommaso went off to fight in the Greek Isles for the Italian Army. He came home wearing the bars of a sergeant. When Mussolini fell, he joined the Italian resistance fighters, who were loyal to the king, to fight the Germans.

In the years after he returned home from the war, Nonna Valentina gave birth to three more children: Chiara, then Frankie, and finally Nicolo, who came as a surprise some years later.

When Nonna and Nonno were in their eighties, Nicolo and his family moved in to care for them. When both grandparents passed, the house was inherited by all four of their children. Nicolo and Sofia bought out the sisters so they could make it their home. It remained the center of gravity for the family, the gathering place.

Antonio looked around, admiring the restoration work done since his last visit. The kitchen still had well-worn tile flooring, exposed chestnut ceiling beams, and thick stone walls, which provided its old-world charm. But Nicolo and the boys had doubled the size of the island and added the necessary modern amenities. After that was complete, they turned their attention to building an outdoor kitchen. It began next to the house, underneath the overhang of the covered veranda, where they located their wood-burning oven and a gas grill. The rest of the island extended into the open air of the terrazza. Antonio loved that they included an outdoor fire pit for roasting meats. He didn't even try to hide his jealousy. He dreamed of having a kitchen like this. Another special touch was the hand-painted ceramics on the walls and table. A few years ago, Sofia started a side business, painting ceramics for local shops. It occurred to him where Giulia inherited her artistic talents.

*****

Antonio and Aunt Frankie enjoyed a day of resting up. Antonio was dead-tired, but decided not to take a nap. He wanted to sleep well that night, to get his body on Italy time.

No one lifted a finger to cook. They took lunch on the terrazza, a simple affair of bread, cheeses, grapes, and cured meats. They spent the afternoon catching up on family news, mostly about kids and grandchildren. One by one Raphe, Leonardo, and Giulia, arrived home. They all joined them for dinner at the nearby Osteria di Fonterutoli.

Nicolo and Sofia were long-time friends with the owner, so were treated like family. The five-course dinner, highlighted by risotto with shaved truffles, and roasted guinea fowl, was exceptional by any standards. Of course, Italians dine later than Americans. As the evening wore on, and the wine took its effect, Antonio was regretting his decision not to take a nap. He began to nod off at the table. Leonardo, sitting on his right, gave him an elbow every time his eyes started to close. He was having way too much fun with it.

Thankfully, Antonio had slept like a log, and awoke the following morning looking forward to the extended family arriving for their welcoming party. Cars arrived all morning: Aunt Chiara and Sylvio from Montepulciano, then three of their daughters, two of their husbands, seven of their grandchildren, and two great-grandchildren. The house exploded with noise and laughter.

When the family gathered for a dinner like this, everyone helped out with the cooking. While Chiara's daughters made fresh farfalle pasta, Chiara and Antonio went searching within the four-foot-high stone walls of the vegetable garden. They returned with a basket overflowing with tomatoes, carrots, yellow squash, celery, onions, and herbs to make a tomato gardiniera sauce for the farfalle. They washed, and peeled, and chopped. Chiara made Antonio dice the onions. She didn't want to cry, but did anyway as the acids created by the enzymes burned her eyes. She smiled and wiped her eyes with the underside of her apron.

They briefly boiled and skinned the plum-style tomatoes, then sliced them in half lengthwise and removed most of the seeds with their fingers. They sweated the other vegetables in a good amount of olive oil, then added white wine to deglaze the pan. After the wine was reduced by half, they added the tomatoes and let the sauce cook gently for a couple of hours. As it simmered slowly on the range, the tomatoes slowly broke down. The aroma wafted throughout the kitchen.

Aunt Frankie, who loved to bake, teamed up with two of her great-nieces. They baked harvest cakes, made with Moscato grapes from the vineyard, orange zest, and sweet homemade vin santo wine.

Leonardo fired up the wood-burning oven. He and Uncle Sylvio, Chiara's husband, baked fresh bread, and roasted recently picked apples with squash. Raphael and Nicolo had the best job, preparing a shoulder of wild boar. Raphe pulled his phone from his pocket to show Antonio a photograph. It showed him kneeling over the large boar, with its dangerous tusks. He explained with pride how he shot it in the woods beyond the vineyard just before it charged him.

They cut the meat open, laid it out flat, and layered it with boar sausage, fennel, garlic, and herbs; then they rolled and tied it. They put it on to roast on the spit above the outdoor fire pit. As its juices dripped on the hot coals, smoke rose to flavor the meat, turning it a beautiful dark caramel color. Amongst all that amazing food it was the center of attention.

It was a wild and crazy scene, bordering on chaos, but Sofia assumed the role of head chef. She orchestrated it all while serving up grilled crostini, Chiara's homemade sheep's cheese brought from Umbria, and other antipasti to keep everyone happy.

There was never a shortage of wine at these dinners. Throughout the afternoon, they sipped white Vermentino from a neighbor's vineyard, fruity and acidic. When the time for dinner arrived, and they were all seated, Nicolo brought out his homemade Chianti to accompany the primi course, the farfalle with gardiniera sauce. He made his Chianti in the traditional style taught him by Nonno Tomasso, with Sangiovese and Canaiolo grapes. When the wild boar was carved, they brought out three vintages of Vino Nobile from Chiara and Sylvio's winery in Montepulciano for a vertical tasting. *Did I have to try them all? No wonder I had trouble climbing those hills yesterday.* Antonio laughed at himself and his tension eased.

The dinner was like a holiday feast. Even better than the food and wine was the laughter that surrounded the long wooden table. Antonio remembered sitting back and taking it all in. He realized how much he missed this. His mind wandered back through the years, to all of those summer dinners with grandparents, aunts, uncles, cousins, and friends in this house, and later, his own wife and children among them.

He closed his eyes. All of these memories swirled in his head, creating emotions he couldn't even begin to name. He had experienced two wonderful events just days apart: his mother's 80th birthday party, and then the welcoming dinner. For a few moments in time, he'd almost been able to forget about the pain which haunted him these past three years. Now, with Giulia in a coma, those joyful evenings seemed like a distant memory.

*****

Antonio had been on the edge of sleep when Nicolo stuck his head into the room. Antonio opened his eyes and saw that Nicolo's adrenaline had pushed aside his exhaustion.

He pulled up a chair next to the bed, and proceeded to tell Antonio about Sandro Pucci, now suspect number one in what would become known as *the road incident*. Pucci was a local mob boss. His grandfather had given rise to the Pucci mob family, a branch of the Camorra crime syndicate. The secret Camorra society, birthed in Napoli, in Campania, was one of the oldest and largest criminal organizations in Italy. As the loose-knit syndicate grew, families were establishing new territories throughout Italy and the world. The Pucci family had chosen the fertile ground of Tuscany to put down its roots, and challenge the mob families of Calabria who arrived before them. The Pucci family's focus was drugs, but they also had fingers in racketeering, prostitution, and human trafficking.

But Sandro Pucci, a brash and careless man, had made mistakes. His pride made him vulnerable, and it was Nicolo who brought the evidence that put him away for life, or so he thought.

"They haven't figured out yet exactly how Pucci escaped," Nicolo explained. "It appears he had inside help from at least one, maybe multiple guards. It's possible they were bribed, or their families threatened. They think he went out in a truck that was delivering produce. He'd been working in the kitchen. He knew the schedule of the supply trucks in and out."

"I don't know, Nicolo. Is it plausible that he planned and executed that attack in so little time? How could he have known you'd be out on that ride?"

"I don't know. That's been puzzling me. A lot of people know I ride Wednesday mornings. Been my routine for years. But how Sandro could have known troubles me. Possibly a mole in the department. You know he could have planned the whole damn thing before he escaped."

"A mole? Seems unlikely. You know your guys so well."

"Yeah. Seems like a long shot. My detectives have been with me for years. I've known Paolo since he was a kid. Coached him in soccer. We hunt together. I've had all the guys over to our house for dinner. It's unthinkable any of them would betray me."

"What about other officers, the ones who walk the streets?"

"There are some I don't know well, but I don't think they would know my routines."

Antonio had always known of the mob's influence in Sicily and southern Italy. He naively thought that they were losing their power and influence. He was sickened to find out that they were stronger than ever, and taking root in Tuscany. He knew how they could get to cops with money, or fear, or both. This was not the Tuscany he remembered and cherished.

Chapter Six

Friday

After Nicolo left, Antonio had finally fallen asleep but didn't sleep any better than the previous night. When nurse Isabella tried to give him opioids and a sleep aid, he refused both. She came back with Tylenol PM. He was still feeling the effects of the opioids they gave him a day ago, and the all-too-familiar cravings for more.

The pain, and his bladder, awoke him several times. During his fitful sleep he had dreams—vivid dreams—bizarre dreams—filled with fear and feelings of helplessness. Things were all mixed up. Recent events and those of his past were twisted, contorted, and intertwined, playing off one another … falling, falling off a cliff, sounds of metallic crunching, screams, a big truck coming at him under the streetlights of the promenade in Nice, then veering away to pursue others like some evil creature with immense, brightly lit eyes. He saw his wife, Randi, hold up her hand as if to stop him from careening into her and Christina. He watched, unable to move, his feet feeling as though they were encased in cement; his mouth open but no scream emerging. Then he was falling again, Giulia falling beside him, rocks and sea rising toward them, a motorcycle coming at her, then him, then alongside him. A truck driven by a terrorist coming at him. It morphed into the red Alfa. As he sailed past the window of the car, it seemed to be in slow motion. He saw the driver, his roll-neck sweater pulled over his nose and mouth. And he saw his eyes, as though his sunglasses were magnifying glasses. They registered surprise, recognition, apprehension.

When he awoke, short of dawn, he willed himself to remember the dream. He wanted to write it down, but couldn't find paper or pen. When he woke again, sometime after dawn, most of the details had faded, as dreams are prone to do. But one image stuck with him — the eyes of the driver, and the look of shock they betrayed.

*****

Doctor Giordano, in his white coat, strode into his room mid-morning to give him the good news. His MRI showed good results. They expected his release in a few hours, after they treated and re-dressed his road rash wounds. The doctor was walking out when detectives Bianchi and Ferrara waltzed in.

"Antonio. How are you today?" Marcello sounded entirely too cheerful. *Is this the same man I met yesterday?* Either he was not very perceptive, or simply trying to cheer him up. Antonio knew he looked like crap. His eyes were bloodshot, and he hadn't been able to shower; just a sponge bath from a male attendant, who'd been about as gentle as a gorilla. Seeing Gabriella, he was suddenly aware that he could smell his own body odor. If she noticed, she didn't let on.

"We wanted to bring you up to date," Gabriella chimed in. "Two vehicles were found matching the description of the car and motorcycle. They were abandoned on the road leading to a tourist parking lot outside of Siena. They were rented from Europcar, clear down in Roma. The credit cards and matching fake ID they used were from someone who died a month ago."

"How do you explain that, huh?" added Marcello. "We'll be working on that this afternoon."

Gabriella continued, "The vehicles are being inspected by our forensic team. But you know how rentals can be, there could be fingerprints and DNA from several individuals. And our DNA lab usually takes weeks, sometimes months to get us results, especially if it's not a murder case."

"Let's hope it doesn't become that," Antonio said. *Why would you even consider such a scenario?* he asked himself, thinking of Giulia. As far as the DNA, he knew that timely results were a problem in the states also. He wondered if it was better or worse here. *Thank God it isn't August when everything in Italy grinds to a halt, when half the country takes off for the coast.*

*****

Just before lunch, he heard a cheerful voice in the corridor. *Nah, can't be, I'm hearing things,* he thought, just before his big sister, Alessia, waltzed into the room.

"Antonio! We've been so concerned about you. And worried sick about Giulia!"

She lit up the room even in her worried state. Alessia was the kind of person others were drawn to like moths to a flame. Not because she craved the attention; she just had a rare charm, beauty, and confidence. She liked to be bossy sometimes. But now, instead of acting like a bossy mother, she put on the role of a nurturing mom.

He smiled at her impulsiveness. He didn't mind it so much. They had always been close, much closer than he was with his brother, who was between them in the birth order.

"Long time no see, sis!"

She laughed that elegant laugh that always turned heads. He realized his mood was improved.

Alessia and her husband, Matthew, lived in the exclusive community of Medina, on the east side of Lake Washington. Their home sat on two acres on a bluff overlooking the lake and the skyline of Seattle beyond. It was only a week ago that they hosted the 80th birthday party for their mother, Elena.

Alessia explained that she arranged a flight the moment she heard about the accident. Mother insisted on joining her. She was at the house resting. Antonio was not surprised the two of them had come. Loyalty ran deep as the Pacific Ocean in his family, a quality he believed he inherited.

She turned serious. "How are you, little brother?"

"I hurt like hell. You?"

"Better than you, I'd say." She paused a long moment. Her eyes showed the effects of jet lag but she didn't complain. "This isn't why you came to Tuscany, is it?"

"No ... it's not."

She locked her eyes on his. After a moment, he looked away, worried she would see he was broken inside.

"Maybe this will cheer you up." She pulled a container of gelato from her oversized purse. "I hid this in case the nurses wouldn't approve." She knew that gelato was one of his greatest weakness. It was a rare day in Italy that he did not find a gelateria. She even remembered his favorite flavor, frutta de bosco.

He chuckled. "That was smart. Nurse Isabella rules this floor with an iron fist. Don't cross her."

"Oh, I think I can hold my own."

"Yeah. What was I thinking?" He laughed. Then grimaced, from the sharp pain in his ribs.

*****

For Antonio, walking out the front door of the hospital was like a release from prison. He had spent far too much time at Hoag Hospital in Newport Beach after sustaining the injury that ended his detective career. He deeply inhaled the fresh air. Sofia and his sister, Alessia, were by his side. The family put their foot down, insisting that Sofia go home to rest. Aunt Chiara and Leonardo would stay overnight with Giulia.

Raphe pulled up in his small SUV, a red Fiat 500X. The air had cooled and the roads were damp with a misty rain. Raphael looked at the sky with concern. "We need to harvest the grapes," he told them, "After they have a chance to dry out. There's a big rainstorm coming in a few days. The grapes will soak up too much water."

When they arrived at the house, Raphael grabbed Antonio's arm and pulled him aside before he could follow the others into the house. "I'm worried, Antonio." He spoke rapidly. "Father refuses to keep his hands out of the manhunt. He's out to get Pucci. Even after the magistrate tried to warn him off. I've never seen him in such a state."

"What do you expect? You are too. We're all in a state." He let that sink in. "I don't think you need to worry so much, Raphael. Your father's a smart man, and an excellent detective."

"Wish I was as confident as you. He has his way, you know. Seems calm on the outside, not like me. But I'm afraid his anger is getting the better of him this time. I think he's taking advantage of his friendship with Marcello to keep himself in the middle of it."

He stared at Antonio; eyes unblinking, looking for an ally.

He went on, "Earlier today he went to visit the accident site. And he's already working his informants, trying to find out where Pucci is hiding."

Antonio's first inclination was to dive right in. *I'm in no condition,* he thought. *Right now, I need a shower, a good meal, and most of all, an uninterrupted night's sleep.*

"He knows the limits, Raphael. I don't think he'd do anything to compromise the case." But even as he said it, he wasn't so sure. He knew what anger, revenge, and the desire to protect the people you love could do to a man. They are powerful forces, for good and evil alike. He'd seen and experienced it himself.

"I'm just as worried about you, Raphael. I don't think you're handling this well."

Raphael stared at him hard, then turned and walked away.

As soon as I get some rest, I'll join the search, he thought. *And keep an eye on Nicolo and Raphael.*

*****

Mother Elena was up from her nap and already taking control of the house. Antonio could see she felt completely at home here in the house she grew up in. She and Aunt Frankie were making a simple dinner, much of it leftovers from their big feast three days ago. They added to it fresh-baked bread brought by the neighbors, who also lavished them with fresh eggs, croissants, and homemade jam for breakfast. Other neighbors brought apples, late-harvest peaches, ripe off the trees, and homemade ricotta.

Antonio knew this was how people were here. Sharing was a way of life, especially in time of need.

Elena looked tired, and older than she had at her party, but she was a woman of formidable spirit. He could see how much it meant for her to be here in this time of family crisis. She was the matriarch of the family now, a role she didn't take lightly. She would use that influence to lighten the load on Sofia and Nicolo. She hugged Antonio too hard. He almost cried out in pain. Then she held him away from her, looked at him with concern, and sent him off to shower. She went about her business, making sure he and the others would be well fed and tended to.

The mood at the table was sullen at dinner. Gone was the laughter, replaced by furrowed brows and bloodshot eyes. Raphael hardly spoke, except a few words meant to comfort his mother. He didn't touch the wine Alessia poured for him, and left the moment he finished eating.

Antonio went easy on the wine himself, and then disappeared off to bed. He had been relocated to Leonardo's bedroom, who would be staying with a friend to make room for the extra guests. The boys lived in an apartment just steps from the main house. They had begun construction on the building before his last visit, but didn't finish it until a few years later. Leonardo gave him the grand tour, obviously proud of the work they had done.

Nicolo and the boys did most of the work themselves. Nonno Tomasso taught Nicolo how to work with stone when he was just a boy. He, in turn, taught Raphael and Leonardo. The stonework looked nearly identical to the main house. The apartment occupied the top floor of three levels—two above ground, and a cellar below. The apartment was complete with kitchen, a large sitting room with a big-screen television, and two bedrooms, each with its own bathroom. It was the perfect bachelor pad. The ground level was a massive garage with room for parking cars and their small tractor, an area for bicycle storage and repairs, and an area for their winemaking equipment. Below this level was the wine cellar where they did their barrel-aging and bottle storage. Antonio wondered how they ever survived without it.

Chapter Seven

Saturday morning

Antonio barely crawled into bed before falling asleep. Somewhere in the night, the dream returned. He awoke in a cold sweat. He turned on the lamp, found paper and pen in Leonardo's bedside table, and wrote down everything he could remember. Back in bed, his mind replayed the dream over and over, like a scratched vinyl record.

This was not the first time he'd had dreams like this, dreams of falling off cliffs, dreams of the terror attack in Nice, of being unable to move. The dreams were never quite the same, but there was one constant … a feeling of complete helplessness. Anxiety began to grip him. It came often when he couldn't sleep. And the anger rose again, like bile in his throat. He needed a distraction. He found his phone and paired it with a Bluetooth speaker Leonardo kept on his side table. He put on some music, choosing his mellowest playlist, a mix of genres. He read for a while, comprehending little, but it carried his mind away. When he finally drifted off, he slept like the dead for the first time in days. When he awoke, it was mid-morning.

*****

It hurt like hell to move his body. He made his way slowly to the kitchen where he was greeted cheerfully by his mother, looking much spryer. He kissed her on both cheeks, holding her arms this time so she couldn't give him a painful hug.

He was famished, and like all good mothers she knew it intuitively. She brought him two eggs, cooked sunny side up the way he liked them, two croissants with homemade red currant preserves, and fresh fruit. She poured him coffee and set cream in front of him. He rather enjoyed being mothered this morning. After eating, coffee, and a few Tylenols he began to feel like a new man. At least the fog was clearing from his mind. It helped that the sun had returned. The world felt fresher and cleaner.

Elena poured him a second cup of coffee and one for herself. She sat down and stared at him until he looked up. "You need to help Nicolo find out who did this. You know he won't let it go." Her voice was strong and determined. "You have to make them pay for what they did to Giulia."

Her tone of voice reminded him of when he was a teenager. She had been a strict, no-nonsense mother, never knowingly allowing her kids to step out of line. Of course, like most kids, they got in plenty of trouble she never knew about.

"Don't worry, Mother. Badge or no badge, I still remember how to be a detective."

She kept her eyes locked on his.

"I just need to work smart. I don't want to create any backlash that could come back on Nicolo or compromise a case."

She gave him a trusting nod. "Do what you have to do. You were an excellent detective, maybe even better than your father. And you know how good he was."

Antonio didn't reply. His relationship with his father, Anthony, had been complicated. Anthony was a detective in San Pedro, California, no easy beat, for nearly thirty years. Before that he was an MP in the army for nearly a decade. He'd met Elena while stationed at Camp Darby in Tirreni, on the Tuscan coast, south of Pisa. They married in 1960 after a whirlwind romance. A few months later they moved to Southern California. Elena's parents were not happy when Anthony took her home to America. They had hoped they would settle in Italy.

Anthony was killed by drug smugglers, just weeks before he planned to retire. He never got the chance to enjoy all the plans he'd been looking forward to for so many years. Antonio regretted that he had not been more forgiving.

*****

Aunt Frankie helped Antonio re-dress his wounds. She had a stomach for such things. She had been a nurse in her younger days and taught him the right way to do it so he could manage on his own. She and Pasquale moved to California in the early 70s so Frankie could live near her big sister, Elena. She attended nursing school at Long Beach State, then worked for years at St. Mary's Medical Center in Long Beach, before returning to Italy. They had always wanted children, but finally gave up after years of trying.

Now clean shaven and re-bandaged, Antonio poured a third cup of coffee, a luxury he rarely allowed himself. He needed a clear mind. He took it outside to sit in the warm late-morning sun.

He pushed aside his anger as best he could so he could think straight. In his mind, he visualized a puzzle, an old trick of his. Not many pieces were in place. Not nearly enough for a picture to develop. He began to ask himself questions:

Is it likely Pucci or his thugs did this? It seemed plausible, even probable. Pucci had expressed his desire for revenge.

But could he have put this together in such a short time? Not even a relevant question. He could have had it fully planned and communicated to his people before his escape.

Would Sandro Pucci have played a direct role in the attack? Possibly. Why else would it have come so soon after his escape? It seemed foolish though. Any sane person who escaped prison would lie low for a time before leaving the area. But Nicolo told him that Pucci was brash and reckless.

How would he have known to expect Nicolo on the road that morning? He figured this was not that difficult. It seemed like half the community knew this. The first pass by the Ducati was probably done to confirm Nicolo was riding, and on his most usual route.

Could it have been someone else? Of course. Nicolo was the Commissario, the lead detective in Siena, where he had worked for over thirty-five years. He would have plenty of enemies. But for now, you play the cards you're dealt and see where they take you.

The warm sun, a cool breeze, and the third cup of coffee revived him. Thankfully, the effects of the opioids seemed to be wearing off. He hated those things! He'd rather deal with the pain.

*****

Antonio finished his coffee and called Nicolo. Nicolo had sent Leonardo home and spent the night in the hospital with his sister Chiara, sleeping in chairs next to Giulia's bed. In a groggy voice, Nicolo told him that Leonardo and Sofia were returning to the hospital to relieve them, and that Leonardo was taking Alessia to Europcar on the way. She wanted to rent a passenger van, large enough to ferry the family around.

Antonio said "*Ciao!*" and hung up so he could hitch a ride. He wanted a car of his own, something small, easy to park and get around on the narrow roads. When they got to the car rental place, he ended up with a two-door Lancia Ypsilon. It was definitely small.

He drove to the hospital, found a parking spot, and went up to find Nicolo. Nicolo looked like he'd aged ten years in these last two days. His eyes were red, his shoulders slumped, and the wrinkles on his forehead looked like they'd been etched with a chisel.

Nicolo wanted coffee. They walked to his favorite espresso bar in this part of Siena. *He needs a lot more than coffee,* Antonio thought, *like a shower, some real sleep, clean clothes, and a shave.* But he remembered how people were kind to him when he looked worse, so he kept his mouth shut. They took a seat at the bar. Nicolo ordered a double espresso. Antonio settled for mineral water.

"So much for us being able to enjoy your visit," Nicolo said.

"The best laid plans of mice and men. Don't worry about me. The question is, how are you?"

"Stupid question."

"Yeah. Sorry." *Why do I ask the same question I hate so much?* "Fill me in on what's been going on."

Nicolo pulled out a packet of photos to show him. They were of Pucci and other members of the family, including bodyguards and other guys known to do his dirty work. He knew Antonio hadn't gotten a good look at the attackers but was still hoping something might trigger. It didn't.

Antonio decided to tell Nicolo about his dream, especially the part about flying past the car window and seeing those eyes.

"I don't know if it's my mind making it up. You know how dreams are. Or if my mind is trying to show me what's hidden in my subconscious. If I see those eyes again, I might recognize them. And it seemed that when the driver saw me up close, there was a spark of recognition ... like he suddenly realized I wasn't you."

Nicolo's blank stare told him he didn't know what to think.

Nicolo changed the subject. He told him about the other murder cases he was working. The magistrate had called him again, admonishing him to focus his attention on those and stay out of the road incident. There had been three murders in a single week. Highly unusual for Siena.

"They all appear to be drug related," Nicolo said. "Two of the victims were street guys ... pushers. The third was a mid-level distributor. I think he was their supplier. We didn't find his body until Wednesday morning. That's what called me away. The gendarmes were called to an apartment by a neighbor who caught wind of the horrible aroma. The body was pretty ripe by then. He'd been dead at least four days."

Antonio knew that aroma all too well. The stench of death. A smell you never forget.

"I have to ask, Nicolo. Are you in any state of mind to be working these cases? Maybe you should take some time off."

Nicolo's glare told him his opinion wasn't welcome. "Yeah. I've mostly got my team working on them. You know Paolo Benevente. Remember we went hunting together on your last visit? I don't know if you've met the other guys, Vincenzo Mancini, and Salvatore Giordano … goes by Jordy."

"I met Mancini on our last trip when you and I came to the questura. Is he still as intense as he was then?"

"Maybe even more so … always uptight. I remember you guys meeting now. Anyway, the first two murders appear to be related. The magistrate doesn't think the third one is—different MO—but I disagree. Too coincidental. The first two murders were similar, an overdose of heroin. Same drugs they were selling. We thought the first was just an OD. But the second one showed signs of a struggle, and the guy being restrained. That prompted us to take a second look at the first victim. We found signs of struggle there too. Just not as obvious. Everyone missed it. Even the coroner. Both syringes were clean. No fingerprints. Not even the victims.

"The third victim was the guy we found in his apartment. Different MO, like I said. Killed with a gun. Whoever did it probably used a silencer. Neighbors claim they never heard anything, or they're just too afraid to tell us if they did."

"Any idea who the victims were working for?"

"That's what we're trying to figure out. Probably mob. Just not sure which family. We've got some competition going on here."

"What's next?"

"I've got a full day ahead. I want to follow up on my CIs. I've put pressure on a couple of them to find out the word-on-the-street about Pucci ... if he ordered the hit on me." He paused. "Also, about these murders. Haven't heard anything from them yet. Probably because they're afraid of Pucci, especially now that he's out. I need to make them more afraid of me."

Antonio knew there were lots of ways to make that happen, mostly threats of busting the informants on charges for whatever low-to-mid-level crimes they were involved in. In more extreme cases, you could threaten to put the word out on the street that they were a snitch. Always a last resort. You'd probably never see them again. It was not something he could picture Nicolo resorting to, at least not under normal circumstances.

Nicolo downed the rest of his espresso. He looked at the barista and raised a finger for another. "Then I need to check in with Paolo. I asked him to head up these cases in my absence. He's so sure this is a family feud that I don't think he's being objective. It's certainly possible, but there's no real evidence. Seems like he's being uncharacteristically sloppy. After that, I'll check in with Marcello Bianchi to see what progress they've made."

"What can I do, Nicolo? I'm not gonna sit around licking my wounds like a stray dog."

"Keep me sane for starters—make sure I am going in the right direction. My brain is mush. Is that how you Americans say it?" Antonio smiled at the colloquialism, probably something he'd heard in a forty-year-old

American gangster movie. Nicolo was still rambling, "… lack of sleep, anger, desire for revenge. Don't let me do anything I'll regret."

"I thought I would go visit the site of the road incident, see if it shakes loose any memories. And go into Castellina," Antonio said. "It's a long shot. Maybe someone saw the guy on the motorcycle without his helmet, or saw the car in town after, and who was driving it."

"Not a bad idea. You never know. Just be careful. If the magistrate catches wind of you sniffing around, it could cause a stink."

"I know. I know. I'll keep a low profile. Just promise me one thing, Nicolo … that you'll take Sofia home tonight and sleep in your own bed. You both need it. Alessia and Frankie are planning to take the night shift. Alessia says she's still on Seattle time anyway, and Frankie is anxious to do her part."

Nicolo nodded but his mind was already somewhere else.

*****

Before heading out, Antonio went back to the hospital. He asked the girls to go get some coffee so he could have a few minutes with Giulia. He felt like his emotions were all used up. He hadn't cried since the memorial service for Christina and Randi. Today would be no different.

He held Giulia's hand and spoke with the assumption she could hear him. "We want you to come back to us, Giulia. I want you back—fully back—no brain damage—no crippled body. I can't lose another person I love. Understand?" *God, please make it so.* He sat for a while, holding her hand and listening to the rhythmic sound of the ventilator.

The girls returned. Sofia spoke softly, "I forgot to tell you, Paolo came by earlier to see Giulia. He's taking this really hard. Our families have been friends for years. Giulia calls him Zio Paolo. His wife, Gemma, and I are good friends. They have a five-year-old daughter, Bettina, who adores Giulia, and vice-versa. I can't imagine what she's thinking."

Chapter Eight

Saturday afternoon

Antonio liked driving the nimble little Lancia on these winding country roads. His first stop was in Fonterutoli on his way to Castellina. The heart of the village lay across the two-lane road from the trattoria where they enjoyed their family dinner, and where he and Giulia stopped to have coffee on the morning of their ride.

Fonterutoli means *rolling fount*. He loved the way it rolled off the tongue. It was the nearest town, a tiny hamlet really, to where Nicolo and Sofia lived. It was a winery village. Most of the people who lived there worked for the Mazzei family, owners of the Castello di Fonterutoli winery. Not many years ago, they replaced the old winery with a state-of-the-art facility, located down the hill from the village. Antonio and Randi toured the winery on their last trip. He found a couple of things particularly fascinating. The grapes are brought into the huge central courtyard. There they are hand sorted and dropped down chutes into the cellar below. The walls of the cavernous cellar are carved into the limestone. Natural spring water—the fount—drips down the walls forming stalactites and stalagmites, which provide natural cooling and humidity.

The winery is one of the oldest in Italy, traceable back to the eleventh century. One of the more infamous members of the family tree was Philip Mazzei, whose stylized portrait appears on one of their wine bottles. He enjoyed his reputation as a "citizen of the world", befriending the likes of Benjamin Franklin, George Washington, and John Adams. Family history tells how he helped Thomas Jefferson plant his vineyards at Monticello. Sofia is a distant relative and grew up there.

Antonio started in the wine shop which fronts the road, then crossed the road to the trattoria, asking if anyone had seen the car or motorcycle. No luck.

Returning to his car, he caught sight of the old gardener, Anselmo, his copper-brown skin weathered by the elements. He appeared to be heading home for the day. Antonio knew him from years past. He had been the gardener there for as long as he could remember. After a warm greeting and re-acquaintance, Antonio asked him about the car and motorcycle.

Anselmo's mouth formed a sly smile. "Come with me," he said. They wove their way through the hamlet and under the ancient wisteria which forms a natural arbor connecting the two-story guest houses on opposite sides of the lane. The bees were hard at work collecting pollen from its lavender flowers which hung like clusters of grapes. They turned left before reaching the small chapel and arrived at a finely crafted wrought iron gate. Anselmo unlocked it and they entered the courtyard in front of the family estate house. Antonio could see why they chose this spot to build the house, with its sweeping view of the rolling hills and vineyards. Siena was visible to the south, bathed in the early afternoon sun. Looking left, you could see the road, winding its way through the vineyards which lay above and below it, leading off toward Castellina.

"Over there." Anselmo pointed to a pull-out, barely visible along the road, more than a hundred yards distant. "A car, a red Alfa Romeo Giulia … beautiful cars … was parked in the turn-out. A man was standing by the car for a long time. He was wearing a hat and sunglasses. I did not recognize him, but I remember he was slender, and had a neatly trimmed beard. He was wearing a charcoal roll-neck sweater. I thought he was a little 'pazzo', dressed like that on a warm morning."

Antonio smiled. He hadn't expected such dumb luck. Anselmo was an observant man.

"He was leaning against his car, having a cigarette," he continued, "like he was waiting for somebody. Then I saw him toss his cigarette. Why do they do that? He answered his cell phone, it was a short call, then he took off like a rocket toward Castellina."

Antonio asked about other features … height, age, ethnicity.

"I'd say he was about average height, like you, maybe a little taller."

Antonio was 5′11″, typical for Italian males. Men from the south were often shorter.

"He had dark hair. Maybe some grey on the temples. Hard to say from this distance. But he looked Italian to me."

Antonio thanked him generously. He got his cell number and asked if he could come back and bring some photos for him to look at. "Were you on your way home, Anselmo?"

"No, no … I was just going across the road for my afternoon espresso." Antonio thought of the espresso he and Giulia had enjoyed there. Seemed like a lifetime ago now. "I'll be working a few more hours. If you don't find me, call me. We live in the house near the horse stable."

Anselmo was eager to help. He was clearly enjoying this.

As they made their way back through the village, Antonio had a new optimism. He walked up the road to the turn-out where the Alfa had been parked. He knew tire tracks would be useless if they'd already found the vehicle. He'd suggest they look at them for confirmation.

He looked around for other clues, including cigarette butts. He found two. They were different from one another. One was smoked all the way down and looked to be days, or weeks old. The other was only smoked about halfway. Antonio guessed that was the one but collected them both. He used his fingernails, wishing he had gloves and an evidence bag. He would ask Nicolo for both in case other evidence presented itself.

*****

Antonio returned to his car, feeling a sharp pain in his rib cage as he climbed in. He hated bruised ribs. It took weeks for the pain to go away. He drove to the place where he and Giulia were run off the road. He walked up and down the pavement, replaying the events in his mind. It revived the anger he felt at himself. He should have spotted the trouble sooner, and reacting to protect Giulia. He pushed his guilt aside. He had work to do.

He put the events together in sequence. The motorcycle rider did a reconnaissance mission on the road to confirm that Nicolo—or so he thought—was on the road, and how far into the ride. From there, he stopped next to the highway in Castellina, waiting for them to pass. When they did, he called the driver of the Alfa Romeo, who was waiting this side of Fonterutoli, to let him know they were passing through Castellina. That put them about seven kilometers, or just over four miles away. *Did they know exactly where they wanted the incident to happen?* The logistics would be complicated. It turned out to be almost mid-way from Castellina.

*****

Antonio drove on to Castellina and checked in at each of the businesses fronting the road that might have seen the man on the motorcycle, or the red Alfa afterwards. His first few inquiries were dead ends, but his luck returned when he found a woman in a pizzeria who had noticed the motorcycle and wondered about it. She told him she always wanted a Ducati so it caught her attention. She was somewhere past her prime. His mind conjured an image of her full-framed body on a Ducati with her grey-streaked ponytail blowing in the wind. It made him smile. She was eager to share the story with him, not even knowing who he was or why he was asking. She spoke English with a heavy accent and grand gestures of her hands. It sounded like she was from the south, possibly Naples.

"I wondered why the man did not take his helmet off, or get off his bike, eh? He just kept starin' up the road for a long time. I was workin' … cleaning the tables before we opened. I wasn't watchin' the whole time, but every time I looked it was the same thing. Must have been twenty minutes. I figured he was waitin' for somebody. Then I saw him open the visor to use his phone… took his glove off to dial. After he finished his call … he took off that way." She pointed south.

More dumb luck? he wondered, *or help from above.* He tended to believe more in providence than luck.

"Did you get a look at his face while his visor was up?"

"Not much. he appeared to be on the young side of middle-age, maybe a little shorter than you, probably Italiano. And I think he had a mustache."

Antonio thanked her. She also enjoyed playing detective.

They chatted for a few minutes. He found out she and her husband owned the place. He ordered a salsiccia pizza with mozzarella di bufala for a late lunch. He ate half and took the rest in a box. It was fabulous. The crust was perfect and the locally made sausage was perfectly spiced. He had owned his own pizzeria for almost nine years now, but he still never tired of good pizza.

*****

Antonio had one more thing to do before heading back to Siena. He asked where he might find a tabaccheria. She told him there were two in town and sent him to her favorite. "It's owned by an honest man," she said.

He walked the few blocks, past the market with its beautiful produce on display outside, past a trattoria where diners were enjoying a late lunch al fresco, and found the tabaccheria, its name etched on the glass door surrounded by a weathered wood door frame. The bell rang when he entered. A tabby cat brushed past him, heading out the door. The aroma of tobacco hung in the air. The stooped and greying proprietor looked him up and down, then nodded. Antonio showed him the cigarette butts and asked if he knew the brands.

The man eyed him curiously. "Why?" he asked gruffly.

"I'm investigating an altercation ... trying to find a man. He hurt a young woman, then fled. I think one of them belongs to her attacker." Antonio knew that Italian men, particularly older ones, were men of gallantry. Hurting women was not something they condoned. He was right. The demeanor on the old guy's face transformed.

"This one that is smoked most of the way down—with no filter—it looks like a Camel. Popular in Italy. This one … it looks like a Muratti Multifilter, an Italian brand. Not so common."

He pulled out a pack and opened it for comparison. They looked identical. Antonio bought the pack, thinking that forensics could confirm. He thanked the man. As he headed for the door he heard the old man's voice behind him, "If you find this man, you let me know. Me and my friends … we'll take care of him for you."

Antonio smiled as he stepped into the sun. He had found a few pieces of the puzzle. Walking to his car, he phoned Nicolo. They agreed to meet up at the tourist parking lot outside Siena, near where the car and motorcycle were found. It was an in-between spot, and Nicolo wanted to check it out. Antonio knew that Nicolo was continuing to overstep his bounds but decided not to press the point.

Driving into the afternoon sun, Antonio got that old rush of adrenaline that often came over him in his detective years. He realized how much he missed it—the drama, putting together the puzzle pieces, without the benefit of the picture on the puzzle box to assist you. You frame the edge, then fill in the pieces. You rarely find them all. But you just needed enough to see the picture, enough to find and arrest the bad guy, and convince a judge and jury that they are guilty.

Chapter Nine

Saturday late afternoon

ntonio found Nicolo huddled with Paolo Benevente. Paolo wore a scowl and barely acknowledged him. Antonio remembered him as a much friendlier fellow. He wrote it off. Maybe it was his concern for Giulia, or pressure from Nicolo about the murder investigations, or because Nicolo was involving him in things he knew he should keep his nose out of.

He thought back to the hunting trip that Nicolo reminded him about. It was five years ago, the last time he, Randi, and the kids visited Tuscany. Paolo bagged a roe deer with a single, perfectly placed shot. The following day he brought some of the venison to the house. They used it to prepare a meat ragu which they tossed with hearty, homemade pici pasta. Antonio remembered it as one of the best pastas he had ever tasted.

Nicolo interrupted his thoughts. "Find anything?" There was weariness in his voice, and his tone didn't sound hopeful.

"A lot more than I expected, actually." Antonio told them everything he had found out. He gave Nicolo the cigarette butts, and the pack of Muratti Multifilters, now in a small plastic bag he'd gotten from the tabaccheria. He knew DNA from saliva could often be collected, but had his doubts about these because of the light rain which had fallen. Nicolo gave Marcello a call and told him about the cigarette butts and the tire tracks.

"Marcello wanted to know how you came by the cigarette butts. I told him you're a better detective than he is." He laughed. "Nah. But I did tell him the truth, and about your other findings. I think he was more angry that they missed all that, than about you being out there playing detective. He told me to remind you to be careful."

"Tell him even commoners have a right to nose around as long as they don't break any laws."

"You really want me to tell him that?" Nicolo flashed a tired but impish smile.

Antonio asked Nicolo if he could borrow the photos he showed him earlier. He wanted to go back and show them to Anselmo and the lady in the pizzeria. She said that she would be working into the evening. Nicolo handed him the envelope. "Keep them. I have extras."

Nicolo had news of his own, "One of my informants told me that the three murdered men were all working for the 'Ndrangheta, a Calabrian mob family. Have you heard of them?"

Antonio shook his head.

"Not surprised. Most Americans only know about the Cosa Nostra, the Mafioso made famous by your movie producers. At one time they were the reigning mob. No longer. Now days the 'Ndrangheta and the Camorra families have grown more powerful. We don't know much about the 'Ndrangheta operations here in Tuscany. Or who leads them. They planted roots quietly in Firenze several years ago. A couple of years ago they expanded operations to Siena. Apparently, they were trying to take back some of Pucci's territory with him in prison. I arrested one of their guys several months ago for trafficking and prostitution. He stuck to their code of silence—*omerta* they call it. We couldn't get a thing out of him, even though it might have kept him out of prison."

"You say those guys come from Calabria? And the Camorra family that Pucci is part of comes from Naples?"

"Yeah. I'm afraid Naples is famous for more than pizza these days."

Antonio shook his head, reminded once again that the Tuscany of his youth, and its innocence—or at least how he remembered it—were disappearing.

"After we're done, I'm going to meet an old friend, Marco Calore, a Spaniard, who works for Europol. He's a good man, very bright. We've made him aware of the murders. Now it's time we get them more involved. They have resources we do not have. I'll have Paolo take these cigarette butts and the pack to the forensic lab at the Carabinieri. Maybe we'll get lucky."

"Is there any concern Europol will take over your investigation?"

"No, no. They're not like your FBI. These guys are more of a resource. They don't plow their way in and push the locals aside."

"Will they be working on the murders, or on finding Pucci?"

"Both. But let's not talk about that."

They walked the kilometer or so to where the car and motorcycle had been abandoned. There were no CCTV cameras covering the road there, probably why the attackers chose that spot to abandon them. As they walked back to the parking lot, it occurred to them that someone might have been waiting to pick them up. It was possible that they parked in the lot, which did have camera coverage.

Nicolo looked at Paolo. "When you stop at the Carabinieri, ask Bianchi if they've checked those, and other cameras nearby."

Paolo, still looking grim, nodded and walked off.

Nicolo and Antonio agreed to meet back at the house later for dinner. Antonio was relieved that Nicolo agreed to take Sofia home for the night.

*****

Antonio, found Anselmo still at work in the formal garden in front of the Mazzei estate house. He was trimming the boxwood hedges. The grand iron gates were locked.

81

He called a greeting to Anselmo who turned, grinned, and headed his way. Before he arrived, two brown and white, long-haired dogs greeted Antonio. They stood on their hind feet with their front paws on the gate. Seeing they were friendly, Antonio reached his hands through to scratch them. He didn't know the breed, but they were fine-looking dogs. When Anselmo opened the gate they circled excitedly, but did not jump on him. They were well trained.

The gardens, surrounded by a two-foot-high stone wall, were impeccably manicured. Anselmo took immense pride in his work. The centuries-old stone house featured one of those doors you see in photographs, made of heavy wood with a curved half-circle, known as a lunette, on the top. It was framed by ivy that climbed the stone wall to the second story. Looking around, Antonio saw that the light had changed on the surrounding hills. It was warmer and the shadows more distinct between the perfectly aligned rows of the vineyards. Siena was now awash in the light of the golden hour.

They made small talk for a few minutes, about how Anselmo was getting the garden ready for autumn, and the heavy rain expected in a couple of days. Anselmo's face lit up when Antonio reminded him that he was Nicolo and Sofia's nephew.

"Aaahhh. I know them well. Sofia was just a teenager when I first came to work here. Now I remember you, a little lad, coming with your mother, Elena. Then you came to visit with your wife and family. I hope they are well."

Antonio couldn't bring himself to tell him about his loss right now. Maybe another day. He wondered if his face betrayed him.

Anselmo grew somber. "I heard that Giulia was in a cycling accident with her cousin." A light dawned in his eyes. "That must have been you."

"I'm afraid it was. Please keep her in your prayers. We are very worried."

"We are. We are. My wife and I go to the chapel every night to light a candle for her. We'll do so until she returns from the darkness." Antonio thought of the little village chapel, a long stone's-throw from where they stood. "She's a beautiful and charming girl. Have faith my friend. Have faith. God placed his light in her for others to see. I don't believe he will let it be extinguished yet."

Antonio found unexpected strength in his words. He wished he still had faith like that.

He showed Anselmo the photographs, hoping for recognition, but there was none. But Anselmo reminded him how distant the man had been. Antonio thanked him and was about to leave.

"But I must ask, I've been wondering since you left, what this is about? Does this have to do with the accident? These drivers! They drive like crazy people. They treat these winding roads like their own grand prix course. Did that driver cause this?"

"I think so. The car fits the description." Antonio didn't want to give away too much at this point.

"You find this man, Antonio! I will bury him in the vineyard. Rotting bodies make excellent fertilizer, you know."

Antonio couldn't tell if he was serious or joking. Either way, it made him smile. "*Grazie*, Anselmo, *mille grazie*! You've been a great help."

Anselmo looked at Antonio. He seemed to stand more erect. His eyes glistened as he flashed a crooked smile. Antonio knew that being able to help meant a great deal to him.

*****

Antonio climbed gingerly back into his little Lancia and drove the winding road to Castellina. The sun was near setting now and the partly cloudy sky lit up in pinks, corals, oranges, and multiple shades of purple-grey. A brisk breeze kept the clouds on the run. The stone on the buildings seemed to absorb the colors, giving them a magical feel.

He parked and crossed the road to where the motorcycle had been sitting, something he neglected to do earlier. The woman from the pizzeria came out and leaned on the pole supporting their striped awning. She waved to him and smiled. He found nothing of interest and walked across the street to greet her.

"*Ciao, ciao bell'amico mio!*" she greeted him flirtatiously. He smiled and, when he came near, she hugged him painfully and kissed him on the cheek. "I'm so glad you came back. Not much excitin' happens around here you know. What's this I hear about a young woman bein' harmed?"

Antonio wasn't surprised that she had heard. News travels fast in a small town.

"Was it Sofia an' Nicolo's daughter, Giulia? I've known them for years. I heard she's in the hospital in a coma ... a cycling accident," she said with genuine concern. But then her tone changed, "Was that bastard on the motorcycle involved?"

Antonio wasn't sure how he wanted to answer, not wanting to fuel the fire. He knew he'd never want to cross this woman. She looked like she wanted to find the guy on the Ducati and go after him with a meat cleaver.

"That's what we are trying to find out, signora. I am assisting my uncle Nicolo."

"*Si, si*! You must be his nephew from Seattle ... the detective turned pizza maker. It's a great honor to make your acquaintance." Her eyes twinkled at him and she put her hand on his arm and squeezed, unaware of the serious pain she was inflicting. "I will help you any way I can."

Antonio pulled out the photographs to show her. He knew it was a long shot since she only saw him with the visor up for a moment. She looked through them carefully. For a moment, she pointed to a man with a mustache but then shook her head no. "Maybe him, but I don't think so."

Antonio thanked her, being careful not to let his eyes linger on hers, not wanting to encourage her flirtations. As he was leaving, she called after him, "If you catch this *bastardo,* you let me have first crack at him. I will cut off his balls, put them on a pizza and make him eat them!"

They were both chuckling as he walked back across the street in the failing light of the day. He hoped for this man's sake that he didn't fall into the hands of the locals. But then again …

Chapter Ten

Saturday evening

It was dark, but Antonio knew the road well, so he drove briskly. The Lancia hugged these winding Tuscan roads like a glove. He was desperate for some Tylenol. He'd forgotten to bring any with him. The pain was becoming hard to bear, but had one benefit. It kept his senses sharp.

When he arrived at the house, the first thing he did after taking three Tylenol was clean and re-dress his wounds. By the time he finished, Nicolo had arrived with Sofia and Chiara. This was the first time Nicolo had been home since Elena arrived. Antonio smiled as he watched them together. It didn't take a detective to see how much he adored and respected his big sister. After a warm embrace, she squeezed her fingers on her nose like a clothespin and shooed him off to shower. He heard her mumble, "You boys, it's a good thing I came to take care of you."

The brothers, Raphe and Leonardo, arrived next. Raphael looked haggard, like he hadn't slept, though his clothes looked like he'd slept in them. Leonardo looked marginally better. *I really need to find out what these guys are up to,* Antonio thought.

Alessia and Frankie had helped Elena cook before they left for the hospital. It was a simple dinner: Hunter's Wife's Chicken, one of Antonio's favorites, served over polenta, with a side of sautéed greens with cipollini onions, and pine nuts. The boys brought a box of hazelnut biscotti from the local bakery.

They sat at the table for well over an hour. It was a happy distraction watching the siblings together, listening to their stories about growing up together. They often remembered things differently. There was much good-natured sparring over who remembered the story correctly. Being the youngest, Nicolo always seemed to lose to his big sisters.

Their father, Nonno Tomasso, passed away at age ninety. He'd been strong like an ox until his final months. After the war, he took work as a stone mason. Antonio recalled spending time with him as a child. Nonno would point out work he had done … houses and stone walls he had built. He was a humble man, but when it came to his work, he took great pride. Their own land was contoured with walls he built to terrace the vineyards, olive trees, and fruit trees. In his later years, when his back was too old for such work, he managed vineyards for the Mazzei family. He died of a stroke in his own vineyard. It took a family search party to find him when he didn't come home for lunch. Antonio idolized the man.

Their mother, Nonna Valentina, was just seventeen when she met and married Tommaso. She gave birth to Elena ten months later. She and little Elena lived with her parents while Tommaso was off fighting. She told stories of baking bread to feed the resistance fighters, whom they occasionally hid in their barn. She later confessed that she was raped by a German officer in that same barn one night, a secret she kept from Tomasso long after the Germans left. She carried a knife in her garter for the remainder of the war, and swore it would never happen again, even if it cost her life.

The years after the war were extremely hard. Poverty took its toll, and food was scarce. She told her children she was five foot, five inches in her youth but weighed a mere eighty pounds when the war ended. She grew shorter and shorter over the years. She wasn't much over five foot when she died.

Following the war, little-by-little they built a new life for themselves through toil and hard work. And they always maintained a deep respect for the Americans who drove the Germans from their soil and gave them their land back.

Like most Tuscan women of her day, Nonna Valentina was an exceptional cook. They had the uncanny ability of creating something wonderful with extraordinarily little. The simplicity of the cuisine, born from necessity, later became known as *cucina povera*. Nothing was wasted. Every part of an animal was used. And stale bread always found its way into other dishes.

Antonio learned to cook, tied to the apron strings of his nonna and aunts. Cooking and hospitality became a natural part of him. He knew this had a lot to do with his decision to open an Italian restaurant. It was a dramatic shift from the twenty years he'd spent as a policeman and detective. But he loved it.

Nonna ruled the kitchen until her final months, still making homemade bread, pasta, and ragu, despite the arthritic pain in her gnarled fingers. When summer came to an end she would gather with friends and neighbors to preserve that which they grew in their gardens. She was a force to be reckoned with.

Valentina surprised Antonio when at age ninety-three she traveled to Seattle for the memorial service for Randi and Christina. She was a devout Catholic. Her faith was unshakeable. He recalled how she came to him after the memorial service. She placed her weathered hands on his cheeks and looked him in the eyes, "You know that your girls are with God now, in a place full of joy and laughter." Her tone changed, "It's nonsense what people say … *they're in a better place.* It is so much more than that! They are in a paradise we cannot imagine, better than the garden of Eden. Soon I will go to be with them. I'll be young and beautiful again. And someday, hopefully many, many years from now, you will come to be with us."

She died peacefully less than a year later. Every now and then, an image would come to his mind—of Randi, Christina, and a young, beautiful Nonna Valentina, laughing together in a garden, the morning sun burning away the mist. He wondered … were these images just his imagination, a fantasy concocted in his mind, a heart reaching for comfort? But they seemed so real. Could they possibly be a gift to help him believe … to get past his anger with God? He didn't know the answer, but he found hope and comfort in them, and courage to get out of bed in the morning.

*****

After dinner, Sofia tried to do the dishes, but Raphael and Leonardo kicked her out. She settled on clearing the table and wiping a few counters but then Antonio and Nicolo chased her off from that too. Antonio smiled at the scene. She spent a little time with Chiara and Elena, then wandered off to bed.

Nicolo, Antonio, Raphael, and Leonardo opened a bottle of homemade vin santo and retired to the living room. They figured it would be just the guys, but Chiara and Elena showed up with empty glasses to join them. They wanted to know what was going on with the investigation.

Nicolo let Antonio explain about his discoveries. Then Nicolo brought them up to date about the murder investigations, and about the meeting with Marco Calore. Marco committed Europol's resources to help. He also had new information received from his detectives, Paolo, Mancini, and Jordy.

"My guys called on the Guardia di Finanza. They handle most of the major drug smuggling operations in Italy." He looked at Antonio. "I'd been hesitant to involve them. I've worked with them in the past. They're a real pain in the derriere—but useful, and in this case necessary." He dipped his biscotti in vin santo. "They found out some new information about the 'Ndrangheta family and their operations in Siena."

He took a bite of biscotti then continued, "The local Laganà clan are members of the larger 'Ndrangheta family of Calabria. Their Tuscan base is Firenze. Recently they've begun to expand their influence southward to Siena. They're involved in all the usual: drugs, racketeering, loan sharking, money laundering. A few months ago, they had a major setback when investigators discovered they were laundering money through more than a dozen restaurants they owned in Firenze. They shut 'em down."

"How do you think this ties in?" Elena asked. Antonio smiled at his mother's tenacity. Her mind was as sharp as ever.

"That's what we're trying to figure out. Paolo has put two theories on the table: one, that the Pucci family has gone to war with the Laganà clan. The second, that the Nigerian mob is involved. The Nigerians have made significant inroads into Italy and Tuscany in recent years. Their focus is human trafficking and prostitution, mainly Nigerian girls. But they also pipeline drugs, mostly heroin from Afghanistan. The rise of their influence, and other immigration concerns—legal and illegal—has brought about quite a political backlash."

Chiara nodded, "He's right. It has caused a political swing to the right, and the government to adopt a closed-door immigration policy."

Antonio knew Chiara had a keen interest in Italian politics, no easy task in a country whose political landscape is in a near-constant state of flux, bordering on insanity.

Antonio added his two cents, "Both theories seem to have credence. But if the families are at war, you would think there would have been revenge killings by now."

"I agree," added Nicolo. "Possible they are planning something even now. Could get ugly."

Raphael and Leonardo had been quiet, glancing at each other occasionally. Antonio could tell they had something to say. He marveled at how these two got along as adults, considering they fought all the time as kids. Their personalities were like fire and water. Raphael, the tall lanky one, was serious and quick tempered; Leonardo, a fun-loving, talkative, free spirit. You could see it in his hairstyle, short on the sides and long and wavy on top, and the eclectic clothes he wore. He was about three inches shorter than Raphael. Little seemed to bother him. That is, until someone put his sister in a coma.

When Nicolo paused, Antonio looked at them and asked, "What have you two been up to?"

Raphael spoke first, "Leonardo and I got up early this morning and made a trip to Roma." He paused until everyone was looking at him. "I had asked Marcello

Bianchi if they talked to the Europcar agent who rented out the vehicles. He said the employee had been off duty and hadn't been answering her cell phone."

He looked at Leonardo like he was passing the soccer ball. "We went to the Europcar rental place. We had to wait a few hours for the woman to come on duty. But we got a description of the man who rented the car and motorcycle. Only one problem. The description is pretty generic ... Italian male, mid-to-late thirties, about 5'10", medium weight and build, neatly trimmed beard, no obvious birthmarks, scars, tattoos. Describes half the guys I know."

"You get her name and number?" Nicolo asked.

Raphael nodded. "And her schedule too." He held out a piece of paper with the description and the other information.

"*Rigazzi pazzo!*" Nicolo tried to give them a stern look but his smiling eyes betrayed him. "Give me that. I'll follow up ... pass the info to Marcello. He's not going to be happy, but that's his problem. They need to get someone down there to show her photographs; and if none are identified, have her meet with a sketch artist. But listen, you guys need to talk to me before you do any more detective work. Got it?"

They nodded but Antonio had a feeling that wasn't going to happen.

Elena asked a string of questions: Did they agree with Paolo's theories? Had they considered other possibilities? Or were they working with the assumption that the murders and the road incident were related, and that Pucci was responsible for both? She added, "I've heard you both say, 'You have to consider all possibilities, that it's not always the most obvious, that if you focus on proving your theory you might miss the real truth.'"

Antonio remembered that his father used to preach this.

Nicolo just nodded, looking tired and overwhelmed.

Then Chiara asked, "How do you manage an investigation with so many agencies involved? My God, it seems impossible."

"Yeah, it's a mess," Nicolo acknowledged, "but there are reasons why it is set up this way." He briefly explained the agencies and their roles. "When problems arise, it's usually egos, or lousy communication, one hand not knowing what the other is doing. Usually both. Someone wants to grab all the glory, so they don't share what they know."

He paused. Antonio saw he was starting to fade.

"One reason I've been successful is I've made friends in every agency. I keep 'em close … cook for them, take them hunting, share my homemade wine. I take good care of them and they take care of me." He stood up, ready to go to bed.

Before he left the room, Elena had the final word. "I'm worried about you guys. Please be careful. This is the Mafioso you're up against. Killing is sport for them. We don't need any more of you in the hospital ..." she added a pregnant pause, "or the morgue. I've been to enough funerals lately."

*****

Antonio headed for bed. He mused about how impressed he was with his eighty-year-old mother, her insight, sense of justice, and family loyalty. From somewhere in his imagination, an image popped into his head—his mother, standing in front of a mob boss, a .38 in her hand—telling him, "Don't mess with my family." He laughed out loud.

Moments before his head hit the pillow, he got a call from his son Jonathan. He wanted to know how he was, and how Giulia was doing. Antonio was happy to hear his voice. Their relationship was strained for years. It finally took a turn for the better when Jonathan married Leah.

Antonio gave him the brief version, too tired to elaborate. He asked him if he could call Shane and fill him in. Shane was Alessia's son, and the manager of Antonio's restaurant. "Let him know I'll probably be gone longer than the two weeks I planned."

"I will. And Dad, I've been worried about you. I know you're hurt, and now you've got yourself involved in this investigation. I hope you and Zio Nicolo will be careful."

"We will be, son. We will. Give my love to Leah."

Antonio went to bed in good spirits. He slept better, though it was difficult finding a comfortable position to sleep in. No matter how he lay, something hurt. If he had any dreams, he didn't remember them.

Chapter Eleven

Sunday morning

Antonio woke early, stiff and sore but feeling more rested. He opened the curtains and the French doors of the second-floor bedroom and was welcomed by brilliant rays of sunlight as the sun peeked over the hills. The world felt like a more hopeful place than it did a day ago.

He decided to try some push-ups. He did two and collapsed in pain. His ribs screamed bloody murder. *God, that was stupid*, he thought. *I guess I'll go for a walk before breakfast. I need to clear my head and think.* He showered and re-dressed his wounds. They were beginning to look better. There was a chill in the morning air so he donned a collarless shirt, lightweight charcoal sweater, and a clean pair of blue jeans. He'd need to pre-treat the ones he wore yesterday to get out the blood stains where his bandages leaked.

He headed east from the house, downhill on a gravel path which took him past the vineyards, to the hills beyond. He loved the way the vineyards, olive groves, farmland, and woods all intersected here. Agriculture in Tuscany was not like the huge conglomerates which had taken over America, focused on producing huge quantities of cheap food. Italians had a deeper respect for the land. They nearly always left a portion of land natural. He took heart that a reversal was taking place in America, with smaller, organic farms cropping up.

Starting out, he was joined by Nicolo's hunting dog, Bella. She was just a puppy on his last visit, falling all over herself. He knelt down and scratched her neck under the chin. She sat contentedly. Nicolo trained her well. She was of a breed known as Bracco Italiana, an Italian Pointer. Her medium-sized body was beige with large milk chocolate spots. She had long brown droopy ears and eyes that reminded him of a Basset Hound.

She wandered all over, ahead and behind Antonio as he walked. He was happy for the company, one who would not distract his thoughts with words. The walking began to work out some of his soreness.

Climbing a hill into the woods, and out the other side, gave him a commanding view of the countryside. He could see Fonterutoli to the south, and Siena miles away beyond that. To the north, he could see Castellina in Chianti. Here and there wineries and small hamlets sat atop hilltops. A soft breeze kicked up, bringing a faint smell of wood smoke. The coolness of the breeze made him glad he'd opted for the sweater.

Morning light on a sunny morning was his favorite. There was a purity about it. Soon the autumn would bring morning mist and fog with its own unique beauty. From this vantage point, it seemed that Chianti and Tuscany still had her purity and innocence. It was how he'd always thought of it, especially when he was away. Had it truly possessed that innocence, or had he just been young and naïve? When did the ugly side invade it? The sordidness of drugs, murders, human trafficking, and prostitution were like a huge, repulsive boil on a beautiful woman. But humans have a way of scarring the most beautiful of God's creations.

He sat down on a rock and thought about his life, now so different than he'd imagined it. His genes and upbringing had given him a natural optimism. It miraculously survived his years as a detective. But things can change in a heartbeat. The first serious challenge came with the injury that brought his detective career to a sudden halt. But that was nothing compared to the loss of Randi and Christina. And yet, the way his family, friends, and even people he hardly knew came alongside him reinforced that most people are essentially good.

Randi and Christina's death occurred at the hand of a Muslim extremist. Antonio's first reaction was extreme anger, bordering on hatred toward people of the Muslim faith. But he knew down deep that wasn't right. A week after the memorial, when all his family had returned home, his Iranian Muslim neighbors, Hassan and Dilshad, showed up at his door. They brought meals and compassionate hearts. That was the day he knew he could not hate someone just because they believed differently than he did.

One important lesson this life had taught him was that all men have the potential for good, as well as evil. He remembered one of his favorite quotes, by Sitting Bull, a Native American, who said, "Inside of me there are two dogs. One is mean and evil and the other is good, and they fight each other all the time." When someone asked him which dog wins, he answered wisely, "The one I feed the most." Antonio believed this was true of all men. We all make our choices, what we value in life, how we let ourselves think. Those beliefs lead us down the paths of life. None of us is all good, nor completely evil.

On his way back to the house, Antonio circled around through some of the vineyards. He rarely came this time of year. He thought it might be his favorite, with the ripe clusters of grapes, and the celebration of harvest.

The loop took him and Bella to the road which ran near the property—the small, lightly traveled road which ran through Fonterutoli and on to Castellina. They were just within view of the house when Bella stopped her sniffing and pawed at something on the ground by a tree. She didn't want to give it up, so Antonio bent down to see what it was. He picked up a cigarette butt. It looked identical to the one he'd taken to the tabaccheria, a Muratti Multifilter. It seemed just a few days old. A chill ran down his spine. *Someone was watching the house. Possibly the same man. Was he watching when Giulia and I left on our ride? From this distance, he could easily have mistaken me for Nicolo.*

*****

When he arrived back at the house, he was welcomed by the aroma of coffee. Croissants, fruits and jams were laid out for a light breakfast.

Sofia and Nicolo were moving slow. He suspected they had not slept well. Lines of worry creased their faces. It felt so different from the joy and energy that usually filled this home.

Nicolo told him he had already called Marcello Bianchi and Marco Calore with the descriptions Raphael and Leonardo gave them. It would be Marcello's job to keep the Guardia di Finanza in the loop.

Antonio poured some coffee and loaded a plate with croissants and fruit. "Call them again, Nicolo. I found this alongside the road, at the one spot in view of the house. Actually, it was Bella who found it." He handed him the cigarette butt which was wrapped in a tissue from his pocket.

*****

Sofia insisted that she and the family go to mass before returning to the hospital. "We will go and pray," she said resolutely, "and light a candle for Giulia." The whole family was going so Antonio decided to join them. He told himself it was out of respect. He was not Catholic but had deep respect for their faith. There were many Catholic churches in the area, but Sofia was partial to the little chapel in Fonterutoli, where she grew up, and was known by all.

They arrived and took their seats in the wooden pews. Antonio looked around. Across the chapel he saw Anselmo with a silver-haired woman he assumed to be his wife. She carried her chin high and her posture so erect that she looked statuesque. He remembered what Anselmo had told him, about lighting a candle here each evening. *I must remember to tell Sofia.*

It felt awkward to be in a church again. He once considered himself a man of faith. But his trust in God had been shattered, along with his heart. He realized he had not stepped inside a church since the memorial service.

Outside after mass, it seemed like every person there came to Sofia and Nicolo to give hugs, and tell them they were praying for Giulia, and for them. Antonio stood aside, watching politely. When the crowd was gone, he rejoined them. He related to Sofia what Anselmo, told him about the candles. She looked at him, her eyes wet with tears. "He's right, you know. The light is still in her. I can see it. I know she will find her way home to us."

*****

After mass, the entire family went to the hospital. They brushed past the nurses who tried to stop them, promising most of them would be gone soon. The family surrounded Giulia. They said prayers and spoke words of love to her—telling her how much they missed her and wanted her back with them.

The doctor's prognosis remained grim. It didn't matter to Sofia. She had found her peace. She said it came upon her when she lit the candle at mass.

Antonio took a last look at Giulia before leaving. He thought about what Anselmo told him about the light in her. It was still there—but barely a flicker. *God, please, please. I'll do whatever you want me to do. Just re-kindle the light in her.*

Chapter Twelve

Sunday afternoon & evening

Sofia and Elena planned to spend the afternoon at the hospital. The brothers offered to take the evening shift so the rest of the family could have Sunday dinner together. Alessia drove aunts Chiara and Frankie back to the house. Raphael and Leonardo left to have lunch with a friend. Antonio's gut told him they were up to something.

Sofia would have preferred for Nicolo and Antonio to take a day of rest. But relaxing was out of the question for them. They put their heads together, discussing what could be done. There was no way to get information from forensics today, and Marcello and Gabriella were taking the rest of the day off. Nicolo decided they would go to the questura to pick up the files on Sandro Pucci.

Nicolo was driving his personal car—a classic red 1960 Alfa Romeo Giuletta Spider Veloce—an exceedingly rare car. There were only 1,200 produced. It was his baby. He kept it in immaculate condition and only took it out on nice days like today.

Winding his way through the back streets of Siena, Nicolo told Antonio about the rest of his conversation with Marco that morning. "Europol is monitoring phone and internet communications, looking for clues as to Pucci's whereabouts. They're also doing cross references with companies thought to be connected to the family, looking for any information—properties owned— anything. Details. Details. That's what Europol is good at."

Nicolo downshifted and slowed around a corner onto a narrow street immersed in shadow. "They found something else quite interesting. There's a ship scheduled to arrive in Livorno on Tuesday from Colombia. They've intercepted suspicious internet chatter. He thinks there might be drugs onboard. There could be a connection. The Puccis have been known to bring in cocaine from Colombia. He suggested a joint sting operation with the Carabinieri and Guardia di Finanza. With luck, they might catch Pucci or members of the family. If it's not them, it could be the Camorras. Either way, they might capture a sizable cache of drugs before they hit the streets."

Nicolo parked near the questura. They walked a block down a sunny avenue to get a panini to tide them over until dinner. Antonio ordered one with prosciutto, fresh mozzarella, and arugula. The bread was very fresh. Walking back to the questura, they saw Paolo driving away. It did not appear that he saw them. Antonio thought it odd.

"Does Paolo usually work Sundays?"

"I don't know. I hardly ever come here on a Sunday. But I've heard he stopped going to church with Gemma and Bettina. Maybe he comes to work while they're at church."

Why would he stop attending church with his family? Antonio wondered, before considering the hypocrisy of his question. *Like I should talk.*

Inside, Nicolo collected the case book and signed it out. Being Commissario allowed him access to files otherwise tightly controlled. They would take this back to the house. Before heading back, they walked past the panini shop to Nicolo's favorite gelateria. The staff knew him by name. Nicolo ordered pistachio. It looked good so Antonio broke tradition and ordered the same. It was delicious, but he missed his frutta di bosco.

*****

The cool, crisp morning turned into a perfect afternoon. They decided to work on the terrazza, with a bottle of Vernaccia di San Gimignano wine on ice. Antonio loved being outdoors, and the terrazza, with its view, was possibly his favorite place in the world. Nicolo and the boys had enlarged the area paved in stone, and built low stone walls. It was Sofia's touch that turned it into a masterpiece though, a slice of Italian heaven. There were pots of dwarf lemon, and kumquat trees, herbs, geraniums, and other flowers. On one end, honeysuckle vines climbed up an arbor, which led to a short gravel path. The path wound its way to a wooden gate, the entrance to the walled vegetable garden, where statues of majestic angels stood guard against evil. Antonio thought about the summer when Nonna Valentina talked Nonno Tomasso into building the wall to keep the deer and rabbits out. Antonio, just ten years old at the time, spent hours each day sweating alongside him. The memory made him miss his grandfather.

Adding to the serenity was a fountain just off the terrazza. The soft trickle of water, often accompanied by the songs of the birds who came to bathe in it, could soothe a troubled soul.

There were two outdoor tables: a large rectangular table of weathered wood, and a smaller table for more intimate gatherings. The small table was inlaid with ceramic tiles, hand-painted by Sofia. Nicolo and Antonio now sat at the larger table, giving them room to spread out.

"Hardly feels like work, sitting out here drinking wine," Antonio said.

Nicolo grunted as he opened the thick file.

They each took a stack of papers to delve through. Antonio occasionally asked Nicolo for clarification. His Italian was rusty after five years away. It didn't help that every detective has their own secret codes—abbreviations, and comments particular to their culture.

As they worked, they could hear the sounds of the women cooking. Chiara made her way to the garden to harvest Swiss chard and cherry tomatoes. She told them they were making chard-ricotta gnocchi, to be served with a sauce of grilled cherry tomatoes, the last of the season, with basil and extra virgin olive oil.

Alessia came out and barked orders like General Patton, "When you guys get done, clean out the fire pit under the grill and be ready to start a fire while I pick up Sofia and Elena. I made a trip to the butcher. You're grilling Tuscan beef tonight."

Antonio crossed his arms and stared at her until she got the message. "Pleeeease," she added sarcastically.

Antonio nodded and smiled.

Not much was discovered in the files. Nicolo wrote down the names of some known associates, most of whom ran seemingly legitimate businesses thought to be money laundering fronts for Pucci.

Antonio found a hand-scribbled note. "Tell me about this, Nicolo. It says, *Pucci-mistress-Mirabella Antonelli*. There's an address in Siena, and a phone number."

"I forgot about her," Nicolo said, with interest. "We never needed to call upon her in our previous investigation."

Nicolo phoned Marco, apologizing for bothering him on a Sunday. He gave him the information about the associates and their businesses. He also told him about Mirabella. He gave him her last known address and cell number and asked if they could monitor her phone activity.

All afternoon a question was nagging at Antonio. He finally got up the nerve to ask. "Nicolo. All three murders occurred while Pucci was in prison. Are you after him because he escaped, or because you think he's the reason Giulia is in a coma? If it's the latter, shouldn't you leave it alone and let the Carabinieri handle it?"

Nicolo scowled, "You don't need to keep reminding me that I'm pushing the edge on this. Pucci may or may not have hurt Giulia. And he may or may not have ordered these murders. Or maybe he's just hiding out. Whichever it is, I'm going after the bastard until someone stops me."

Antonio locked eyes with him, gauging his frame of mind. "I'm only doing what you asked me to do."

"I know. I know. But look who's talking. You haven't exactly been lying low. We'll be fine as long as we don't let our emotions get the better of us ... do something rash."

"Agreed. Are we going to check out this mistress?"

"Tomorrow. But we should ask Marcello and Gabriella if they want to join us. They should. But that might leave you out."

*****

Antonio and Nicolo finished the bottle of Vernaccia as they grilled the beef. They talked about the grand adventures they had together as kids. The evening meal turned out spectacular. The flavor of the homemade gnocchi was so fresh and vibrant. The beef, from the Chianina cows of Tuscany, was just to Antonio's liking, with a beautiful smoky char, and a pink, juicy interior, and so tender you could almost cut it with a fork.

The mood had begun to shift. The difficult circumstances were drawing this already- close-knit family even closer together. Sofia's newfound courage seemed to strengthen them all.

They talked about Giulia more than they had, telling many stories of her childhood. Antonio laughed as they recounted her attempts to date boys who were most often scared off—or just plain scared of—her big brothers. *Poor girl*, Antonio thought.

Sofia looked at Antonio, as if to apologize for what she was about to say. "You know how much she loved Randi and Christina. She looked up to Christina so much. She wanted to be just like her. After you guys would go home to Seattle, she would mope around here for days. That trip we made to Paris to visit her," she paused, "it was all she could talk about for months. They were probably the happiest days of her life."

"She told me that over coffee," he hesitated, "the morning we went riding."

Antonio looked at his mother, Elena. She dabbed at a tear that ran down her cheek. She bit her lip and raised her chin. In the midst of his own pain, he often forgot how close the bond can be between grandparent and grandchild. Now that he was going to be a grandfather, he was beginning to understand, and he hadn't even met them yet.

Chapter Thirteen

Monday morning

Once again, Antonio awoke to pain. He pulled off his bandage wraps and frowned, seeing that his left leg didn't look right. He was afraid it was getting infected. He found Aunt Frankie and showed it to her. She agreed and told him to soak the leg in warm water for about twenty minutes, clean it thoroughly, and treat it with alcohol. It was going to hurt. She was right.

Before re-bandaging he showered, doing his best to keep the stinging spray from making a direct hit on his wounds. He shaved for the first time since arriving. He typically only shaved two to three times a week. Every now and then he tried growing a beard but got annoyed at how grey it was, so always ended up shaving it off, except for the soul patch on his chin.

The kitchen was quiet. Frankie was nowhere to be found and the other ladies had yet to show their faces. Nicolo sat at the table, staring into his cup of coffee, looking marginally better. As Antonio poured himself a cup, Nicolo told him he had received a call from Marcello.

"Their forensics team finished analyzing the car and motorcycle. I'm going to meet him and Gabriella at the forensics lab to go over the results, and pass along the other cigarette butt Bella found by the road. I told him about Pucci's mistress. That got his attention. They're going to meet us for lunch later, then we'll pay her a visit."

Antonio heard his stomach growl. He found some grapes, a few paper-thin slices of prosciutto, and a day-old croissant. It would have to do for now. As he was scrounging for food, he heard Nicolo phone Paolo and ask him to arrange a team meeting with Mancini, Jordy, and himself later that morning.

Nicolo ended his call and poured more coffee in his cup. "I need a favor," he said. "Alessia slept late. I need you to take Sofia and Frankie to the hospital to relieve the boys."

Antonio nodded silently, but felt like he had been shuttled to the sideline.

*****

The Lancia was cramped with the three of them. Antonio parked and followed the ladies up to see Giulia. He almost made it into the room when the brothers stopped him in the corridor. Leonardo looked around to make sure no one was listening. He spoke quietly.

"Remember we met a friend for lunch yesterday?" Antonio nodded. "He's the chef at Osteria Giovanni, a restaurant in Siena." Leonardo leaned in and lowered his voice even further, "He thinks the restaurant might be owned by Pucci."

His eyes darted around and his voice sounded conspiratorial, causing Antonio to question what he was hearing. "What makes…?"

"He's been the chef there about a year. Before Pucci went to prison, he ate there two or three times a week. The guy who runs the place is Giovanni. Luca assumed he was the owner … you know … the name. But whenever Pucci showed up, Giovanni always pandered to him—never charged him for his meal—even if it was a large group, which happened pretty regularly. Pucci acted like he owned the place. Luca didn't know who Pucci was until he saw his picture in the newspaper after his escape."

It sounded like a movie plot, but Antonio knew those usually had some basis in reality. "Maybe he does own it. Or maybe it's one of those situations where the mob extorts a business, for protection."

Raphael came into the conversation. "We thought about that, but there's more. Luca called us this morning. Giovanni told him to plan on a private dinner for twelve important guests in the banquet room tomorrow night. He asked him to prepare porchetta, and spinach and ricotta gnocchi among other things. Luca says that was one of Pucci's go-to dinners. Since he heard about Pucci's escape, he thinks he might be attending."

Antonio lips curled up. Raphael narrowed his eyes at him, "What's so funny?"

"Nothing. A mob family meeting at an Italian restaurant is so stereotypical in American movies and TV. It struck me as humorous."

Raphael wasn't amused. "Luca told us one more thing. A couple of months ago, he saw a hand-written sales ledger that Giovanni left sitting on the bar. The numbers were a lot higher than he expected. He thinks they may be laundering money through the osteria. But he's smart enough not to ask questions."

"How do you know this Luca guy?"

Leonardo answered, "We went to college together. Raphael got to know him through me. He rode on my cycling team for a couple of years. He's a trustworthy guy."

"Why did you decide to go see him? You must have had a reason."

"He said something a couple of days ago when we were out with the old team for a beer. He was kind of joking about it, but I had a feeling it was no joke. So, we invited him to lunch."

Raphael joined in again. "He's appalled at the idea of working in a restaurant run by the mob. If it's true, he said he doesn't give a damn about losing his job. He just doesn't want to put himself at risk. He thinks it would be better if the restaurant got shut down than to quit. He's afraid that might call attention to himself."

"He sounds gutsy to me. But he's right to be cautious."

*****

As Antonio was walking out the door of the hospital, he got a call from Nicolo.

"Can you meet for lunch in a couple of hours? Marcello, Gabriella, and Marco will be joining us. I thought we'd eat at ..."

"Wait, hold on. You and I need to meet first."

"Why? What's up? I have the meeting with my detectives next."

"There's something you need to hear. I'll call you back in a few minutes." He hung up before Nicolo could object.

Antonio used Google on his phone to look up a restaurant which sounded exactly right. It was highly rated and located a few doors away from Osteria Giovanni.

He called Nicolo back. "Let's meet at La Taverna di San Clemente. I'll explain why when you get there."

"I suppose. I'll tell the others to meet there at 12:30." He sounded annoyed. "I'll try to arrive an hour ahead. It might be later though."

"I'll meet you out front when you get there. We need to take a walk before lunch."

*****

Antonio was leaning on the wall outside the taverna when Nicolo arrived. He led him a half block away to a small piazza where they took a seat on an empty bench.

"In a minute you'll understand why I wanted to meet here." He told him the whole story that the boys had related. "I think there's something to it."

"You may be right. Those guys would make good detectives. Not that I want that. I just wish they'd keep their noses out of this."

"Yeah, well they feel the same about you." He looked for a reaction but got none. "I thought we could take a casual walk by Giovanni's. It's just around the corner. I considered us having lunch there, but if they figured us for cops, might set 'em on edge."

They did their little stroll, chatting casually as they walked. It turned out the osteria was closed. The sign on the door said they were closed Mondays. Not unusual. The walk past didn't tell them much, but they circled the block which gave them the lay-of-the-land. There was a narrow street which ran behind it, more of an alley really. They arrived back at the taverna about twenty minutes before the others were due. Nicolo asked for their most private table which could seat five. A man, who Antonio guessed to be the owner, brought them to a round wooden table in the back corner. Over antipasti of fried vegetables and artichokes, Nicolo filled him in on the forensic findings.

"The car was wiped clean, no fingerprints. They found some hair fibers, but they appear to have come from three different people, probably different renters of the vehicle. One of them may or may not be from the driver in the road incident. DNA could take weeks. I snuck in and personally appealed to the lab guy, Federico. I used to coach his soccer team when he and Raphael played together. Must have been twenty years ago. He promised to get it done as soon as he could."

"The motorcycle?"

"Clean. These guys were pros."

Antonio nodded. "Any idea how they got the ID of a dead man?"

"No clue."

"How was your meeting with your detectives?"

"Okay, I guess. I don't know really."

"That's a clear-cut answer."

"I kind of lost my cool." Nicolo sighed and shook his head. "They don't seem to be getting anywhere on these three murders. We talked about strategies to get them moving. I'm losing patience. Maybe the stress and lack of sleep are getting to me."

"Or maybe you should have your sons on the case," Antonio said with a half-smile.

"Yeah. They'd probably make more progress. Even though my guys have decades of experience between them."

"They're pretty damn sharp, alright," Antonio said. "Obviously got that from their mother."

"Yeah, thanks." Nicolo smiled knowingly, then narrowed his eyes. "After lunch we're going to check things out at Pucci's mistress. Marcello, Gabriella, and two of their officers will come along in case Sandro is there.

Not likely, but if he is, he'll probably have some of his guys with him."

Chapter Fourteen

Monday afternoon

Nicolo stood to greet Marco when he arrived. Antonio followed suit, and Nicolo made the introductions. Antonio could see right away why Nicolo liked the tall Spaniard. He was handsome, with dark hair and eyes, a warm smile, and impeccable manners. Antonio saw no wedding ring, but doubted the man had trouble getting a date. He looked to be about forty. His frame was slim with a muscular build. His posture spoke confidence, but with no evidence of cockiness.

Marco was just settling in when Marcello and Gabriella arrived. They rose to their feet again. Antonio felt a spark when he saw her. She let her hand linger in his as she leaned in to greet him with a kiss on each cheek. It had been so long since he'd felt any desire toward a woman. She looked even more beautiful than the last time he saw her, and carried the fresh scent of her morning bath or shower. She took the seat next to his.

None of them had eaten at this restaurant before. They opted for the daily specials. Everything was served family-style. They started with a tureen of zuppa di minestrone with the local cannellini beans and late summer vegetables, followed by a large platter of bucatini all' Amatriciana, prepared authentic to its origins from the town of Amatrice in the neighboring region of Lazio. It was delicious.

Over the meal, Nicolo and Antonio told them about Luca and the osteria. They all agreed on the same conclusion. There was a very good chance Pucci would be there.

They round-tabled their options. They could simply watch the place, and if Pucci showed up, arrest him. But if they could plant a listening device in the meeting, they might be able find out a lot of useful information. Maybe enough to take the whole family down. They knew the family might sweep the room before the meeting, so planting bugs ahead of time was too risky.

It was Gabriella who proposed the idea, "What if we had a listening device come in with the food?"

The others nodded approvingly.

"Chef Luca might know the best way to do it. I'm just concerned it might put him at risk," she said. "We'll need to ask him if he is willing."

"I'll call Leonardo, and have him ask Luca," Nicolo said. He dialed, looking around to make sure no strangers were listening in.

"*Ciao*, Leonardo. Antonio told us about your friend Luca, and the meeting. It sounds like he's a brave young man—or maybe *pazzo*! We would like to see if he is willing to talk to us." He paused a moment while Leonardo spoke. "We saw the osteria is closed today. We need to plan an operation. We would like to plant a listening device. Hold on …" He paused while a waiter walked by the table. "Anyway, we think there is a good chance they'll sweep the room before the meeting, so we're thinking it would be best if it could be brought in with the food somehow. He may know a good way to do that." There was quiet while he listened to the reply. "*Grazie*! Why don't you text me his reply? We may be busy. Oh, and ask him if he can meet up with us tonight … **yeah, at the house** … if he's willing to help."

"Leonardo will call him right now," Nicolo told them after hanging up. "I'll let you know as soon as I hear."

"We'll need approval from the magistrate," Marcello said. "I'll give her a call." He stood and walked outside to make the call. The four of them made small talk until he returned. "She gave us the go ahead," he reported. "We just need to do the paperwork for her to sign." He looked at Gabriella. She nodded.

Marco spoke, "Our people can assist with this, if you'd like. We can provide the bugs and listening van. I have one in Roma. I can have it here by morning." Marcello seized upon his offer. Marco continued, "I'll also have my team research the osteria's business license to see who is listed as owner, and see if we can get some tax records."

Marcello reported that they had mostly been doing paper trail work and checking with every source and informant they knew, looking for clues to Pucci's whereabouts. Nothing yet, but they had found out some interesting things in the process.

"The 'Ndrangheta family from Calabria, run by the Laganàs locally, has apparently been really ticked off ever since Pucci crossed into their territory." Marcello pressed his fingertips together as he spoke. "Instead of focusing on other opportunities such as prostitution, Pucci went head-to-head with them in the drug trade. After Nicolo put him in prison, they'd been trying to take back some of the ground he had intruded on. Seems to me that the murders could be tied to this family feud. There hasn't been much of that in recent years, at least not in Tuscany … feels out of place and time."

"Yeah, seems like the families have been more civil to one another in recent years, considering the amount of overlapping activity," Marco added. "But these are big egos we're dealing with, and piles of money. That can lead to anything. I think every so often the families have to fight it out before making a truce to restore the peace."

He hesitated to let that sink in, "That leads me to the subject of the ship coming into Livorno. I gave you bad info. It's not slated to dock until late Wednesday afternoon. If it has cargo for Pucci's clan, the timing of their meeting tomorrow makes sense."

They discussed a plan to observe the off-loading of the ship. Even if they arrested Pucci before then, and possibly other family members, there's no way that the cargo would be left on the dock. Someone would see that it was retrieved.

"Whatever the case," Marcello said, "the magistrate needs to be kept informed on that as well. I'm sure she'll want to involve the Guardia di Finanza. I'm surprised that the GDF chose not to get involved with the investigation of the drug murders. An operation like this is different. If they get left out, they're sure to raise a stink."

Nicolo asked, "Do you mind calling her again, Marcello, and asking her to contact the Guardia di Finanza? They'll need to pull the operation together quickly." Marcello nodded.

Marco rose a finger to the waiter, calling for the check. "I've got lunch," he said. "I have the biggest budget, backed by the entire EU."

*****

While waiting for the check, Nicolo and Marcello confirmed their plan to meet at a parking lot two blocks from where mistress Mirabella's apartment was located. Marcello's two additional Carabinieri would meet them there. It was just a few blocks from the Porta Camollia, the northernmost gate of Siena, which the Florentines rebuilt after destroying it in the siege of 1555. They inscribed it in Latin, "Siena's heart expands to let you in." It was still insulting to the Senese. To this day, there remained a strong competitive spirit with their northern neighbors.

"Can I join you?" Antonio asked, looking at Marcello, knowing it was not really his place.

"You may come along," Marcello said. "But it wouldn't be safe for you to enter the apartment unarmed. We have no idea what we'll find. But it could be helpful to have you stand watch on the street for us."

Antonio knew it was useless to ask for more. He would make the same decision. Nicolo told him he could ride with him.

As they walked to the car, Nicolo had a silly grin on his face.

"What are you smiling about, Zio?"

"You haven't noticed, Antonio? The way Gabriella seems taken with you? The way her eyes light up when she greets you? There is genuine affection there. And if I am not mistaken, I see that you are taken with her as well." Nicolo looked over and laughed. "She is a beautiful woman, Antonio. And you have more in common than you know. She is a widow. And her daughter died of leukemia when she was just fourteen. She and Giulia were friends. It was incredibly sad."

Antonio didn't tell Nicolo that he already knew all of this. He didn't want to fuel the fire.

Chapter Fifteen

Monday afternoon

They arrived at the parking lot where they were met by the two additional Carabinieri. Marcello gave instructions. They proceeded on foot to the apartment, located in a 13th century building on Via Camollia, a quiet street running southeast from the Porta Camollia gate into the old city.

Nicolo looked at Antonio. "If I had Pucci's money, I think I'd treat my mistress to something better than an old apartment—probably a villa in the hills."

"You planning on taking a mistress anytime soon?" Antonio smiled wryly, "Past your mid-life crisis, aren't you?"

"You know I'd never take a mistress. Sofia has told me more than once, 'If you ever sleep with another woman, I'll castrate you! And remember, I'm a better detective than you.'" He paused and laughed, "I think she's serious."

Marcello gave Antonio a radio in case he saw anything suspicious on the street.

As a senior detective, Nicolo carried a gun; so, all four of those who would be entering the apartment were armed. The Carabinieri carried Beretta 92FS handguns. Nicolo carried a newer model Beretta, the APX Compact— smaller, and easier to carry unnoticed.

It was about 2:00 when they arrived. Antonio began his watch from a half block up the street with a good view of the front entrance to the old building. Gabriella took up a position near the rear entrance. It was more likely to be used if Pucci or his guys happened to show up. Antonio moved about occasionally, trying not to appear obvious.

Nicolo, Marcello, and the two uniformed Carabinieri entered the front door of the building. Moments later, Antonio watched a well-dressed man come out and walk leisurely up the street. They had been inside less than five minutes when Marcello radioed him and Gabriella.

"There will be an ambulance arriving in a few minutes. Don't be alarmed. We're all fine. Direct them up to the apartment."

Antonio saw the flashing light bouncing off the stone buildings before he saw the ambulance round the bend in the road. Gabriella came to the front entrance and led them up. Antonio maintained his watch as curious neighbors gathered—gawking, pointing, and wondering aloud. Antonio saw a man duck behind some others when he made eye contact. It was the same man who came out of the apartment building after the team entered. He looked directly at Antonio, then turned and walked the other way. He was a handsome man—about thirty years old. He appeared to be from the south, standing about five foot-eight, and stocky, with his dark mustache neatly trimmed. He wore perfectly pressed charcoal slacks, a black button-down shirt, and expensive grey blazer. Antonio wormed his way through the onlookers to get a closer look. The man had vanished. He walked farther up the street but saw no sign of him.

Some ten minutes later, the medics came out the front door rolling a stretcher on wheels. It was a woman … face swollen …. nose looking broken … makeup running down her face. Mirabella, he guessed. He'd be surprised if she didn't have a concussion, or worse. She appeared to be in her late twenties. Gabriella was holding her hand, speaking kindly, reassuring her that everything would be okay.

Nicolo followed them out and walked Antonio's way. "Damn! We missed Pucci by less than an hour. He and one of his guys were up there. Looks like they came unannounced. They found her with another man. Shot the guy three times in the chest and once in the crotch. Probably used a silencer. Then Pucci nearly beat Mirabella to death, but not until after he raped her. She was unconscious when we arrived … thought she was dead at first. We managed to wake her enough to get that much information."

"Who is the man they killed?"

"Haven't been able to ID him yet. She's in bad shape so we didn't press it. His body will need to stay there until forensics is through. We'll wait to interview her in more detail, until after the doctors tend to her injuries."

Nicolo phoned Paolo. He asked him to stand guard with her at the hospital and let him know when they could come and talk to her. She would be taken to the Quinto Lotto Policlinico Hospital, where Giulia still lay in her coma.

The two uniformed Carabinieri were dispatched to interview the neighbors. Marcello called his forensics team to go through the apartment. He would stay until they arrived.

*****

Nicolo, Gabriella, and Antonio went to the questura to check out the CCTV footage. There were cameras inside and out of the Porta Camollia gate. The southside camera covered part of the street, but the curve in the road prevented them from seeing the apartment entrance.

They rewound the recording to noon, then fast-forwarded, until they spotted three men wearing sunglasses. The man in the middle was wearing a white suit and a fedora.

"Looks like Pucci." Nicolo pointed at the man in the middle. "When he takes that hat off, he's nearly bald. I'm guessing those goons are his bodyguards."

They saw Pucci and one of his guys stop and light a couple of cigarettes, while the third man went through the gate. He walked a block, looking all directions, then came back. Then all three entered the gate.

The time log showed 12:51 PM. The man who had been the scout continued straight, toward the front of the apartment building. Pucci and the other guy turned right, toward the rear, then disappeared off camera.

Based on what they were seeing here, and the little they'd found out from Mirabella, they speculated that the two men went up together. After Pucci shot the man, the other bodyguard was probably sent down to watch the rear entrance while Pucci had his way with Mirabella.

"Reckless of Pucci to come to the apartment," Nicolo said. "They could have picked her up and brought her to him. He always has been an overconfident S.O.B."

"My guess is they didn't want her to know where he's hiding out," Antonio added.

"Bastard!" Gabriella spat out. Antonio had never seen her angry. He caught her eye and nodded.

At 1:33, Pucci and his henchmen showed up again on the CCTV cameras, laughing as they walked back to the gate and beyond. They checked other cameras and were able to follow them for some distance, but not all the way to a vehicle. They probably knew the location of the cameras and parked in a blind spot.

Before they got that far though, Antonio saw someone he recognized. It was the man he had seen earlier. It appeared he was following them from a distance. Antonio waited patiently while they tracked the three as far as they were able.

"Rewind the tape about two minutes, Nicolo." He pointed when the man made his appearance. "See that guy? I saw him twice while I was on the street. He came out of the building just after you guys entered. Later, I saw him behind the crowd when the ambulance arrived. We made eye contact. Then he ducked behind some others. I went to get a closer look and he disappeared. Back the recording up some more. I think he was following them."

A survey of the tape confirmed it. He had followed them both in and out.

"But wait a second. I saw him much later than that. He must have doubled back."

A fast forward of the tape substantiated it.

"Who do you think he is?" Antonio asked. "And why was he following them?"

"Maybe he's from the 'Ndrangheta family—the local Laganà clan?" Gabriella suggested.

"As good a guess as any I can come up with," Nicolo added. "Or a rear guard?"

"But why double back?" Antonio added.

"I'd like to know the answer to both of those questions," Gabriella said. "One thing we now know for sure. Pucci's still in Tuscany, and probably staying near Siena. I can't wait to see if he shows up at the osteria tomorrow night. It's time to put that bastard back behind bars."

Chapter Sixteen

Monday afternoon & evening

Marcello caught up with them. "Forensics is still working the scene, but hasn't found anything we didn't already know." They filled him in on what they'd found on the CCTV footage.

They listened in while Marcello phoned his commanding officer, General Peluso. They confirmed a team meeting for tomorrow where they would finalize plans for the observation and possible raid of Giovanni's osteria. Marcello had spoken to him earlier. The general was recruiting extra forces from Firenze, where he himself was stationed. If the dinner meeting was what they thought it was, there would probably be four or five family capos. The rest would be bodyguards. They wanted to outnumber them at least two-to-one.

Marcello made a second call, to Fiero Belluci, the commanding general of the Guardia di Finanza in Siena. He arranged a second meeting to discuss plans for the Livorno drug smuggling operation. Both meetings would take place at the Comando Provinciale Stazione Carabinieri Siena, located north of the old city.

*****

Nicolo dropped Antonio at his car. He wanted to spend a few hours with Sofia and Giulia. Sofia insisted on staying the night with Giulia. Nicolo would stay into the evening. Then Alessia would come and take his place. He needed sleep. Tomorrow would be a big day.

Antonio picked up Aunt Frankie to take her home. She was quiet. Worry lines creased her forehead. He had never seen her so serious. As they climbed into the Lancia, his phone rang. It was Leonardo. He asked if they would stop at Il Forno di Francesco bakery to pick up fresh bread to accompany dinner.

When they walked in the house, the delicious smell of the warm, fresh bread Antonio was carrying mingled with a bouquet of other welcoming aromas. He suddenly forgot that he had eaten a sizeable lunch. Leonardo and Raphael were cooking a simple dinner of rabbit stew, grilled polenta, and sautéed broccoli raab. Chiara had made a dessert. She and Elena ate their dinner early then retired for the night. Antonio was surprised when Frankie joined them. She appeared to get a second wind. As they set the table, Antonio heard the deep vibration of a motorcycle in the drive. Moments later a young man strolled in, a broad smile on his face, looking like he owned the place.

"*Ciao, Ciao*! Everyone, this is our friend, Luca," Leonardo intoned with affection, "the world-renowned cyclist, and chef, from Giovanni's Osteria."

Antonio rose to greet him. He liked Luca right off. He exuded the kind of energy that rubs off on you, and the smile of someone always looking to stir up a little trouble. He wore his wavy sun-streaked hair in a ponytail. He looked nineteen, though Antonio guessed he was probably more like thirty.

Raphael handed him a bottle of wine to open. He did so with a flourish. The bottle, a Sangiovese, was from niece Teodora's winery. Teodora was Alessia's daughter. She and her husband, Tomas, owned Chateau Teodora, a small production winery not far from Healdsburg in the Sonoma Valley of California. They specialized in Italian varietals. Most of their vines were planted from cuttings smuggled home from Tuscany. One exception was their Primitivo — the DNA ancestor of Zinfandel. Those cuttings came from Apulia, passed along by a long-time friend of Nicolo.

Teodora was one of Antonio's favorite people. He was also impressed with their wines which seemed to match her vibrant personality. Somehow, in addition to running the winery, they found time to raise three young daughters, four dogs, a couple of horses, and various other farm animals. She had a lot of her mother in her. This often created friction between her and Alessia. The distance between them helped.

Leonardo interrupted his thoughts. "I texted my father to let him know Luca agreed to plant the listening devices for us. He has an idea on how to make that work."

Luca spoke, "I think we could put the bugs into holes drilled into two bread boards. I can serve the crostini and antipasti on one, then bring in the other with bread and fruit on it when I serve the other courses."

"Sounds like a great idea," Antonio said. "They'll need to test it though, to make sure the bugs will pick up the sound through the wood."

They ate slowly and lingered at the table. Luca was a talker. He told Antonio about his culinary school training; and they talked about everything from cooking, to running a restaurant, to cycling, to motorcycles, and the upcoming grape harvest. The brothers were expecting an excellent vintage.

The conversation was engaging, but Antonio was losing steam. He was about to call it a night when he heard the downshift of Nicolo's Alfa Romeo coming up the drive. He stayed to greet him. He poured Nicolo a glass of wine, but no more for himself. Too much wine before bed almost always messed with his sleep.

Nicolo took a sip and exclaimed, "Aaahhh, bravo! Teodora's wines are getting better all the time." Raphael warmed a bowl of stew for Nicolo, and they sat again. Frankie brought them each a slice of Chiara's dessert, a black currant jam tart, and sat down at the table with them.

The brothers introduced Luca, who Nicolo now remembered he met before. Luca explained his idea. He showed him the two thick cutting boards he brought with him. If it turned out to be workable, he wanted them back by noon tomorrow so he could bring them with him when he headed for the osteria.

Nicolo phoned Marco, who said he'd call their tech team to make sure it would work. Time was short. Nicolo's phone rang ten minutes later. Marco had already spoken to the lab and called Marcello. Marcello and Gabriella would pick the boards up in the morning. The team at the lab wanted them by 8:30. If their sound test showed good results, they said they could have them ready by 11:00.

Raphe, who'd been quiet, spoke for himself and his brother, "Is there any way we can be involved?"

"I'm afraid not," Nicolo said. "I understand you wanting to. I do. But the Carabinieri will never go for it. Far too dangerous."

They nodded. Raphael looked sullen, though Antonio was sure this was the answer he'd expected.

Nicolo continued, "Because of Antonio's detective experience, Marcello has agreed to let him be in the surveillance van, but no more."

This was news to Antonio. He wondered why Marcello was putting so much trust in him. He was surprised but pleased.

"There will be a lot of people involved in this operation. The Carabinieri are bringing in extra help from Firenze. Plus, we'll have Paolo, Mancini, and Jordy. You and I, Antonio, will be in the surveillance van, which will double as a command post, with Marcello, Marco, and one of his comm guys. Also, the Carabinieri will have a chopper in the air and available if needed."

He turned at Luca. "And, Luca, you need to find a safe place for you and your staff to hide when you hear trouble brewing."

Luca smiled and nodded. He appeared to be excited for a little dangerous adventure.

*****

As the sound of Luca's motorcycle faded away, Nicolo told them he'd gone to see Mirabella as soon as the doctors gave their okay.

"Whatever loyalty she'd had to Pucci—or fear of him—is gone. Her anger has taken over. She told me everything she knew about him, including places he has taken her. I doubt he'll be at any of those places though, not after what he did to her."

"Agreed," Raphael said. He was eager to remain involved somehow. "But is it possible he thought she was dead?"

"Maybe, but Marcello doesn't want to go searching yet anyway. He'd rather let the meeting go ahead."

"Hmm. Risky, isn't it?" Antonio asked.

"Yeah. But he'd rather take the chance in order to gather intel. He and General Peluso want to take down the whole family."

"What about the dead guy?" Raphael asked.

"If you're asking about the guy that was with Mirabella, they haven't identified him yet. Just some guy she met in a wine bar, according to Mirabella. They ran the name he gave her but found out it wasn't his real name. Imagine that. Looks like they took his wallet. Hopefully, his fingerprints will turn up a match … much quicker than DNA." He paused and took a sip of wine. "Mirabella was able to ID Pucci's bodyguard, the one who came up with him. She gave me enough to put him away with her testimony."

Frankie jumped in, "Do you really think she'll be willing to testify?"

Nicolo looked at his big sister and flashed a tired smile, "I asked her. She said she's willing if we can put her in witness protection. I think the magistrate would agree to that. But threats to her family could always change her mind."

Chapter Seventeen

Tuesday morning

Antonio awoke with the sunrise. It occurred to him that his body was beginning to heal. For the first morning in a week, it wasn't screaming in pain. Mornings were the worst. A few pain killers and movement always helped, though certain movements would still make his rib cage scream at him.

But his mind felt unsettled. It was that old detective feeling he knew too well. It often came after a sound night's sleep when his brain was processing away. He felt something wasn't right with the case. But which case? They all seemed muddled together. He knew they were missing something. They were dealing with few solid answers, mostly suppositions. But either way, Pucci needed to be apprehended and sent back to prison. And if they could make a major impact on local mob operations, so much the better. He hoped they would know more answers by the end of the day.

He took another morning walk with Bella, his favorite way to think. He thought he should get a dog just like her. He wondered if they had any plans to breed her.

The morning was crisp and cool, with just a few clouds, like puffs of cotton, moving across the sky. He paused to take in the view from the house. He breathed in the panorama. A misty fog sat in the valleys, obscuring the lower vineyards. The hills looked like they were floating on a sea of white.

They wandered down the hill into the small dell. The mist chilled his body, but thinned as they began to climb the opposite side. He knew it would slowly disappear as the sun gave warmth to the tiny dew drops. As they climbed, a pair of pheasant skirted away. Bella, proving she was a well-trained hunting dog, took up a pointer stance instead of chasing them. Something else moved in the brush. He hoped it wasn't a wild boar. They were nasty creatures. But he was sure Bella would have warned him, so he relaxed.

His mind wandered from the case. He realized it was the first day of autumn, sparking another remembrance. Today was Randi's birthday. She would have been fifty-three. She so enjoyed coming here. She loved his family, both the near family at home, and the extended family here in Italy. She felt at home with them. She was especially close to Sofia. He suddenly felt a deep ache for her. For a passing moment, he thought he felt her presence, a feeling he'd had before.

He remembered a morning much like this one, when they had taken this very same walk. On that morning, they returned to the house to find Christina and Giulia up early, making breakfast—an American-style breakfast of pancakes with maple syrup—Giulia's favorite when she visited them in Seattle. The kitchen was a mess but everyone laughed at the shapes the girls made with the batter: misshapen hearts, Teddy bears, and Mickey Mouse. He smiled at the memory, but it made him ache all the more—for Randi, for Christina, for Giulia. Would Giulia return home to the land of the living? Fully return? He wondered if the rest of his life was destined to be consumed with grief.

He started down the hill, whispering a prayer as he walked. He wondered if God heard him, and if he could trust Him. He had at one time. He desperately wanted to believe there was a loving God, and that Randi and Christina were with Him, just like Nonna Valentina had told him.

*****

When he arrived back at the house, he found Nicolo, Marcello, and Gabriella, leaning against the kitchen counter drinking coffee. He poured himself a cup. Gabriella gave him a gentle squeeze, and an affectionate kiss on the cheek. He had a sense that she could read his sadness this morning.

Antonio caught himself staring at her. He found it hard to ignore his growing attraction, and the comfort a relationship with her might bring. Then he immediately felt guilty about it. For three years he'd been telling himself he could never love another woman after Randi. Aside from that, what good could come from falling for a woman who lived half a world away?

His thoughts were interrupted by some delicious aromas wafting their way, and the sound of Frankie's voice. She walked into the room with a round platter holding the biggest frittata he'd ever seen—must have been a dozen eggs in it—made with leeks, greens from the garden, tomatoes which had been dried in the sun, and Chiara's fresh homemade sheep's cheese. A second platter held freshly baked almond pastries. His stomach rumbled. Gabriella heard it and laughed. His feelings of guilt abated.

Marcello and Gabriella tried to say no to eating, telling Frankie they needed to get to the lab to drop off the boards.

"All this work I did! Cooking for you! If you don't have some of my frittata, you will be on my *merda* list. I may never forgive you!" Antonio tried to stifle a laugh. Such a dramatic performance spoken with an uncharacteristic sharp tongue.

Her intimidation tactics worked. They smiled and made amends by wolfing down a slice of frittata, complimenting her after every bite. Frankie smiled coyly, wrapped a couple of pastries in waxed paper, placed them in a brown paper bag, and shooed them out the door, mumbling to herself the whole time.

Antonio took the time to relish every bite. He ate two hefty pieces of Frankie's frittata and a couple of warm pastries. Between bites, Nicolo explained that Marcello and Gabriella arrived just after he left for his walk.

"They wanted to go over their plan for the osteria op before the team meeting, to make sure we're on the same page. They sent a tech team to the alley behind the osteria yesterday evening. They hid wireless infrared video cams on both ends of the alley. They figure the dinner guests will likely come through the rear entrance."

"And if they don't?"

"If they come in the front, we'll have eyes on them. Our van will have a view of the front from a block away. The street lighting is good. We can observe without infrared. They also checked the CCTV cameras on the main road to make sure they're working."

"I see why you trust these guys."

"It's going to be a full day—two planning meetings. One at the Carabinieri Stazione this morning—a final planning meeting for tonight's op. Then a meeting after lunch, for planning the drug intercept. It got moved to the GDF. Belluci likes to operate on his own turf."

"The GDF is running that op?"

"Yeah. I doubt they'll allow you to be a part of it. I'll try to bring you into the planning meeting if I can. Do you want to bring your own car, or ride with me?"

*****

They took separate cars and arrived about ten minutes before the meeting. Once assembled, Marcello thanked those in attendance for being there.

"We managed to pick up a couple more officers from Firenze, so now we have twenty-six total including the surveillance team. From the Polizia Municipale in

Siena we have Nicolo, Antonio, Paolo, Mancini, and Jordy. Joining myself and Gabriella are eleven Carabinieri from Siena, and six from Firenze. We very much appreciate your assistance," he said, looking at the Firenze group.

Antonio glanced their way. They looked pleased to be involved. Most police are adrenaline junkies. They like to see action. Marcello introduced his regional commander, General Peluso, who was sitting in.

Marcello moved on, "The operation has been approved by our local magistrate, Ms. Capra. The purpose of the op is to do surveillance on a dinner being held at Osteria Giovanni. We have reason to believe it is a meeting of the local branch of the Camorra family, and that Sandro Pucci may be in attendance. We know the dinner is for a dozen people. If Pucci is in attendance, our goal is to apprehend him, preferably alive, as well as his bodyguards. There is the possibility that this is something else. If it's not a crime family meeting, we'll call it a night and go home."

"But," he paused, "*if* it is what we think it is, we will wait until the end of the meeting to arrest Pucci. Two reasons: first, we want to hear all that they have to say. We'll have listening devices in the room. This could provide valuable intel, not only on Pucci, but on other family business as well. Secondly, it's probably a safer time to attempt capture, fewer people on the streets."

Antonio was struck with how organized Marcello was, and how confidently he spoke.

"If this is a family meeting, and Pucci is in attendance, we will have reason to arrest the other family members for aiding and abetting. It's possible our surveillance may give us additional grounds. The magistrate has given me the go-ahead to make those decisions based on what we hear. She'll be on standby if we need to consult her."

"Questions on what I've covered so far?" The only question was about the listening devices. Marcello declined to explain. Antonio assumed it was to protect Luca in case there was a mole in their midst.

"We have live infrared video cameras concealed on both ends of the alley, and we will have two men on the roofs, one at either end." He pointed out the two Carabinieri, who raised their hands. "These men are trained snipers. They'll also have low-light cameras with telephoto lenses. We'll try to get good photos of all in attendance, but if a firefight breaks out," he looked at the two, "to hell with the cameras. Be prepared to support with sniper fire."

They nodded.

"The alley behind the restaurant is about 300 meters long. The rear service entrance to the restaurant is about 75 meters from the south end. We will break up into three teams of five, with one team covering the south end, and one the north. The third team will cover the front."

"All teams will be driving our armored Jeep Grand Cherokees. I want everyone clothed with full body armor; helmets included. We'll keep the teams at a distance until we know everyone has arrived and entered the meeting. Then we'll move you in closer, but still out of view. They'll almost certainly post bodyguards outside to keep watch."

Marcello showed them on the map where he wanted them to stage initially, and then relocate to once the meeting began.

"If Pucci exits the rear, which we think he will, we'll move the Cherokees into position to block the two ends of the alley. The third team will remain on the street in the front of the restaurant. I'd like to keep them there in case Pucci or anyone else tries to escape through the restaurant. If we need support at any of the points, we'll have Paolo, Mancini, and Jordy held in reserve here." He pointed at the map. "I'll make that call." He paused to make sure they got his point. "But in order to make a good decision, I'll need good communication from our team leaders."

He paused, took a drink of water, and checked his notes. "Commissario Nicolo Zaccardi, detective Cortese, and I, will be in the surveillance van with Marco Calore from Europol and one of his comm experts." Antonio glanced at Nicolo in surprise. He hadn't heard himself referred to as "detective" for nearly ten years. Mancini glared at him. It was obvious he did not like the reference.

Marcello continued, "I almost forgot a key point. We'll have a helicopter in the air in case we need them." There were nods of approval from the group.

"Let me reiterate, we'd like Pucci taken alive and for this to be a quiet capture, if possible. Do not, I repeat, do not open fire unless fired upon. Each team leader will have an LRAD, long-range acoustic device. When the meeting breaks up, and they begin to exit, we will call for Pucci to surrender. We'll ask the others to stand-down. Hopefully, they're smart enough to take our advice.

"Each vehicle is equipped with a floodlight. Use them to illuminate the alley. This will blind them. But keep your distance from the lights because if they start shooting that's the first thing they'll aim for.

"A couple of cautions: watch your rear in case there are other family members stationed on the perimeter that we don't see. Also, if this turns into a shootout, aim your shots carefully. We'll be in a crossfire situation. I don't want any of our own to go down by friendly fire.

"Okay, team leaders will be Major Gabriella Ferraro, and Lieutenant Aurelio Russo from Siena, and Captain Cesare Cattano from Firenze. Gabriella, your team will cover the front, Aurelio the south end of the alley, Cesare the north." Marcello went on to assign teams, keeping people with those they had a relationship with.

"Any questions?" He paused. "No? I guess I must have been thorough. We'll meet back here at 7:00 for arms and body armor checks. And to issue your Beretta assault rifles. Godspeed to us all."

Chapter Eighteen

Tuesday mid-day

Marcello, Gabriella, Nicolo, Marco, and Antonio, went with the comm expert to check out the surveillance van. Walking over, Antonio asked Marcello about his introduction as "detective".

"It was the only thing I could do, unless I excluded you. Some would chafe at having a civilian involved. I really don't know why the hell I've let you." He stopped and looked at Antonio. "Actually, I do know. It appears you have a calming effect on Nicolo, and I think you can be an asset. Just don't do anything stupid or you'll put my job at risk. Keep your head down. Stay in an advisory role and don't get otherwise involved." His eyes bored into Antonio's and held them for a few seconds.

Antonio nodded. He knew the risk Marcello was taking, and he didn't want to do anything to screw it up.

*****

They had a couple of hours until the meeting with the GDF so Nicolo and Antonio grabbed some quick slices of pizza and headed to the hospital to visit Giulia. Nicolo was feeling guilty about spending so little time there. Frankie and Sofia were with her.

Sofia told them the doctor had stopped by. "He says her vital signs are weak. He told me if we don't see improvement soon, we may be faced with a tough decision." Nicolo turned pale. Antonio felt his knees go weak.

"He also says there's been an increase of the swelling and pressure on her brain. He's worried it could affect her cognitive function if she does come out of this."

Despite the bad news, her trust in God appeared unwavering. She confirmed it, "I suppose I should be afraid. But God has given me assurances." Antonio hoped she was hearing God correctly. Without her faith, he didn't believe he'd have a shred of hope.

Sofia suddenly turned serious, "Nicolo, Antonio … please be careful tonight. You know these men are dangerous. I'll be worried sick all night. Watch out for one another."

Everyone keeps telling us to be careful, Antonio thought. *I hope we haven't been taking the danger too lightly.* He knew all too well that a desire for revenge can make men careless.

*****

The Guardia Di Finanza Comando Provinciale Compagnia Siena, was located north of the Basilica Caterina San Domenico. On the way, Nicolo warned Antonio, "Remember, General Belluci is a bit of a pompous ass. He and I have had our run-ins. There is no love lost. If you're not allowed to remain in the meeting, don't make a fuss."

Nicolo rarely spoke poorly of anyone. He knew this guy had to be a piece of work.

They entered the meeting room, where they found Belluci and two of his men, a captain, and a lieutenant, along with Marco Calore, Marcello Bianchi, and Gabriella. They walked into a haze of smoke. All three of the GDF people were smoking. Italy has anti-smoking laws similar to the U.S., but he knew they weren't always taken seriously. It depended on who was in charge. Nicolo did not allow smoking within the walls of the questura. Obviously, that wasn't the case here. Gabriella opened a window and stood next to it. Belluci gave her a look of annoyance and she gave it right back.

Antonio understood immediately why Nicolo didn't care for Belluci. His chin was constantly raised and he did not offer a single word of welcome. By contrast, Nicolo was a professional and a diplomat. He could work with almost anyone. It seemed Belluci was the opposite, an egotistical man who seemed to care little about getting along with anyone. *A classic "almost winner" … "I'm okay, you're not" kind of guy*, Antonio thought, thinking back to a book he'd read in college.

Belluci was about five-ten, thinning hair, cut short, with a mustache and goatee. He was clad in a perfectly pressed and tailored general's uniform. Antonio guessed him to be under forty and wondered how he made general at such a young age.

Marcello took it upon himself to initiate introductions. When they got to Antonio, Belluci asked who he was, wondering why he had never met him. When he figured out he was a man with no official capacity in Italy, he glared at Nicolo and waved his hand toward the door, commanding Antonio to leave.

Antonio raised his palms in surrender and walked out. He found a small piazza near the San Domenico convent, and a place to sit in the sun. He texted Nicolo where to find him after the meeting.

*****

Nicolo found him half-asleep. Nicolo had a sour look on his face. "Told you," he said. Then he brought him up to date.

"The operation will be run by Belluci with Marcello second in command, since he'll have people involved. Marco, Gabriella, me, and my team will be in a support role, observers mainly, unless trouble arises. It came across clearly that we're just pawns on his chessboard. It's a good thing Marcello is a level-headed guy. Belluci treated him as an underling and was dismissive of every concern he raised."

"Why does that not surprise me?"

"Yeah. Right. Anyway, Marco says the ship is scheduled to dock at 6:00 PM. He offered to have drones in surveillance of the ship upon its approach and when docked and unloading. The GDF will use their own people for surveillance at the docks. If it appears drugs are being transferred, they'll follow the transport vehicle. They're more interested in taking down the heads of family than simply recovering the drugs and arresting the couriers."

"Makes sense on one level. Riskier though."

"They're aware of the risks. But if the couriers figure out they're being followed, they'll just move in on them. Not likely they could lose them on the roads from Livorno."

"But won't it be easy to spot a tail on those dark country roads?"

"They plan to use multiple tracking methods. They'll rotate unmarked vehicles. Belluci wants my guys to do one of the rotations. I was tempted to say no, just to be bullheaded, but thought better of it. Marco also offered their drones for tracking, in case we lose contact. They have the range. The GDF will also have a helicopter keeping a safe distance, available if needed. As much as Belluci annoys me, it's a solid plan."

"Did you or Marcello let them know that Pucci could be in custody by then?"

"Yeah. But as we said before, there's no way they'll leave millions of euros of drugs sitting on the dock. While Pucci was in prison for a year, someone was obviously running their drug ops."

"Seems crazy that these two things are happening on back-to-back nights. You're probably right about this being the reason for tonight's meeting."

"We'll know soon enough."

*****

After the meeting, Marcello and Gabriella found Nicolo and Antonio. Marcello was in a worse mood than Nicolo.

"We heard from our DNA people. We've been pushing 'em hard. That cigarette butt you found near Fonterutoli?" He looked at Antonio. "It did not appear to be waterlogged from the rain, yet there was no DNA on it, no fingerprints, nothing. Like it was never touched by a human."

Antonio stared at him with his mouth open. "Something's not right."

"No shit. I hope we'll find out about the other one soon."

Antonio and Nicolo decided not to go home for dinner. They stopped for gelato, then, with an hour to spare, they walked to the espresso bar three doors down. They wanted caffeine to keep their senses alert. Antonio could see Nicolo's mind was preoccupied.

"Are you okay, Nicolo?" he asked. Nicolo's eyes looked everywhere but at him.

"Just thinking about Giulia." His eyes followed a young woman walking by outside the window. He didn't speak for a long time. Finally, he turned his eyes to Antonio, "I'm scared, Antonio—scared of losing her." There was a tremor in his voice. "I've been so angry, so focused on finding who did this, wanting revenge. I wouldn't let it ..." His voice trailed off. He took a sip of his espresso, then fixed his gaze back on Antonio. "I don't know what I would do. I don't know how you ever made it this far."

Antonio had no idea what to say. He reached out a hand and placed it on his shoulder.

*****

They assembled at 7:00 as planned, and though Nicolo and Antonio were to be in the surveillance van, they still donned body armor. Nicolo wore his Beretta sidearm and placed two extra clips in his vest. "A precaution," he said. He was all business now. Antonio felt naked being unarmed.

The surveillance van moved into position early, about sixty yards up the street from the restaurant. It was a tall Mercedes Sprinter van with a decal on each side ... *Marcello's Old-World Renovations* in Italian. The Jeep Cherokees were kept at a safe distance along routes not likely to be taken by the family. In case they were spotted, they placed themselves in locations that would not seem unusual. Comm checks were completed with the vehicles and team leaders. Camera checks were completed. The snipers were in position. Marcello verified that the helicopter was on standby. It would not go airborne until it was confirmed that this dinner was what they thought it was.

The listening devices in the boards were working perfectly. They could hear chopping and banter in the kitchen, only slightly muffled by the wood. Luca was keeping the mood light as he and his kitchen staff prepared dinner service. The restaurant would open at 8:00, with the private party at 9:00.

Antonio felt the butterflies that go along with an operation like this. He could smell the distinctive aroma of danger brewing. Now all that was left to do was wait.

Chapter Nineteen

Tuesday evening

Shortly before 9:00, the first sign of the family appeared. A black BMW 745 passed the van, circled the block in a counter-clockwise direction, looking for signs of trouble, then pulled into the alley. From the van, they watched the eerie infrared image as four men stepped out. Three of them entered the rear of the restaurant, while one remained outside as a lookout. Antonio could see by the cut of his suit that he was packing. A couple of minutes later, a black Mercedes SUV came from the opposite direction and circled the block clockwise, then entered the alley as well. Three men got out. Two went in. One joined the man outside. Almost immediately, a silver Maserati Levante GTS came directly in and entered the alley. Two men exited and entered the back door. None of those who had arrived so far were Sandro Pucci, but Nicolo recognized at least one man from each vehicle as family members. The tension was building. They knew this was a family meeting in progress.

About 9:10, a red four-door Ferrari came into view. "That's a Grand Lusso," Antonio said to Nicolo, "the GTC4. Probably the twelve cylinder. They run about three-hundred grand in U.S. dollars." Nicolo whistled and nodded. They circled the area twice before finally pulling up to the front of the restaurant. Two men got out and entered the front of the restaurant.

"I'm sure that's Sandro," Nicolo said, pointing to the screen. This video feed was not infrared, but the old city lights made it look surreal all the same. The guy he pointed at was wearing a white suit under his overcoat. His hat was pulled down and his collar turned up.

"Leave it to Sandro to go in the front door," Nicolo said. "The same recklessness which got him caught the first time."

The car moved to the back alley and the driver entered the rear door.

*****

They were blind for a few minutes, only hearing clatter from the kitchen. Then they heard voices change as Luca carried the antipasti board into the private dining room. Things went quiet. Then Luca introduced himself and explained with gusto what they would be enjoying for their evening meal. If he was nervous, you couldn't hear it in his voice.

"Tonight, gentlemen, you will be enjoying a dinner of epic proportions. We'll begin with a variety of crostini: chicken liver pâté, homemade ricotta with lemon zest and extra virgin olive oil, and panzanella. This will be followed by zuppa—cream of leeks, topped with crispy cotechino salami. The primi piatti will be spinach and ricotta gnocchi with a pecorino fondue sauce and shaved black truffles. For the piatti secondo we will be presenting two options: porchetta from a small suckling pig, served with roasted fennel; and Tuscan beef braised in a fine Brunello di Montalcino, served with roasted fingerling potatoes with fresh herbs. These courses will be accompanied by fresh fruit, and Tuscan bread, baked fresh today by Il Forno di Francesco, the finest bakery in all of Siena." Luca paused to catch his breath. "But save room for dolce. We will serve gianduia semifreddo with Piemonte hazelnut nougat and a Baileys reduction." With the panache of a circus ringmaster, Luca added, *"Buon appetito, signori!"*

The group gave Chef Luca a hearty applause and a "bravo, bravo chef," which prompted Antonio and Nicolo to look at each other and smile. Luca made the meal sound so amazing that Antonio wished he were dining with these guys. Crooks or not.

There was no business discussed over the next ninety minutes, only amicable small talk about politics, immigration problems, local soccer news, and raves about their dinner. Nicolo identified Pucci's voice for Antonio. Unnecessary, he had figured it out already. He was the loudest, most boisterous voice in the room and seemed to dominate every discussion. *A real know-it-all*, Antonio thought.

After an hour, they watched the cameras as two of the bodyguards traded places with the guys outside, presumably so they could eat. As the meal progressed, and the wine took effect, the talk grew louder and livelier.

But once dolce was finished, and they had grappa in their glass, the talk turned to business. Marcello moved his teams into closer position so they would be able to close off the alley quickly when the time came.

Antonio was surprised that it wasn't Sandro's voice that took charge after dinner. They had been working on identifying the other voices and it seemed there were four men who did most of the talking. They knew these would be the family members, but Nicolo was unable to identify which voice belonged to whom. The voice that took over now was serious and began to pepper Sandro with questions.

"Tell me Sandro, the murder of the three dealers from the Laganà clan of the 'Ndrangheta family? Did you order those hits?"

"No. Why would I do such a thing?"

"We've heard from the Laganàs. They seem to think differently. They believe you're a reckless man, that you don't care about keeping the peace and tranquility here in Tuscany."

"You don't believe me? You believe the Laganàs, when I tell you to your face it wasn't me? He let loose some expletives. They're lying. I don't give a damn what they think about me. I had nothin' to do with those." They sensed Sandro turning red in the face. "Maybe it was you, Lorenzo. Stirring up trouble while I'm rotting away in some lousy prison cell! You've been jealous of me since we came to Siena. You'd like nothing better than to be capo of this family."

Nicolo noted Lorenzo's name as he rubbed the stubble on his chin. Antonio imagined a stare down.

Sandro's voice quieted a little. "If they were so sure we did it, they would have struck back by now."

"I don't think they want to start a war unless they're certain." Lorenzo's voice was calm. "Have you made any effort to reach out to them?"

"Why would I bother? Those sewer rats aren't worth wasting my time. Besides, they've obviously been talking to you. They don't give me the time of day."

"To keep the peace among families, Sandro, to keep the peace. They may be rivals, but no need to create bad blood."

"Hmmph! Whoever clipped those guys did us a favor."

"See, there you go again. This is w…"

"Go again what? You think I care about the well-being of the Laganà family or their street dealers? You sound like you've gone over to their side!"

"You may not like them, Sandro, but they've been operating in Siena longer than we have, and they have a bigger crew here than we do. Do you want to end up in a gangland war with them?"

"You know that if I called home today, I could get another two dozen soldiers here by tomorrow."

"I wouldn't be so sure of that."

"That's because you don't know a damn thing, Lorenzo."

Lorenzo's voice remained even in the face of Pucci's bombastic attacks. "Tell me, Sandro. The accident with the daughter of Commissario Zaccardi and the American? They also believe it was you. At least, that's the word on the street."

"I wish it were. I spent months dreaming of ways to get back at him! But I didn't want to cause trouble for the rest of you. His day'll come. I guarantee he won't walk away when it does."

Nicolo looked at Antonio. He raised his eyebrows and smiled.

"So, you've become considerate of the rest of us suddenly? Why so vengeful towards the detective, Sandro?" Lorenzo continued to poke and prod at Pucci. "The man has his job to do. You're just ticked because you got caught with your hand in the biscotti jar. You were reckless."

"Now you're the one being reckless, Lorenzo."

"Who attacked them if it wasn't you? Funny, you break out of prison, and then that happens."

"I have no idea! You think you're so smart, you figure it out. If I knew, I'd give them a medal."

"You think it wise to hurt a man's family, Sandro? A daughter? They probably have every cop in Tuscany looking for you! That puts us all in danger."

If they only knew, Antonio thought.

"I swear I had nothin' to do with it. I spent my first days out of jail laying low—someplace I wouldn't be found."

Antonio and Nicolo looked at each other again. It was Antonio's turn to raise an eyebrow.

A new voice, deeper, more resonant, entered the conversation, "How can you say that, Sandro? You were at your niece's christening, Sunday morning after you escaped. You call that hiding?"

"Listen, Salvatore. I could care less what comes out of your tiny brain. I'm not accountable to you. I'm her godfather. Her christening was the reason I took the risk of escaping. I refused to miss it just because of a little thing like prison."

Nicolo wrote the name Salvatore on his pad. He scribbled a note and showed it to Antonio. "Sounds like a coup taking place." Antonio nodded.

The voice of Salvatore pressed on, "Then you venture out to see your old mistress? And kill a man in the process!"

"I should have killed her too! I went soft."

"We're not talkin' 'bout your manhood, Sandro. And we aren't like that anymore. This is no game. We don't kill people for the hell of it. You've been watching too many mob movies. It draws unnecessary attention. It's bad for busin ..."

Sandro didn't let him finish, "How did you know about that anyway? Have you been watching me? You're a little nobody, Salvatore! You know that?"

Antonio looked at Nicolo and jotted a note, "The follower we spotted?" Nicolo nodded.

"Watch yourself, Sandro." It was Lorenzo's voice again, more forceful than before.

"My turn to ask you a question, Lorenzo. Why are you the one to bring my inquisition? Did you make yourself capo of the family in my absence?"

"I have no ambition to clean up your mess, Sandro. But you make our partnership difficult." Lorenzo's voice returned to calm. It was obvious he had far more self-control than Sandro.

Pucci blew a fuse now. Antonio pictured him rising from the table as he spat out a string of purses. "You ungrateful…! I'm the one who has made this partnership successful. Without me you'd still be stealing bread on the streets of Napoli."

"Speaking of Napoli, a decision has been made, Sandro. Not by me," Lorenzo said. "By the family council at home. You will no longer be head of the family here in Tuscany."

There was silence for several seconds. Then Salvatore's voice came in again. "Your uncle Matteo is coming to take over, Sandro. It has become obvious to the family that you were too young and brash for the responsibilities given you. Since your father's death, support for you has been falling away. You have proven to be a careless man. The three of us played no part in this decision but we support it. You've crippled the family business here with your recklessness."

Antonio looked at Nicolo. He was expecting another outburst from Sandro, but none came. The silence was deafening.

After a full minute, a fourth voice joined the conversation, in a tone like that of a nurturing father, "The family has asked that you return to Naples, Sandro. As soon as possible. They fear you will be captured and imprisoned again. In Naples you can have a fresh start, a new identity. Buy a little villa on the coast, live a quiet, comfortable life, maybe raise a family. Matteo has already arrived in Tuscany. He will personally take charge of the merchandise arriving tomorrow night."

Nicolo turned to Marcello and Marco and gave them a thumbs up.

Sandro said nothing in reply. Instead, he gave an instruction to his driver. "Get the car, Piero. I am clearly an unwanted guest in my own osteria."

Marcello sprang into action. He radioed his team captains that Pucci could be coming out anytime. He made sure they understood what vehicle he would be leaving in.

Chapter Twenty

Late Tuesday night

Tensions were high. With all eyes on the monitor, they watched the driver pull up. Sandro's other bodyguard was first to exit the rear. He looked up and down the alley, then motioned over his shoulder. Sandro followed.

Marcello gave the word. On the monitors, in macabre infrared light, Antonio saw the teams race their Cherokees into position on opposite ends of the alley. They turned on their flashing lights, then their floodlights. The infrared cameras were blinded. All detail lost.

From outside the van, they could hear the command from the LRAD, long-range acoustic device, instructing Sandro and his bodyguards to surrender, and the other family members to stand down.

Hell broke wide open. Antonio heard gunfire—three shots—two more—five more. He had a habit of counting shots, and trying to decipher which weapons they came from. His ability to identify the weapons wasn't working. The van muffled the noise beyond recognition.

The radio crackled, "Sandro and his men are back inside the osteria!"

"Gabriella, be ready," Marcello radioed. "Team one, secure the rear exit of the restaurant. Team two, move in closer as backup. Order the other family to exit with no weapons."

Less than a minute later, Pucci and his guys burst out the front door, bodyguards first. Antonio could now see them on the third video monitor. Instead of the crazy colors of the infrared, it looked like an old black and white movie scene. They lurked in the shadows of the front entry portico, barely visible, looking for a way to escape. One of them was holding his side. He appeared to be injured.

Marcello radioed Paolo, Mancini, and Jordy to be ready. They were south of the restaurant, just yards from the van. Nicolo piled out to join them, keeping low. Seeing the movement, one of the bodyguards laid down random cover fire their direction. It sounded like a submachine gun. Antonio saw people on the street running for cover. It was pandemonium in motion.

Pucci and his two guys turned to run north, then saw the Cherokee and Gabriella's team. The submachine gun rattled again; sparks flew as the bullets bounced off the armored Jeep. It was a short burst, coming from the injured bodyguard. Moments later, Antonio saw him lurch forward, taken down with three well-placed shots from behind. It had to be Nicolo or one of his guys.

Pucci was moving … running … crouching … shooting a handgun … looking like a man who would rather die than go back to prison. His other bodyguard laid down cover fire—sounded like an assault rifle—and then followed. Antonio saw Gabriella and two others leapfrog along the wall in pursuit. Then one of the other Jeep Cherokees appeared, having moved from the alley, cutting them off. Marcello had given the order after the other family members surrendered. A new sound joined the cacophony. It was the sound of the chopper, amplified by the stone walls. It cast its floodlight on the scene, making things looked even more surreal.

Pucci and his last standing bodyguard turned back, running toward the van. Gabriella's team moved also, behind them on the opposite side of the street. Antonio saw Gabriella pause, trying to help a civilian who was crouched where a building edge protruded. Pucci turned and fired three shots. Antonio heard a scream and saw Gabriella fall. "Oh God," he said out loud. He barreled out of the back of the van before Marcello could stop him. In the bright floodlight, he saw Gabriella in an exposed position about a hundred feet from where he was.

Gunfire continued. Without warning, the second bodyguard dropped his weapon and threw his hands up. He knew he was dead otherwise. *Sandro's screwed,* Antonio thought. But Pucci took advantage of the distraction. He snatched up the submachine gun and headed toward Gabriella. *Shit, he's going to try to take her hostage.*

Antonio saw Pucci's body jerk, then realized he was wearing body armor under his suit. But it slowed him down. Antonio's adrenaline took over. He ran headlong toward Gabriella. Pucci rattled off a short burst which just missed him, throwing rock chips from the building beyond. Antonio threw himself headlong into a baseball slide, landing in front of Gabriella. The air plunged from his lungs and the excruciating pain of his ribs and scabs hitting the pavement almost caused him to black out. Her gun was on the ground next to her. He grabbed it and rolled to fire. But it was too late—not for Antonio—but for Pucci. Bullets hit Pucci in the chest, causing his body to jerk, then caught his right arm, sending the submachine gun clattering to the pavement. He went down screaming, clutching his bloody right arm with his left. The gun battle lasted about two minutes, start-to-finish, and then it was over.

*****

It didn't take long for two ambulances to arrive. It turned out Marcello had them on standby. The flashing red lights, mixed with the helicopter's floodlight, added to the surreal feeling as they bounced off the centuries-old buildings, old world meeting new.

Breath slowly returned to Antonio's body. He put down Gabriella's gun, pushed aside his searing pain, and turned to her the moment Pucci went down. He saw where one shot had hit her in her body armor. She'd have a nasty bruise. But the real concern was the shot which had penetrated her thigh and exited her buttocks, about ten inches from the entry wound. There was a lot of blood. He hoped it had missed the femoral artery. He put heavy pressure on her posterior. One of the Carabinieri team arrived with a first aid kit. They rolled her on her side and used thick layers of gauze to pressure the wound, front and back. Marcello showed up moments later and began to loosen her body armor. Within a minute, the medics pushed them aside and took over.

One of Pucci's bodyguards was dead. Besides Gabriella, and Pucci, another Carabinieri had also been shot—a leg wound. *So much for a quiet capture*, Antonio thought.

*****

With guns now silent, and ambulances on-site, the curious onlookers began to poke their heads nervously out of their windows. Others started to come around on foot. The Carabinieri pushed them back and cordoned off the area.

Gabriella and her team member were being loaded into the first ambulance. The paramedic confirmed that the bullet missed her femoral artery. Pucci was being loaded into the other ambulance, along with the covered body of the dead bodyguard. Before the medics covered him up, Antonio saw that one of the rounds caught him in the neck. It appeared to have severed his carotid artery. He would have died quickly.

As Pucci was being loaded in the ambulance, he turned his head and looked at Gabriella from his stretcher. Antonio saw recognition on his face. Then Pucci spoke hoarsely, barely loud enough to hear, "I'm sorry, Gabriella. I didn't know." She simply nodded.

As the medics were sliding Pucci into the ambulance, Nicolo stopped them. "Wait!" he said.

"Sir, we can't …"

"Yes, you can! Thirty seconds." He looked at Pucci, barely controlling his rage. "Is it true you had nothing to do with the road incident, the one that put my daughter in a coma?"

Pucci appeared weak. Pain creased his face. But he looked Nicolo in the eye. "I had nothing to do with it! I swear. I knew you'd pin it on me, but I swear on my mother's grave, Zaccardi. I am telling you the truth."

Nicolo turned to the medic, "Get him out of here!"

Nicolo turned toward Antonio, asking if he was okay. He probably saw the grimace of pain on his face. Antonio nodded, then grabbed the bar on the back of the ambulance and pulled himself up and grabbed his side. "I'm going to the hospital with Gabriella."

Nicolo shook his head as his worried scowl almost disappeared into a half-smile.

Chapter Twenty-one

Early Wednesday, just past midnight

The staff at Quinto Lotto Policlinico Hospital swung into action the moment they were notified that gunshot victims were coming in. They called in their best surgeons. Gabriella was the most seriously hurt of the three. She had been in and out of consciousness as the ambulance maneuvered through the shadowy streets. Antonio held her hand and tried to keep her focused.

Gabriella was in surgery for over two hours. Antonio was getting sick of this place. He was in a lot of pain himself but didn't bother anyone about it. He paced the floor, as restless as an alley cat, fretting about Gabriella, trying to settle his nerves and sort through the conflicting feelings he was having.

Once more, a woman he cared about had been in danger. For once he didn't blame himself. He'd been able to do something about it. He was thankful he didn't have to fire on Pucci. He would have. But he knew it would have created big problems.

His mind was a snake pit of questions. *How does Pucci know Gabriella? Why did he tell her he was sorry? Do I believe what Pucci said about Giulia ... that he had nothing to do with the attack? It sounded genuine. But if it's true, who's still out there that wants to harm Nicolo? And why?* He'd suspected as much all along.

Nicolo wandered into the waiting room sometime after midnight, still looking high-strung. "Have you heard anything about Gabriella?" he asked. "Is she alright?"

"One of the doctors came out a while ago. She's still in surgery. But he thinks she will recover fine."

"Thank God. I needed some good news. What a mess out there tonight! A gunfight on the streets of Siena. I really didn't think it would come to that. Thank God no bystanders were hurt. Remind me not to read the newspapers tomorrow."

Antonio nodded. Tension strained Nicolo's face … his voice was somber. "This will be all over the news. There will be inquiries."

"Remember, Zio, this was Marcello's operation."

"I know. I don't want problems for him. I'm glad the magistrate approved the operation, and General Peluso. I should have seen it coming … should have known a guy as reckless as Pucci would not go down without a fight. Especially after they deposed him as head of the family."

"Stop blaming yourself, Nicolo."

He nodded and moved on. "You were pretty stupid out there. Or brave. I can't decide which."

"My body says I was stupid." Antonio said with a half-smile. He couldn't think of anything else to say.

"I didn't even think about your injuries. Is that blood on your clothes yours or Gabriella's?"

"Mostly hers, I think. But I probably ripped off some scabs. I'll be fine. Would've been worse without the body armor."

Nicolo looked him up and down. "We've arrested the other family members. Booked 'em for aiding and abetting. Most will be out on bail by morning. I doubt any of them will face serious jail time. Hope I'm wrong about that. But now we know all the key family members. We'll be able to dismantle most of what they've built up here and monitor their future activities. We never let on that we had the room bugged. We don't want them to know that we're aware of tomorrow's drug shipment. We're not telling anyone what we heard in there until afterwards."

Antonio nodded. They both stared at the floor, fatigue and adrenaline fighting one another. Neither of them spoke for a while.

Nicolo finally broke the silence, "Luca and his staff are fine." His tone was more cheerful. "The restaurant will be closed down. Luca's not heart-broken. He's already out celebrating with Raphael and Leonardo, who were apparently only a block away during all of this," he said with a scowl that almost turned into a smile. "Luca said it's the first time in his life he's walked out and left his kitchen a mess." He laughed. It seemed to relieve his tension.

"So, what do you think about what Pucci said — about the road attack? Do you believe him?"

"I think I do."

"Yeah. Me too. You know that puts us back to square one. It means whoever wants to harm you is still out there."

Nicolo nodded. "I was so sure it was him," he said. "So sure." He closed his eyes and leaned his head back.

*****

With Gabriella still in surgery, Nicolo asked Antonio if he wanted to go with him to see if Mirabella was awake. She was. They lucked out. The nurses were tending her. Antonio cringed when he saw her face. He hoped she didn't notice. It was still puffy and discolored. Nicolo told her about the arrest, and that she would be free to live her life without the need to go into witness protection. She smiled for the first time since he had met her. Somehow that made the ugliness go away.

"I'm leaving Siena," she said. "Going home to Roma. My family came to see me. I told them the ugly truth," she paused, a tear ran down her cheek, "about the life I've been living. I know I've disappointed them. They want me to start over, do something good with my life. I want that too. I'm going back to school. I'd like to become a teacher."

This made Nicolo smile. He told Antonio afterward that he had seen too many like her. Many never escaped the trap until they were all used up and kicked to the curb. Her words brought a spark of life back to his eyes.

On the way past the nurse's station, Nicolo spotted nurse Isabella. He stopped and stared at her until she looked up. "Nurse Isabella, I need you to tend to my nephew again. Seems he's always getting himself into a scrape. I think his wounds may need cleaning and fresh bandaging."

She looked at Antonio and rolled her big brown eyes. She took his arm and led him to a room to tend to him. "What happened to you?" she asked. "Why is there blood all over your clothes?"

"Not mine. At least, not most of it anyway." He told her a bare minimum.

She made him strip down to his underwear. She carefully cleaned his wounds and put ointment on them, humming what sounded like Nessun Dorma as she worked. She was being more gentle than last time she had tended to him.

"I heard about what happened out there. So, you like to play the hero, huh?" she said, as she wrapped fresh bandages around his wounds, "Save the ladies, just like Popeye saving Olive Oyl."

He laughed, which hurt, and asked himself, *how does a young Italian woman know anything about Popeye?*

She saw him grimace. "How are your ribs?" she asked.

"They hurt like hell."

"I'm going to wrap them for you. That should help the pain." She wrapped him up, and went and found him a few Tylenols.

"*Mille grazie,*" he said with a pained smile. "You're an angel of mercy."

"*Prego,*" she laughed. Then added, "*Pazzo Americano*! Next time you tear your scabs off you can bandage them yourself."

He caught the glint in her eyes as she headed out the door. It seemed wrong to put his bloody clothes back on but that was all he had.

*****

Sometime around 2:00 AM, Marcello arrived after handling the booking of the other family members. The three of them huddled. "The magistrate is at the station now, overseeing the questioning," he told them.

They were interrupted by the surgeon entering the waiting area. "Good news," he said, glancing from one to the other. "Gabriella's out of surgery. The bullet passed through her hip and exited her buttocks. Missed the bones, but the soft tissue and tendons were pretty torn up. We did what we could. She's damn lucky it missed the artery! She'll recover fully in time. We'll need her to stay in the hospital about 36 hours, assuming no infection. Always a risk with gunshots. She'll need physical therapy but should be back on the job in a couple of months."

He turned to Marcello, "Your man, Sanguinetti, the bullet went through his calf, mostly muscle and soft tissue damage. He'll be fine. His recovery should be quicker, three or four weeks I'd say." Marcello breathed a sigh of relief.

"What about Pucci?" Nicolo asked.

"He'll live. Still in surgery. His arm looked worse than it was. They're trying to patch him up well enough so you guys can get him back to prison. We really don't want him here. He may be able to go back tomorrow. The prison infirmary can tend to him."

"I have a man standing by to guard his room," Marcello said. "Please let me know when you move him."

"Will do." He turned to go but Antonio put his hand on his arm. "Doctor, will Gabriella be coming around anytime soon?"

"She's in the recovery room. Probably within the hour."

Marcello looked at Antonio, "Why don't you go home? You're a bloody mess. Get out of those clothes and take care of that body of yours. After that baseball slide, you must be hurting like hell." His voice betrayed genuine concern. "I'll be here when she wakes up."

"I want to stay."

"Thought you might." He put a hand on Antonio's shoulder. "I'm glad you were there tonight. When you took off out of the van, I thought you were crazy. Thought I was crazy. That's probably true. But *grazie. Tante grazie* for watching out for my partner."

"Just glad I didn't have to fire her gun. Do you know who shot Pucci?"

"Paolo," Nicolo said.

"What about the dead bodyguard?" Antonio asked.

"Mancini and I were both firing at him," Nicolo said. "Could be he took bullets from both of us. Forensics will let us know." He stared off into space, taking no joy in the fact that he may have helped kill a man.

"Since we're all still here, I thought you guys might be interested in a couple of things," Marcello said. "We figured out who Lorenzo and Salvatore are, and the other voice. His name is Ottavio. They're all cousins. Lorenzo has a different last name, Ricci. He is the son of Pucci's aunt." He stopped and rubbed his face. "Matteo, the guy who has come up to take charge, is an uncle, as we heard earlier. We don't know a thing about him. Sounds like a family power struggle. We're hoping Marco can find out enough about Matteo and their operations for us to put them all away for a while."

Antonio turned to Nicolo. "Have you gone to see Sofia yet? She must be worried sick."

"I was just heading there. I sent word with a nurse earlier that we were okay. I didn't tell her about your heroics yet."

"Will you go home tonight? You have another big day tomorrow."

"No. I'm going to stay with Sofia. She needs me."

Antonio nodded. *And you need her,* he thought.

"Can you take Alessia home when you're done here?" Nicolo asked.

"Yeah. Sure."

*****

It was about 3:00 AM when Gabriella awoke, groggy and incoherent. She smiled at the two men standing by her bedside. Her eyes took in the blood on Antonio's clothes and she frowned. Then her eyes closed again. Antonio hoped to stay until she was more coherent, but the nurse chased them out of the room, telling them she needed to rest.

Antonio went to Giulia's room. Sofia rose and gave him a hug, ignoring the blood on his clothes. She stepped back, grabbed his hands, and looked him in the eyes. Her body looked limp, ready to collapse, but her eyes smiled at him. "It's going to be okay, Antonio. All of it. I know it. Have faith."

He pulled her close for a longer embrace. Maybe, just maybe, he was starting to believe her.

*****

On their way out, Antonio and Alessia found Nicolo and Marcello talking in the hallway. Marcello turned to Antonio. "I was just telling Nicolo. We found an ashtray full of cigarette butts on the table at the osteria. Some were Muratti Multifilters. My investigators just called me. Apparently, those belonged to Sandro."

"*Merda*!" Antonio said, "Something to cast doubt on Pucci's denials."

Nicolo shook his head, looking even more weary, and pushed past them to be with Sofia.

*****

When Antonio and Alessia reached the car, she reached the driver's door first and spoke, "Give me the keys."

"I'm fine. You're not on the rental agreement."

"Ask me if I care. You're not driving. Not in your condition." She planted her feet and glared at him until he gave up the keys. She flashed a victorious big-sister smile.

He mumbled something about bossy sisters as he gingerly folded himself into the passenger seat.

"Now tell me everything that happened," she said. "Every detail."

Chapter Twenty-two

Early Wednesday

It was after 4:00 AM when he made it to Leonardo's room. Sleep would be impossible for a while. The adrenaline was beginning to ebb, but his body was in pain, and his mind was racing as fast as a Ferrari. The apartment was dark and quiet, devoid of life, just himself and his jumbled thoughts.

He went to the kitchenette and found an open bottle of wine. He poured a glass, hoping it would settle his nerves. He didn't like to drink before bed. It usually woke him up in the middle of the night. But that logic held no water now. It was well beyond the middle of the night anyway. At this point, any sleep at all would be welcome.

He didn't want to drink on an empty stomach, so he rummaged through the refrigerator. Behind some outdated milk, and cheese that was either moldy, or gorgonzola—he didn't know which—he found some Sopressata salami and a medium-aged cheese that looked like it might not send him back to the hospital. They smelled safe enough.

He went to bed with his wine and a plate of food. He tried reading to distract his mind, but after a couple of pages he realized he couldn't remember a single word. He decided to try some music, his "Blues Rock" playlist—a little Susan Tedeschi and Stevie Ray Vaughan would surely change his mood. For some strange reason, blues music always made him feel better.

He'd been in gun battles before, but none so intense as what he'd experienced tonight. The scene kept playing over and over in his head like a video loop, intertwined with thoughts of Gabriella, and what Pucci said to her, and what he told Nicolo about the road incident.

Like birds on a telephone wire that fly away one by one, his tension ebbed away. He finally turned off the music and lights and fell asleep, probably close to six in the morning. He slept deeply for about three hours.

He awoke feeling more alive than he expected, but his body hurt even more than it did last night. He took some Tylenol, an extra-long, hot shower, followed by a blast of cold water, and hoped some movement would help. He did not regret what he had done. It may—or may not—have saved Gabriella, but he knew he had done everything he could to protect her. For once, the pain was worth it.

*****

Antonio opened the French doors, leaned on the railing, and thought about the day ahead. He would have nothing to do with the surveillance of the ship coming into Livorno, and the bust he hoped would follow. He would go to see Gabriella and Giulia later. He had no idea how to spend the rest of his day so decided to take another of his morning walks. After the insanity of last night, he longed for the peaceful serenity of the Chianti countryside. But not before he had some much-needed coffee. He limped his way to the kitchen. As he poured his coffee, he smelled something delicious baking, and heard laughter. He didn't feel like talking yet, so snuck out and whistled for Bella. It appeared she'd been waiting for him. He could tell she looked forward to these morning walks as much as he did.

Passing down the gravel path alongside the vineyard, he heard voices and more laughter. He looked up and saw Raphael, Leonardo, Luca, and a few others harvesting grapes. There were already several large baskets filled to overflowing in a trailer attached to their small tractor. They greeted him warmly, "*Buon giorno*, Zio Tonio!" They seemed no worse for having celebrated last night. For a moment, all felt well in the world.

"Would you like to help us with the harvest?" Raphael asked. "We usually have the whole family, but with everything going on we called in the reserves." He pointed to his friends, smiling. He was more animated than usual, not his normal, serious self.

"The harvest is late this year. August was cooler than usual," Leonardo explained. "We'd like to give these grapes a few more days but the rain is coming tomorrow afternoon."

He heard a cheerful voice behind him, and Aunt Frankie showed up with a basket of warm almond pastries and thermoses of hot coffee.

"You only get a pastry if you help the boys out, Antonio," she said playfully. *I don't think she has any idea of my condition,* he thought. *Oh hell, why not. My walk can wait.* He wolfed down a pastry, then snuck another behind her back, realizing how famished he was. He washed it down with more coffee.

He grabbed an empty basket. It took him twice as long to fill it as the young guys. Every bend hurt. Every twist made his ribs scream. Finally, he begged out, "I'll leave the rest to you young Italian stallions."

He found Bella sniffing around the woods nearby and whistled for her. She bounded to his side and they headed up the hill beyond the vineyard. He realized he was limping as he tried to keep pace with her. He noticed her long, milk chocolate ears getting dirty as they dragged the earth, moist with dew, every time she sniffed the ground, which was pretty much all the time. He laughed, which felt good, despite the pain.

Antonio wanted to forget everything and just enjoy his time here. He had come to be with the family he loved, and find some measure of peace. He'd been stuck in his grief so long it was hard to see past it. He knew it was time to move forward. But he couldn't. Not as long as Giulia lay in a coma, a victim of senseless violence. And for what? His desire to find out who and why consumed his thoughts.

He forced himself to focus on the case. What was he missing? Maybe it really was Pucci, and he was just one hell of an actor. Who else had motive to go after Nicolo?

He'd been a detective in Siena for well over three decades, so who could count how many bad people he'd arrested. But the same question kept plaguing him—who would have known his patterns, and expected him to be out riding that morning? Was his life so predictable that anyone could figure it out?

He knew Nicolo and Marcello would be tied up today. And Gabriella, well, she'd be out of the picture for a while. *Forget protocol. I'm going to find the answers. Someone has to work the case.* He made a mental list of things to follow up on.

There was one person he knew would be available—Gabriella. He hoped she would be clear-headed after a lack of sleep, and the influence of pain killers. He was sure they gave her opioids. Maybe she could answer some of his questions.

*****

Back from his walk, he found his Aunt Chiara in the kitchen. He greeted her with a hug and a kiss. He had always liked Chiara. She was quieter and more serious than her sisters. He thought of her as a bit of a freedom fighter, always taking up one cause or another. She was also a woman of the land. She loved working in their vineyards and taking care of their animals. They had a milk cow and a few goats. She used their milk to make homemade cheese, and taught the occasional class on cheese making. It didn't take much effort to sweet-talk her into frying him a couple of eggs. While she was preparing them, he found another almond pastry. *God, I'm gonna get fat!*

He phoned Nicolo. He answered on the first ring, *"Pronto.* Elena and Alessia are on their way to the hospital to take over for us. I'm going to bring Sofia home to rest."

"Good. Glad she's taking a break. But hasn't Alessia been there a lot? She just got home about seven hours ago."

"She insisted. Who am I to argue with your sister?"

"Good call."

"After I drop Sofia off, I'm heading over to meet Marcello. We have to be at the GDF at 10:30 for a final briefing."

"Well, while they have you guys tied up making drug busts, I'll be working our case. I'm starting over, from the beginning."

"Okay. Just ..."

"Just nothing, Nicolo. I know the damn rules! If I break any, you'll never know."

There were a few seconds of silence. "Be careful, Antonio."

"Yeah, yeah. Listen, I hate to beat a dead horse, but tell me one more time about your riding habits. Does every soul in Tuscany know when you're out on your bike?"

"I've been thinking about that. I ride most Wednesday mornings. I go in late. Usually, the same route you rode with Giulia. A lot of people know that: friends, co-workers, people I see en route. I almost always stop in Fonterutoli, and sometimes in Castellina."

"The circle gets bigger every time I hear you tell it. Who else wants to harm you, Nicolo? Or see you dead?"

"God, I wish I knew. I've been racking my brain half the night. Hardly slept at all."

"Not surprised. You'll be in great shape tonight. I managed to get a few hours' sleep. Listen, have you heard anything more about the DNA for the other cigarette?"

"Not yet. I'll ask Marcello when I see him. If he's got it, I'll give you a call."

"What about Pucci?" Antonio asked. "Will you question him again today, knowing what you now know about the cigarettes he smokes?"

"I should have a chance after our meeting," Nicolo said. "But I doubt he's going to change his story."

"Watch his body language, Nicolo. That will tell you. *Ciao*."

*****

His eggs were almost cold by the time he got to them. But his aunt knew how to cook them exactly right. The bright orange yolks stood so tall he wondered if she'd plucked them herself from under the chickens.

After eating, he headed to the hospital. It was a beautiful late morning for driving. Coming around a sharp bend he nearly rear-ended an Ape full of grapes. They didn't have the horsepower to move very fast.

Alessia and his mother, Elena, greeted him with hugs. "I've been hearing stories," his mother said, "about last night, about how you dove in front of Gabriella. Sounds like you were pretty brave, or stupid." Alessia laughed. He didn't.

"Why does everybody keep saying that?" He acted mad but wasn't.

"Lighten up, little brother," Alessia said. "We were actually just talking about how courageous you were."

He gave her a half-smile, "I don't really think I was either. I just wasn't going to see another woman I …"

"I what?"

"I …" he paused too long.

"… that you care about. Right? God, it's about time you admit it to yourself."

"Okay, sis. Yes, I care. I care a lot. Are you happy now that I said it?" He could see them both smile. "Women! Always trying to be matchmakers."

"In our DNA. Get used to it. How's your body feeling? Hurting, I'd guess."

"Yeah. Kind of set me back a few days." *Probably more like a few weeks.*

"Hey, I almost forgot. Sofia told us that Giulia stirred a little last night and murmured, more than she has seen until now. She's convinced she's going to come out of this soon."

He looked at her still, ashen form in the bed. *God, I hope she's right.*

Chapter Twenty-three

Wednesday

Antonio took the elevator to the second floor to see Gabriella. She was one room away from where he had been just days before. She was awake when he arrived. She gave him a sleepy smile, motioned him close, and kissed him on both cheeks. He had a strong desire to embrace her.

His feelings for her were growing stronger. He wondered if they were genuine, or his natural proclivity to rescue a maiden in distress? But she was no helpless maiden.

He felt like something inside him was awakening from a malaise. Losing Randi and Christina had changed him in ways he was just beginning to understand. He hadn't even considered feelings for another woman until now. Was he punishing himself? He knew he still blamed himself for not being able to save them. Why did these feelings for Gabriella make him feel that he was being untrue? He knew Randi would want him to move on. She'd even told him as much, the day they were on their flight to Paris. Her timing now seemed surreal—more than coincidental—as if she sensed her days were about to end.

He thought about how different Gabriella was from Randi. Randi was a mix of Norwegian and Scottish descent—a blonde with the hint of red that showed up in the sun. Her skin was fair, with freckles around her nose. He remembered how she used to lather on the sunscreen before she went surfing, then a layer of zinc oxide on her nose and under her eyes for added protection. Her dad taught her to surf when she was a little girl. She grew up in Newport Beach, in a house on a quiet finger of the bay. Her parents were wealthy but somehow managed not to spoil her. She was quiet, shy, and never knew how beautiful she was. *And nice to a fault* he thought. *She never wanted to hurt anyone's feelings. But she had never been that way with me. I was the one person with whom she could say whatever she felt. That wasn't always easy.*

Gabriella was as Mediterranean as you could get, with full dark hair and olive skin. She was outspoken, expressive, confident, decisive. But bringing balance to her toughness was a soft, vulnerable, feminine side. She had a compassion that was rare, except with those who have experienced the hardest things in life. Hardship does that to some, but not everyone. Many allow bitterness to take root, building a stone wall around their heart to protect themselves.

"Hey, hello, Antonio. Where did you go?" Gabriella asked.

"Just thinking," he said, looking back at her. "I'm glad you're okay," he took her hand. "I guess turnaround is fair play. Now I get to see you in a hospital gown. It looks a whole lot better on you. Just be careful walking around the corridors." He thought he saw her blush. It was the first time he had seen her with her hair down.

"Antonio. I wanted to say thank you." He knew what she was referring to, but wanted to hear it.

"For what?"

"Don't be an idiot! You know what for."

"It was nothing."

She looked him in the eyes. "No. It was something. Something I won't forget."

He nodded, deciding not to blow off her gratitude.

"It must have caused you a lot of pain."

"A bit." He didn't want to tell her how much. He changed the subject.

"Gabriella, I'm sorry to trouble you about the case. Can I ask you a few questions?"

She punched him in the arm. "You don't have to be so damn nice. Is this how American detectives get things done?"

He held his hands up, palms outward, "Only with beautiful women," he said. She punched him again, harder.

"You, on the other hand, have a mean streak," he said, before turning serious. "Do you know if anyone ever went to Roma to show suspect photos to the rental agent?"

"Yes. Marcello handled it. He sent the photos to our Roma office, the same set you had. They brought them to her. She didn't recognize any of them. Of course, most of those photos are Pucci's associates. So, if he really had nothing to do with this, as he claims, then she wouldn't have."

"Do you have any idea how the person who rented the vehicles managed to use a dead man's ID? It couldn't have been his photo unless he doctored it."

"We asked her about that. She says the man was wearing a hat and sunglasses but looked similar enough that she didn't question it."

"Did anyone ask how he managed to leave with both a car and a motorcycle?"

"She told us that she questioned the guy about that. She had never seen anyone do that before. He told her he had business for which he needed the car, but he also had some personal time and wanted to take a road trip on the motorcycle. He left in the car, supposedly dropped it at his hotel, and came back a while later for the motorcycle. He returned, dressed in his own black riding gear with his helmet."

"Do you know if they sent over a sketch artist?"

"That I don't know. They were supposed to. We'll need to ask Marcello. He's probably in his meeting right now but I'll send him a text."

"*Grazie*! Let me know. If they did, I'd love to get my hands on the sketch."

"So, what … you're taking over the case now?" she said in her best serious voice, but the smile in her eyes betrayed her.

"Somebody has to. You're playing hooky … eating breakfast in bed … and Marcello is chasing drug dealers." He turned serious again. "If I don't find out who did this, I will have failed another person I love. I've lived long enough with that kind of guilt."

Gabriella gazed at him for a long moment. He felt like his soul lay naked.

"I understand. More than you know. But remember, this isn't your territory, Antonio. Don't play lone wolf. We can't let you or your uncle Nicolo be too involved. If you find out anything, you need to take it straight to Marcello. A wrong move could mean justice doesn't happen. You don't want someone walking on a technicality."

Antonio nodded. She was right. But he believed he had enough good sense not to cross the wrong lines. He also knew he would do whatever he had to do to bring justice for Giulia. And justice doesn't always happen through the courts.

He hung around for a while, longer than planned. They talked about all kinds of things. When her lunch showed up, he decided to go and grab a slice of pizza. He'd grown fond of the little pizzeria around the corner from the hospital. Walking in, he was greeted by his favorite aromas, yeasty bread baking with rich tomato sauce, melting cheese, sausage and cured meats. It made him think about his own restaurant. He wondered how they were doing without him. It had been the furthest thing from his mind the last week.

*****

He had just taken a bite when Nicolo called. "Assumptions are your enemy," he said. It was a familiar phrase to Antonio. "We were barking up the wrong tree. We knew that maybe we were, but now it feels like we'll never find out who did this to my daughter."

"Maybe, Nicolo, maybe not. Don't give up. There are still the cigarette butts. Pucci could still be our guy. I'll be more confident if we can get that DNA." He told him about the discussions he'd had with Gabriella.

"Marcello told me she texted him. He gave her a hard time for working from a hospital bed. But he called Roma and it turns out they've had the sketch done since yesterday but never sent it. With everything going on, he neglected to follow up. They sent a digital file of the sketch. I'll text it to you."

"That's something at least. So, tell me about tonight's op."

"As much as I don't like Belluci, it feels like he's anxious to put these guys away. I'm sure it wouldn't hurt his career. He and Marco have put together a good plan. Between them they have all the resources they need. Marco and I will be watching from a distance. There will be two GDF teams there when the ship is unloaded. They've received cooperation from the port authority and one of the teams will be undercover as longshoremen, offloading cargo from the ship. If they identify what appears to be a drug offload, we'll be using a variety of means to follow it to its destination—same plan as I told you—drones—alternating vehicles. There will be backup teams in Siena that can deploy on a moment's notice."

He continued, "The big question I have is who'll be helping this Matteo character? We assume the Pucci family has more guys than those who were at the meeting last night. They may have even brought more from Napoli. We still know little about him … Matteo. Marco is trying to find out more and get us a photo."

"Sounds like a well-thought-out plan. Can I ask a question though?"

"What?" he asked in a clipped voice.

"Why are you involved? It sounds as if the Guardia di Finanza and Carabinieri have it handled. Do they want you involved, or is it your choice?"

"Some of both. They wanted my team to help with the tail and as backup. And they think I might be able to identify some of the people if I lay eyes on them. But as for my own reasons, I still wonder if there might be a connection between the drug running, the murders, and the road incident. It all feels like part of a big spider web."

"You may be right, Nicolo. I hope it goes well. Part of me wishes I could be there with you."

"I understand. But I'm glad you'll be home with Sofia tonight. She's nervous about me being involved in operations like this two nights in a row. Can't say I blame her. She's always been prone to worry. You know what it's like. But since the attempt on my life … you being hurt … Giulia in a coma … a shootout last night, she's worrying even more."

"I'll do my best to keep her mind at ease."

"Thanks. This could be a late operation. Don't wait up for me. I'll fill you in tomorrow when I decide to climb out of bed."

Chapter Twenty-four

Wednesday afternoon

Antonio made an unplanned stop at the gelateria on his way back to the hospital. He bought four cups of Frutta di Bosco. He dropped two cups off for Elena and Alessia, kissed Giulia on the forehead and said he owed her one, then brought one to Gabriella.

"How did you know this was one of my favorites?"

"Lucky guess."

Antonio heard his text notification and checked his phone. He pulled up the file showing the sketch. There was something familiar about the face. Was it the face in his dreams? Someone he knew? The hat and sunglasses made it difficult to recognize.

He showed it to Gabriella. She agreed it looked familiar but couldn't place it either. Both were frustrated by their inability to make the connection.

"Get out of here. I need to rest," Gabriella told him as she finished her last bite of gelato. He admired her forthrightness. As he headed for the door, she stopped him. "Antonio, I'm supposed to be released sometime tomorrow. I was wondering if you would drive me home?"

"Of course." He hoped his eagerness wasn't too obvious. "If I'm not around, just call or text me."

He turned to leave but before he got out the door, a man and woman walked in. Gabriella stopped him again.

"Antonio, please meet my brother, Andrea, and his lovely wife, Bria. They drove all the way from Perugia to see me. Andrea is a detective there. This is my American detective friend I told you about. Or maybe I should call him a restaurateur."

Bria greeted him warmly. Andrea with far less enthusiasm, eyeing him suspiciously. Gabriella chided him. "Andrea. Stop treating my male friends the way you did when I was a teenager. I've been a grown woman for some time, you know!"

Andrea winced. "Okay, sis, okay. You win. I'll play nice. *Piacere*, Antonio." He shook his hand and forced a smile. Antonio had doubts about his sincerity but laughed on his way down the corridor.

*****

Walking to his car Antonio felt more cheerful than he had for a long time. The reason was obvious. *How long since I've felt these feelings?* he asked himself, before hard reality set in. *Don't be an idiot, Antonio! What are you thinking? You can't let yourself fall in love. It makes no sense! We reside in different universes. And as much as I'd like to live in Tuscany, I have my family in Seattle ... Jonathan, Leah, grandchildren coming, Mom, Alessia, Shane, my restaurant, my friends. My whole life.* Then a second realization flooded his mind—Seattle didn't feel much like home anymore either. It hadn't been the same since ...

*****

Antonio didn't think there was anything more he could accomplish today. He headed back to the house. On the drive, he thought about how much Nicolo and Sofia's home felt like a second home to him.

As he drove up the packed gravel drive, he saw the garage doors wide open. He found Leonardo, Raphael, and friends sorting and crushing the Sangiovese and Canaiolo grapes from this morning's harvest. Luca and friends were doing the sorting, hands moving as fast as they could, while the brothers operated the crusher-destemmer. Raphael said they were planning to harvest the single row of Cabernet and Merlot grapes tomorrow before the rain came. The mood was high spirited, probably due to the half dozen empty and half-empty wine bottles he saw sitting around.

Nicolo and his family were amateur winemakers. Whatever extra grapes they didn't use they shared with neighbors or sold to a local winery. They made Chianti, and a Super Tuscan-style blend of Sangiovese, Cabernet Sauvignon, and Merlot. Usually, the whole family got involved in the process. When it came to blending the grapes, they all played a part, but it was Sofia's job to make the final call. They all recognized she had the most refined palate.

In a typical year they made three barrels of wine. Nicolo liked the oak to be subtle, so he bought his barrels from neighbors or local wineries—barrels which had been used for two vintages. Three barrels made about seventy-five cases, more than they would drink themselves. What they didn't drink they gave away or traded with friends and neighbors. This helped create an enviable cellar collection: wines from Chianti, around Tuscany, and other regions of Italy. They also had non-Italian wines, mostly Old-World varietals from France, Spain, Portugal, and Greece, as well as some Washington wines, which Antonio sent them, and wines from Chateau Teodora in Sonoma, the winery owned by Alessia's daughter and husband.

Antonio decided to help the guys for a while. It would take his mind off his troubles. He rolled up his sleeves and began to sort the grapes. It was backbreaking work, being bent over for hours, especially if you had just helped with the harvest. He wouldn't stay long.

The guys were grateful for the help. They poured him a glass of Morellino di Scansano, a red wine from the Maremma in southern Tuscany near the coast. Morellino translates "little dark one". He swirled the wine, lifted the glass to his nose, and breathed deep. He detected notes of dark cherries, pomegranate, and savory herbs. Finally, he took a sip. It was fruity and succulent with a gentle structure.

His stress began to flow away with the juices of the grapes. It felt great to hang out with younger guys. While they sorted, Luca told him the story about the osteria. "I'm going to boast a little and say those guys ate really well before things went crazy. We were taking a break when I heard the loudspeakers. I sent my sous chef and line cook to hide in a back corner of the storage area. I headed to the dining room. We had some guests there and I wanted to get them to safety. Just then Pucci and his guys barreled through the restaurant. I hit the floor … nearly crapped my pants," he chuckled. "Once they were out the front door, I brought the guests back to our hide-out, along with the waiters and bartender. There were almost twenty of us crammed in a little area."

"Must have been crazy," Antonio acknowledged.

"Yeah. A few of them were in a panic. I couldn't get them to quiet down. That's when it got fun. You should have seen it; an elderly woman, older than my grandmother, took charge. She made the sign of the cross, then spoke to them firmly, like they were her children. That was all it took. Damnedest thing I've ever seen," he laughed.

*****

When Antonio entered the house an hour later, with purple stained hands, Chiara and Frankie were getting ready to leave for the night shift at the hospital. They showed him a huge pan of Lasagne Bolognese they had made; homemade spinach pasta layered with meaty Bolognese and béchamel sauces. The aroma wafted through the kitchen. He could already taste it in his mind. It was ready to go in the oven an hour before dinner. Luca and friends were invited to stay for dinner.

But there was a competing aroma coming from the oven, the scent of apples, cinnamon, and warm autumn spices. "Oh my, it smells like autumn in here," Antonio said. Sofia, wearing a simple white apron, turned and smiled. She gave him a peck on each cheek.

"I took a nap when I got home, then decided to make a couple of apple cakes. We need to take good care of our laborers," she said, nodding toward the guys outside. "Besides, baking is therapy for me, relieves my stress."

He nodded as he picked up the wooden mixing spoon and took a lick.

"Oh, something else," she said. "A neighbor stopped by this afternoon with these dark cherries. They're already pitted." She held up two large canning jars.

His eyes lit up. "I've got the perfect use for those," he said, wanting to make a contribution, "one of my favorites." He opened a jar, drained them, and put them on a baking sheet. When she took the cakes out of the oven, he put the cherries in and roasted them until soft, adding another delicious aroma to the mix. While they were in the oven, he turned on the outdoor gas grill, sliced up yesterday's leftover bread, brushed the slices with olive oil, and grilled them for bruschetta. He topped the bruschetta with some of Chiara's goat cheese, and the roasted cherries, and set them aside for now. Later, while the lasagne was baking, he would place these back in the oven to warm, then top them with fresh thyme and a drizzle of balsamic glaze. A simple but delicious antipasti for tonight's meal.

Chiara and Frankie gave him kisses and left. He still had time to kill before dinner. Like Sofia, baking was therapy for him. Besides, it was his turn to contribute to the cooking. He was amazed he still had any energy left for it on so little sleep. He knew it would catch up to him later.

He went to the pantry and found the flour, salt, yeast, olive oil, and a scale. From memory he weighed out warm water, added the yeast, and set it aside. Then he weighed out the flour to give him the hydration level he wanted for his pizza dough. Using his fingers, he mixed salt into the flour. He added a few glugs of the aromatic green oil to the water and yeast, mixed it together, then combined that with the flour and salt. First, he stirred it with a wooden spoon until it began to come together. Then he rolled up his sleeves, wet his hands, and dug into the mixture, mixing it with his fingers. What was sticky at first became less so. He began to use his fingers less and the palms of his hands more, until he had some semblance of a dough ball. The therapy was working. While his hands were a sticky mess, his phone rang. The caller ID told him it was Nicolo. He decided to ignore it and call him back when his hands weren't in the dough.

He sprinkled flour on the stone counter, placed the messy dough on it, and began to knead. He used his weight to push the dough under crossed palms, folded it over itself, rotated and repeated until the dough was a smooth, elastic ball—firm to the touch, showing that the gluten in the flour was activated. He covered it with a clean cloth and set it aside to rest, allowing the rise to begin, and the glutens to relax.

He washed his hands and called Nicolo.

Chapter Twenty-five

Wednesday evening

N icolo answered immediately, "Pucci is dead."

"Huh? What! How?"

"The doctors didn't want to deal with him. They moved him to the prison infirmary this morning. He was found in the infirmary bathroom this afternoon. Someone stabbed him under the ribs into his heart. Not a clean wound. Probably a kitchen utensil."

"What a shock. Do they have any idea who did it?"

"Only conjecture. Could be payback from the Laganà family … the 'Ndranghetas, for the loss of their three guys. Not so sure they bought Sandro's denials. Or it could even be his own family. They obviously saw him as a loose cannon. They might have feared he would turn on them since he was deposed. Whoever it was had someone on the inside, unless they paid a guard to do their dirty work. No weapon has been found."

"Nor will it be."

"You're right about that."

"I'm guessing you didn't get another chance to talk to him."

"You'd be correct."

"Hey, Nicolo, careful out there tonight. Even I'm getting nervous with all this crap going on. These guys don't play games."

*****

Antonio hung up and went back to his dough. It was mindless work, thankfully, because his brain was focused on trying to make sense of this latest news. Murder always bothered him. Even when it was a guy like Pucci.

He cut the dough into eight pieces and formed each into a smooth ball. He placed them on a large baking sheet, lightly oiled them, covered them, and put them into the refrigerator for pizza tomorrow or the next day. He would ask Sofia which day she'd prefer. In Napoli, the birthplace of modern pizza, they made their dough and used it the same day. He liked to proof his dough for at least a day, preferably two, to optimize the flavor development.

Sofia came back to the kitchen, refreshed, and wearing a lovely dark-blue dress with a floral pattern for dinner. Italians like to dress nicely. Antonio thought she was even more beautiful now than in her younger years, despite the subtle lines of age.

He asked her what she had on hand to make pizza sauce. He knew she'd have everything he needed. She went to the pantry and brought back two jars of pureed tomatoes which she said she canned the week before he arrived. Then she went to the windowsill and brought back a potted basil plant that she had moved inside out of the weather. Basil doesn't like cold nights. She picked some tender leaves which she julienned for him. He added the basil along with salt, pepper, and extra virgin olive oil. *Almost forgot the garlic,* he thought. He cut off a head from the braid hanging above the island, pulled off a few cloves, laid them on the cutting board, and smacked them with the side of the chef's knife to loosen the skins. He minced the cloves finely and added them to the sauce. He tasted it, added more salt, then offered Sofia a taste. She smiled, nodding her approval. He covered the bowl and put it in the refrigerator. It would be even better in a day or two.

He decided not to tell her about Pucci yet. She had enough to worry about tonight.

*****

The wine still flowed and the dinner table was loud and boisterous with the boys and their friends. Sofia tried her best to join in and show her appreciation, but it didn't take a detective to see she was feeling uneasy. Nicolo had tried to reassure her, telling her that if they moved in to capture the drug cartel, it would be a team of GDF and Carabinieri. But she was no rookie at being a cop's wife. She knew things can go sideways, just like they had last night.

The boys did all they could to cheer her up and take her mind off her worries. After dinner, despite being dead-tired themselves, they insisted on doing the dishes. Antonio feared they would break some dishes in their present state but the six of them made quick work of it with no disasters.

Antonio found Luca outside having a cigarette afterwards. His light spirit seemed to have ebbed away like the tide.

"I shouldn't smoke these things," he said. "They're bad for my taste buds. Every chef knows that. But tonight, I needed one." He didn't say anything more for a while.

"I heard about Pucci," he said. "Nicolo called Raphael." He went quiet again, staring at the night sky. The stars were out in force and a nearly full yellow moon was rising over the hills in the east. "It's funny," he continued. "I'm saddened by his death. Despite who he was, he was actually pretty civil to me." He took a puff from his cigarette and slowly blew it out. "I loathe all this violence."

Antonio nodded. He felt the same. He'd seen plenty of violence in his life, but he'd never gotten used to it.

"Maybe I should come to Seattle and work for you." He looked at Antonio, probably searching his face for a response. "I don't think I'd like all that rain though."

"You'd certainly be welcome. The rain's not as bad as most people think. Most of it comes in the fall. We get plenty of gloomy days though. And days I call *dry rain* days. It rains all day and you get an eighth of an inch. Some people love it. I have to admit though, I've never quite adjusted to it." He joined Luca in his silence, then added, "Beautiful place for cycling though—and safer than the roads of Tuscany." Luca looked at him again and nodded.

"I live in a town called Woodinville," Antonio added. "About twenty miles northeast of Seattle. That's where my restaurant is. There are dozens of wineries, so a lot of people come there to drink wine. They get hungry."

"I'd like to visit sometime."

"Come anytime. You can stay at my place. It feels pretty empty."

Luca stubbed out his cigarette and looked at him. "I've heard about your wife and daughter. I'm sorry."

Antonio just nodded and turned his gaze to the moon.

A cold breeze passed by. It caused a chill to penetrate his bones. It was the coldest night yet. Luca rejoined his friends as they ate their apple cake, with brandy whipped cream that Sofia whipped up. Then they headed off to celebrate a good day's work. Antonio hoped they all made it home safely.

*****

Antonio brought in an armful of firewood. He started a roaring fire in the tall and wide stone fireplace. He joined Alessia, Elena, and Sofia, as they gathered around.

"Thank you, Antonio," Sofia offered. "A good fire warms more than the body."

The four of them talked late into the night. It was hard for them to think about going to bed while Nicolo was out tracking the operation. It felt comforting to be together.

Sofia asked the same question Antonio had asked. Why was Nicolo involved in this operation? She just nodded when he told her Nicolo's explanation.

Elena and Alessia fell asleep on the couch sometime before midnight. Antonio was nodding off in a leather chair when he heard a text notification go off. It was Sofia's phone.

Sofia smiled and breathed a deep sigh. "All is well," she said in a voice the others barely heard. She showed Antonio the message on her phone … *If you're up, I want you to know I'm safe. On my way home.* It was 1:05 AM.

*****

After hearing the good news, Alessia and Elena wandered off to bed.

When Nicolo arrived home, Antonio was anxious to hear about the operation, but Sofia wouldn't allow it. She told Nicolo to come directly to bed.

Before leaving the room, Nicolo told him only that there had been a recovery of several million dollars of drugs. More importantly, no one was injured or killed. He would tell him about the rest in the morning.

This was enough to ease Antonio's mind. He was curious for more details but forced his mind elsewhere. When he climbed into bed, he pulled out his electronic tablet and went back to his book. It was his habit to read at bedtime. It helped him relax. His comprehension was better tonight, but he knew he wouldn't get far. The book was one of the Harry Bosch detective series, by Michael Connelly, one of his favorite authors. He thought it was funny that this was his favorite genre. He thought he might like to write his own novel someday. A half-page later, he was asleep.

Chapter Twenty-six

Thursday morning

Antonio slept like a bear in winter until mid-morning. He found Nicolo bleary eyed in the kitchen with his hands wrapped around a steaming cup of coffee. It smelled good. None of the ladies had shown their faces yet. Antonio poured himself a cup.

He took a seat across from Nicolo who filled him in on the operation. "As far as a drug haul, it was very successful. But four of the perps got away, including Matteo, the new boss of the Pucci clan."

Nicolo took a sip and rubbed his face. "The ship arrived early, about 3:30. The customs people boarded about 4:00, and had the suspected cargo released by 5:00. The cargo was palletized, three pallets, so it didn't take long to get those loaded on the trucks. It appeared to be wine cases. We found out later that the drugs were inside the bottles. There was real wine in the outer cases of the pallets to appease any nosy customs inspectors. The cases were loaded onto a truck of a wine group known as *La Vendemmia Gruppo di Vini*.

"They left the docks an hour later, took an indirect route, south on E80, then east on SR68 past Volterra, San

Gimignano, Monteriggioni. Trailing the truck went without a hitch. They arrived in Siena shortly after dark at a wine shop called *La Dolce Vino* on Via Esterno di Fontebranda. There were three guys on the truck. They were joined by another five to unload. The cases were taken to their cellar.

"Marcello and Belluci got into an argument about when to move in. Marcello wanted to do it when most of the guys were outside, but Belluci pulled rank. He thought it made sense to wait until they were in the cellar … said he didn't want any more gun battles on the street. In hindsight, Marcello had the better plan. Turned out there was a way to escape the cellar."

"From a cellar? How the hell do you do that?"

"Ever heard of the bottini?"

"The underground aqueduct that runs beneath the city?"

"Yeah. Most of it was built about seven-hundred years ago to bring water into the city, some even earlier by the Etruscans. You can tell when different sections were built by the architecture. The newer tunnels have barrel vaulted ceilings, like you see in wine cellars. Thus, the name."

Nicolo took a drink of his coffee. "It's a perfect escape route, a labyrinth which branches in all directions. Twenty-five kilometers of tunnels with multiple exit points. When our teams stormed the cellar, they headed there like so many tunnel rats. We caught two of them right away, before they got into the aqueduct. Another two were captured in the bottini. My guys and I were with the team that followed them in and made the capture. Shots were fired but they quickly found they were outgunned and gave up. One of their guys was injured. He'll recover."

"Sofia's not going to be happy when she hears there was shooting."

"I don't plan to tell her." He looked up from his coffee cup and stared hard at Antonio. His message was clear.

Antonio nodded. He didn't like it but knew this was no time to cross Nicolo.

"The other four men, including Matteo, were never found. Some of us continued to search the tunnels while others split up in teams and went to cover as many exits as they could. We called in the stand-by units and even extra Polizia Municipale. But no luck."

"At least you and your guys are all safe."

"Yeah. That's what's most important." He took another sip of coffee. "Belluci separated the guys we caught and took them to the GDF for questioning. They clammed up tight. I was there for a couple of hours while they were being questioned but nothing was gained. I'm sure they're afraid to talk. Afraid they'll end up like Pucci."

Antonio nodded, "Can't say I blame them."

Nicolo continued, "But as far as drug busts go, it was big. Marco sent me a text this morning. About 100 kilos of cocaine and 10 of ecstasy. Street value of 60 million euros."

Antonio whistled.

"Did you hear about Operation Pollina in '98, or the Genoa bust in '99? Compared to those this is chump change. Still significant though."

"I remember reading about the Pollina Op. Didn't they get something like 4 tonnes of cocaine?"

"Yeah. And 120 kilos of ecstasy. It was a multi-nation operation. Ninety members of the 'Ndrangheta family were arrested in six countries. I think I told you those guys are bigger than the Cosa Nostra ever were. Same family the Laganà clan is part of. I've heard the families learned a lesson from that. They smuggle their drugs in smaller lots now. That way, if they get busted, they don't take such a big hit."

"I heard something about the Genoa bust too. But don't remember the details."

"Not as big as Operation Pollina but still huge. Confiscated a cargo ship in Genoa with 2 tonnes of cocaine destined for Spain, worth about 500 million euros. It was a group of traffickers known as the Gulf Clan, a Colombian cartel.

"I don't want to downplay this though. It's going to hurt the Pucci family and the Camorra cartel they're a part of. And Marco and his Europol team have already begun following the money trail of the wine group and freezing assets. Between that, and our operation at the osteria, we've put a big dent in mob operations in Tuscany."

Antonio studied Nicolo's face. "Agreed. But can I ask you a question?"

Nicolo flicked his eyes toward him and nodded.

"You don't seem all that excited about these busts."

Nicolo's eyes narrowed and turned dark. "Come on, Antonio! Means nothing to me while Giulia lies in that hospital. You should know that!"

Antonio felt like an idiot. After all, it was exactly how he felt. He set that aside.

Nicolo's anger dissipated as quickly as it flared. "And it got us nowhere on our murder cases or the road incident." He paused and poured them each more coffee. "I'm heading to the questura for an update meeting with my detectives. Do you want to come along?"

"Yeah, I'd like that, but I'll bring my rental. When Gabriella is released later today, I agreed to drive her home."

Nicolo gave him a sly sideways glance and tried to hide his smile.

*****

The sky above Siena was starkly beautiful today. The gathering cumulus clouds billowed tall, making the blue sky look even deeper blue. Antonio had seen the boys out in the vineyard when he left, looking quite hungover.

He hoped they were almost done harvesting the final row of grapes.

When he arrived, Nicolo was waiting for him, leaning against his Alfa Romeo outside the questura. Antonio was surprised he had driven it with the rain coming. They hadn't eaten breakfast, so they walked to a bakery nearby and picked out some pastries. Walking back, Nicolo received a call. He walked away from Antonio and turned his back.

He returned a few minutes later. "Magistrate Mariani," he said without enthusiasm. "She thinks I'm too involved in the investigation of the road incident. She was reminding me again to focus on the murder investigation. She's worried that after the last two nights, and Pucci's death, if we don't solve these soon, a full-fledge mob war could break out."

"She's right to be worried. Did you tell her I had taken over the other investigation?"

Nicolo gave him a stern glare. He didn't have much of a sense of humor today.

"I know, I know—be careful. Don't worry. I am."

Chapter Twenty-seven

Thursday mid-day

When they arrived at the questura, Paolo and Mancini were standing outside. It appeared they were having a heated discussion. When Paolo spotted them, he turned and walked inside. Mancini nodded as they passed, and stayed to finish his cigarette. Antonio looked to see what kind it was. It had no filter. He was keeping an eye on everyone he saw smoking.

Mancini was a handsome man with a George Clooney haircut and a neatly trimmed beard. He was wearing a fine Italian suit, tailored to show off his trim physique. The ladies probably loved him, but the guy never smiled. A minute later he followed them into the meeting room where Paolo and Jordy were waiting, looking as bleary eyed as Nicolo. He remained standing, leaning against the wall with his arms folded across his chest.

Antonio noted how opposite Mancini and Jordy were from one another, and yet they were partnered up much of the time. Nicolo had said they sparred like a couple of brothers but there was an underlying fondness and respect. Jordy was shorter and stockier, with thick black hair and mustache. His attire was far more casual, rumpled, you could say. He also had the sense of humor the others lacked, at least today.

The room was a typical detective room, furnished with a laminate table and plastic chairs. The walls were white except for a single window, and three bulletin boards mounted on the wall. Each had grizzly photographs of the murder victims, as well as copies of coroner reports and other notes. Antonio looked at each board carefully before taking a seat. It soured his mood. Murder is something you never get used to.

Nicolo wasted no time. He was clearly frustrated, bordering on angry as he spoke. Antonio wasn't sure if he was mad at the detectives for their lack of progress, or at the magistrate, or at whoever put Giulia in a coma, or at himself. *Feels like all of it,* he thought. Whatever the reason, it made him focused and intense.

"Good morning, detectives. I need updates on the murder cases. We now have four murders, including Pucci. It will probably be more if we don't get a handle on it."

Mancini spoke, "Boss, we've had no time with these ops the last two days, neither of which brought any clarity." He leaned forward with his hands on the table. Color rose in his face. Still, his speech was refined. Antonio could tell he was well educated.

"Well, we know that Pucci claimed he had nothing to do with the murders," added Paolo. "Though it looks like someone didn't believe that."

"Is it such a problem that these mob guys are killing each other off? It seems like they're doing our job for us," Mancini added with obvious sarcasm.

"Bastards get no sympathy from me!" Paolo spat. His whole body seemed to tense. "They're killing the young people of Siena with their drugs!"

Antonio was caught off-guard by Paolo's outburst. He'd never seen him so emotional.

"I understand how you guys feel. Especially you, Paolo. But you know this is our job. If a mob war breaks out, it's only a matter of time until innocent people get caught in the crossfire."

Nobody dared reply until Nicolo spoke again. "I've been reminded to stay out of the road incident and let Marcello handle it. But my gut tells me they're related. Do you guys see any connections, or am I just chasing ghosts?"

"I don't see it," Paolo said. "The road incident was someone after you. Why would someone who is killing drug dealers also want to kill you, the commissario? Makes no sense. Could have been Pucci, even though he denied it. And didn't you arrest a member of the Laganà family a few months back—that Sergio guy—for the prostitution and human trafficking ring he was running? They've got motive. I'm sure there are a lot of guys like them who would love to take revenge."

Nicolo nodded. Wheels were turning in his head.

"I agree," Mancini added. "And if that's the case, Nicolo, they're probably still after you. I think you should lie low for a while and let us work on this."

Nicolo ignored the comment. "This morning I got some new information from Marcello and Gabriella. The Carabinieri forensic lab came up with DNA for the cigarette butt found near my house."

Mancini and Paolo looked at one another, as if in surprise. Antonio wondered if Nicolo saw it.

"Another cigarette butt?" Paolo asked. Antonio realized they didn't know about the second one.

Nicolo filled them in, then he added, "It appears this is the same brand as the one found on the road near Fonterutoli, not a common brand, so odds are this was the same person."

Nicolo paused, wheels turning in his head again, "We know this was the same brand Pucci smoked. We found his butts in the ashtray at the osteria. But the DNA on the one found near the house was not a match to him. Nor to anyone in our criminal data base. We sent it off to Marco to see if it matches anyone in their system."

"I'm not surprised," Mancini said. "I never thought Pucci would be directly involved in the road incident. So, let's suppose someone *was* watching you leave on your bike—or at least they thought it was you—all the more reason for you to lie low. And I agree with Paolo. I can't see any connection between that and the murders of the drug dealers."

"Back to the murders," Paolo said. "I got one thing done before we headed for Livorno yesterday. We finally received the phone records for the first two dealers. I went through them thoroughly. Could not find a single clue. No pattern changes. No new callers that suddenly surfaced."

"Do you know when you'll receive the records for the third murder?"

"Hopefully tomorrow. If not, we're looking at Monday."

Jordy spoke for the first time. Antonio noted his thick southern Italian accent. It was entertaining to watch how much his hands figured into the conversation. "I ain't so sure that third murder is tied to the other two. MO's different. First two guys were low-level street distributors, kidnapped off the street, shot up with needles. Camilleri was shot in his apartment. The only thing tyin' 'em together is they happened about the same time, and that he was supplyin' the street guys."

"And they all belonged to the same family, Jordy," Paolo reminded him.

Antonio thought out loud, "Is it possible the third murder was the Laganà family cleaning up their own mess? Maybe they were afraid the first two guys gave up information, including who their supplier was. Maybe they didn't trust him to follow their code of silence."

"*Omerta.*" Nicolo sounded the word out slowly. "Farfetched, but possible. Those low-level guys know little or nothing about beyond their direct supplier. But Camilleri probably would have known a lot more."

Mancini broke in. "Maybe it was someone else in Pucci's family. Maybe Sandro denied it because he knew nothing about it. Maybe they were acting independently while he was in prison. Or getting direction from Naples … from this Uncle Matteo guy who's taking over here, or someone else who's pulling strings."

"So many possibilities," said Paolo. "I even considered the Nigerian Mafia. They've been increasing their alliances with the Camorra family of Naples, as well as the Cosa Nostra. That could put them at odds with the 'Ndrangheta."

"I can't see them doing this for the Pucci family, but we'll see what the word on the street is," Nicolo said. "Mancini. I know you were working with the magistrate to get the CCTV access. Have you been through those?"

"Yeah. A couple of times. But you know those street guys are smart, they work the blind spots. I've looked at footage from nearby, looking for anything suspicious— like someone showing their face on the night of both murders—nothing. But my time's been limited by the other ops. With more time and a wider search, I might find something."

"Jordy, tell me about bank records. Did you get them?"

"Yeah, boss. Nothin' there either that stands out. I'll spend some more time on 'em today."

"Actually, I have another idea. I'd like us to look at all this with fresh eyes. I want to rotate it around. Paolo, you look at the CCTV footage. Mancini, you look over the bank records. Jordy, take a fresh look at the phone records."

"That's like starting all over boss," Mancini said, with a frown. He put on his designer glasses and grabbed the bank records from the table by Jordy.

"Exactly."

Nicolo continued, "I'm going to take Antonio with me to take another look at Camilleri's apartment. Then I'm going to hit the street and talk to my CIs, see if anything new has surfaced. Antonio, you'll probably be tied up by then," he said with a smug smile.

"You sure you want to hit the street alone, boss?" Mancini asked. "You have a family to think about."

"Thanks for your concern, Mancini. I'll be careful."

Antonio remembered Nicolo telling Sofia the same thing yesterday, hours before following those drug smugglers into the dark tunnels of the bottini.

"Don't worry boss. We'll be watchin' your back," Jordy said.

Chapter Twenty-eight

Thursday afternoon

Nicolo and Antonio walked to Camilleri's apartment. Nicolo needed the fresh air. Besides which, driving and parking in Siena is no easy task. They passed through the Piazza del Campo, one of the largest piazzas in Italy, and one of Antonio's favorites. He thought of the Palio horse race held here twice each summer. He'd seen it several times, usually with an excellent balcony view because of Nicolo's connections. Each of the city's ten main districts, or contradas, has a horse in the race ... one frenetic lap around the piazza. He loved the pure insanity of it.

It is a rare day that there are not hundreds of people in the piazza. Today was no exception, even though peak tourist season was past. The cafés, with their sienna-colored awnings, and tables that spill out onto the piazza, were packed with people eating lunch. Dozens more mingled about the central area which slopes gently towards the Palazzo Pubblico and its tall narrow tower, the Torre de Mangia, pointing like a finger toward heaven. The piazza felt calm and peaceful. Students, locals, and tourists, intermingled with nuns, a pair of gendarmes, and a wandering dog. Most sat with their face to the sun, soaking up its warmth, which would soon disappear behind the cumulus clouds building in from the Tyrrhenian Sea. A young woman sat playing her guitar with her case open to collect donations. Antonio placed a Euro in it as he passed by.

By contrast, the apartment they arrived at was a dark, dingy place, located on the second floor above a taverna. When they arrived, a charcoal-colored cat sat in front of the door, as if awaiting entry. When they opened the door, she turned and wandered off. Nicolo and Antonio ducked under the yellow crime scene tape. They had no idea what they were looking for, just some missing piece of the puzzle. They'd know it if they found it. They both had a lot of experience with these kinds of searches. Nicolo's initial search was cut short by the fateful call telling him about the road incident. He'd left it to Mancini and Jordy to stand in for him. They found nothing of interest.

Nicolo told Antonio, "I haven't been able to figure out why Camilleri opened the door to his killer. The entry was not forced. It had to have been someone he knew."

It was a tiny apartment, dusty and messy. The aroma of death still lingered in the air. The kitchen, dining area and living room were pretty much one room. There was one bedroom, and a bathroom, not much bigger than an anchovy can.

"Start in the living room, Antonio. That's where Baccio was shot. I was searching that area when I was here before."

There was dried blood on the Oriental area rug where Baccio's body was found. Nicolo showed him crime scene photos. "There were two shots to the chest. A large caliber gun at close range. Both slugs passed completely through his body. The second shot was after the body fell. We could tell by the angle, and it went through the rug and chipped the tile underneath. We didn't find any slugs or shell casings. He would have had to roll the body over to retrieve the one beneath him. This was a pro job."

"Even pros make mistakes. Or so a great detective once told me."

"Trying to butter me up? Yeah, maybe we'll get lucky."

"You also told me good detectives make their own luck. Of course, you were a rookie detective who knew it all when you told me those things. And I was an impressionable teenager uncertain if he wanted to be a cop."

"Yeah, well, they're still true."

"I'm not sure I ever told you, Nicolo. It was your influence that made me decide to join the force. Life with my father had given me a bad taste, even before he got killed."

Nicolo nodded. "I know your relationship with your father wasn't easy. But he was a good man, Antonio."

Antonio didn't want to pursue this conversation right now.

While Nicolo searched the bedroom, Antonio went over every inch of the living room. He'd come up empty until he lifted the rug and noticed a smudge in the dried blood on the tile. He looked closer and saw what looked like a partial fingerprint. It was faint, but he thought it looked like the side of the finger or thumb. It probably happened when the shooter retrieved the slug. *Surprised he wasn't wearing gloves,* Antonio thought.

He called Nicolo over to show him. He agreed with Antonio's assessment. "This really pisses me off," Nicolo said. "I can't believe nobody caught this! I hadn't gotten this far. But the forensic team, Mancini, Jordy, someone should have seen this. Now whether there's enough of a print remains to be seen."

Nicolo called Lieutenant Vitali, the head of forensics. His voice betrayed his frustration. Antonio could hear Vitali apologizing. He said he would come right away. While they were waiting, they finished their search, finding nothing else of interest.

Vitali arrived and took the print. "I'll get on it right away," he promised. "It's more of a smudge than a clean print. Probably why we missed it. I'm not confident we can get a match. We have software which will try to fill in the remainder, but it's not always accurate."

*****

As they exited the building, the cat sat on the steps. She followed them with her eyes. Antonio had a feeling there was a story she wanted to tell them.

On their walk back to the questura, Antonio remembered something. "Nicolo. You said something earlier to Paolo when he reacted so strongly. You said that you 'especially understood how *he* felt.' What's the story?"

"Sorry, thought you knew. You've known him a long time. But you've had your own tragedies to deal with." They rounded a corner. "A little over a year ago, Paolo's nephew—his sister's son—Maximo, died of a meth overdose. I think you even met the kid; he was only eighteen. A few weeks later, his sister, two years older, tried to commit suicide. She would have been successful if Paolo hadn't shown up in time. He found her unconscious. She blamed herself. Knew he was using."

Nicolo stopped cold and looked at Antonio. "The dealer was Riccardo Coppola, the first murder victim. He'd been arrested six months previously by Mancini and Jordy. But they mishandled evidence. It took months to go to trial; the whole time, Coppola was out on bail. Then the judge threw the case out. His attorney, probably provided by the Laganàs, was too damn sharp."

"Not likely the Laganàs killed their own guy, then," Antonio said. "Why would they spend all that time and money on his defense if they planned on taking him out?"

"Good question. I've thought of that. Didn't your mother used to tell that you were too smart for your britches?"

"Yeah. Like forty years ago." Antonio paused, then turned serious. "I don't really want to ask this next question."

"Go ahead. I know what's coming."

"Is it possible Paolo murdered Riccardo? Maybe Ricci too? Or even all three? That's a huge motive."

"Of course, I considered it. But I've worked with Paolo for over a decade, and I've known him much longer. I just can't see it. Besides, he has an alibi for the night. He was with Mancini."

Antonio heard the text notification on his phone go off. "*Mi scusi*, Zio" He looked at his phone. His dour mood lifted when he saw it was from Gabriella.

Will be released in an hour.

He typed, *Great. I'll be there. If you promise your brother won't beat me up.*

Haha. I think you can handle yourself.

I'm too damned sore to fight him. See you in a while.

"I'll see you later, Nicolo. Duty calls."

"You call that duty? Watch out for her overprotective brother."

Antonio gave Nicolo an incredulous look. "How'd you know?" he chuckled. "Oh, by the way, Nicolo, I made pizza dough and sauce last night. I'm not sure how late I'll be. If you want, you can fire up the oven. I told the girls we were making pizza for dinner tonight."

"We?"

"*Mille grazie*, Nicolo! I knew you'd back me up. There are a few things we need by the way." Antonio handed him a rumpled list from his pocket. "I'll keep you posted."

*****

Driving from the questura to the hospital, Antonio considered the conversation about Paolo. He remembered Paolo's sister, Amara, a widow, and her son, Maximo, and daughter, Alessandra. They had come to dinner at Nicolo and Sofia's house the night they prepared the roe deer sauce. They had all seemed so happy around the kitchen island, helping to roll out the pici pasta.

The kids were young then. He remembered Paolo's affection for them. He treated them like his own children. Hearing about what happened to Maximo hit him like a punch in the gut. He could only imagine the impact it had on Amara and Paolo.

Could Paolo have killed one or more of the drug dealers? Had Nicolo seriously considered the possibility? What about the alibi? Was it possible that Mancini was covering for him? Or that they had done it together?

Antonio asked himself if he could kill someone in those circumstances. He had seen guilty killers and drug dealers walk free. It eats you up inside. He could only imagine if the guilty person caused the death of someone you loved so dearly. He knew beyond doubt he could have killed the terrorist who took the life of Randi and Christina, and so many others. But the French police got to him first.

232

He believed in forgiveness. Without it we become angry, bitter people. He'd battled that bitterness. He had tried so hard to forgive that man, if you could call him that. Not for the man's sake, he was dead anyway, and probably rotting in hell. No, he had tried to forgive him for his own sanity, so he could move forward. But so far, he hadn't done a very good job of it. He knew forgiveness would have been near impossible if the man walked away free; if he'd sat in a courtroom and watched the judge dismiss the case. Wouldn't he have been tempted to take justice into his own hands? If Giulia does not recover, will I be able to forgive the men who did this to her?

These questions troubled him deeply. Can a man who has devoted his whole life to doing good, do the ultimate evil? Take another man's life? Many good men have crossed that line.

Chapter Twenty-nine

Thursday late-afternoon

Antonio took the hospital stairs to Gabriella's room. Marcello was leaning against the wall outside her room. He said she was getting cleaned up and dressed.

"I need to talk to you, Antonio," Marcello said. Antonio nodded, wondering about Marcello's fatherly tone.

"I heard the magistrate talked to Nicolo, reminded him where his focus should be … allow me to handle the road incident. I'm going to need your help."

"How's that?"

"Nicolo says he'll keep his fingers out of it if I keep him informed. He still thinks the cases might be related. Maybe they are. If so, our investigations will re-converge down the road. He knows a misstep could compromise everything. But I'm worried, afraid his emotions might overrule his good sense."

"I'll keep an eye on him." *But who's going to keep an eye on me?* Antonio thought. "Just don't hide anything from us, Marcello." He looked him in the eye. "Are we clear?"

Marcello nodded, his eyes flicked away and back. "Watch your steps, too, Antonio. Remember, you're a guest in our country. I like you." He hesitated, to collect his thoughts, "I've given you a long leash, longer than I should have. Don't take advantage of it."

Their fragile alliance suddenly felt adversarial to Antonio. He didn't like being referred to as a *guest* in Italy. This country was a second home to him. He'd try to overlook it. But he was rather good at reading body language, and his instincts told him that Marcello was already hiding something, something he wasn't telling him.

"Don't forget, Marcello. Those guys nearly killed me, too. I'm not going to stop until one of us figures out who it was."

*****

A nurse came out, pushing Gabriella in a wheelchair. Standard procedure he knew, even if not needed. She glanced from one man to the other, sensing the tension. When they reached the exit, they handed her crutches and helped her up. Antonio grabbed her bag. He was ready to get out of the hospital. He had spent way too much time there lately.

It was tricky getting her into the tiny Lancia Ypsilon. He wished he'd thought to trade for the use of the van.

The hospital had given her a pillow. She put it on the seat, but still winced when she sat on her posterior.

She instructed him to drive north to Castellina, and then she would direct him. As he drove, she pulled out her phone and sent a text. He glanced at her.

"My neighbor," she said. "She's been taking care of my dogs. She's going to keep them a few more days but I asked her to bring them over so I can see them. I've missed my girls."

The route took them through Fonterutoli and past the accident scene. The roads were wet from a shower that came briefly and left. Antonio looked in his mirror and noticed a car following them. It had been with them since leaving Siena. He wondered if he was being paranoid. He let out a sigh when it turned off into Castellina's parking area.

He decided to venture a question. "Has Marcello kept you abreast of the investigation?"

Gabriella was tentative in her response. "Yes. He brought me up to date. He's had time to focus on it with the other operations in the rearview mirror."

"I get the feeling he's not telling me something."

"You know, if that's the case, I can't tell you either. But I'll tell you this. He has nothing solid. Just some gut instincts he wants to look into."

Antonio didn't know what to make of that.

They passed through Castellina and Gabriella directed him to take a small road downhill toward the west. He was blinded momentarily by the sun which found a gap in the clouds. The road wound down the hill and narrowed to a single lane. They came to a gravel road which she directed him to turn on.

They passed a few houses. Two of them looked newer, though built out of stone in the Tuscan style. Gabriella pointed to an old stone farmhouse.

"That's my place. The house is nearly two hundred years old. It belonged to my husband's family. They could have taken it back after he died, but they were gracious to me. Renato was their only child. I still see them often. They're very, very good to me. They treat me like their own daughter. I love them dearly."

"Where do they live?"

"They have a small house in Castellina, with little property to worry about, just enough for her rose garden and his little vegetable garden. They can walk just about everywhere. They are in their eighties—married almost sixty years—mostly good health. They seem happy."

He helped her gently from the car and retrieved her crutches. He heard friendly barking, looked up and saw her neighbor coming down the gravel road with two beige and brown dogs with hairy faces and ears.

Gabriella lit up. "My girls! Oh my God, I've missed you!"

She knelt gingerly. The dogs ran to her, pouncy, with tails wagging a hundred miles an hour. He was afraid they were going to knock her over on her injured bottom. He knelt and put his hand on her back.

"Meet Lucia and Gia," she said as she lovingly petted them. "Mother and daughter, purebred Italian Spinone. I bred Lucia a few years ago."

"I've never heard of the breed."

"They were nearly extinct after the war, but saved by enthusiasts. Good hunters. I personally don't hunt, but my father-in-law takes them out. He likes to hunt wild boar and quail. It's thought they are named for the spino, a thorn bush, because they are great for hunting in dense brush."

Antonio petted the dogs and scratched them under the neck. They took to him right away. The feeling was mutual.

Gabriella's neighbor, a red-haired woman of maybe fifty, caught up and eyed Antonio curiously.

"And now meet the lovely Fiorella, my neighbor."

"*Piacere*, Fiorella. *Mi chiamo Antonio Cortese. Sono un amico di Gabriella.*"

"Formal, isn't he?" she laughed, as she looked at Gabriella.

"Fiorella was an English teacher at the high school for over twenty years. Feel free to speak English. She probably speaks it better than you do."

She looked at Gabriella. "I'm so glad you're home. I was worried sick when I heard." She paused and made eye contact with Gabriella. "I made some cannelloni for you, lamb sausage with porcini mushrooms, with my world-renowned tomato-porcini sauce." She laughed at herself. "I put some in your refrigerator and some in your freezer for another day. There are also some beet greens from my garden in the refrigerator."

Antonio realized he was hungry.

"*Grazie*, Fiorella! You are a dear. How can I repay you?" It was more a statement than a question.

"Just let me keep these girls as long as I can. They brighten my days."

"So, they charmed you too, did they? Let me know if you need any help with them."

*****

Antonio was captivated by the panoramic view which rivaled that from Nicolo and Sofia's house. The house sat on a gentle, west-facing slope overlooking a patchwork vista of woods, olive groves, farm fields, vineyards, and hills which rolled gently away for miles. The deciduous trees were just beginning to take on their autumn color. The tall cumulus clouds had opened to a patch of blue sky, but darker ones were moving in behind them from the west. A stiff gust of wind kicked up, then disappeared as quickly as it came. The heavier rain would arrive soon.

Antonio grabbed Gabriella's bag from the car and followed her inside. The house was old and new at the same time.

"Renato did a lot of remodeling on the place before he died," she said. "He was handy with stone and woodworking. But you'll notice a lot of things half done, things he was unable to finish before he was sent to Albania. I've managed to continue a few things myself, like that tile backsplash behind the range. But, as I'm sure you know, time can be hard to come by when you are a detective."

Antonio gazed about admiringly. It had the large wood beams common in Italian farmhouses. The kitchen was well laid out with lots of counter space and open shelves and cupboards of stressed wood.

"I think it's perfect. I could live here in a heartbeat. I mean, I …"

"Oh, shut up. I know what you meant." She laughed at his awkwardness.

"My home is older also, at least by Pacific Northwest standards. It's a work in progress too. Still a long way to make it what I want."

"Is that what they call your area? The Pacific Northwest? Sounds romantic."

"If you like gloomy days, we get plenty. But when the sun comes out there are few places more beautiful. Except Tuscany, of course. I live in a town called Woodinville. My house sits above an agricultural valley with many wineries. I'm also on the west side of a hill, but I don't have near the view that you do. Too many trees in the way. I get great afternoon sun for my garden though."

"What kind of grapes do they grow there?"

"None really, except maybe a few table grapes in home gardens. Too cool and damp. The wineries get their grapes from the east side of the mountains, the Cascade Range. The climate there is continental. It's a young but promising wine region. Cabernet, Syrah, and Merlot grow especially well. And whites such as Chardonnay and Riesling. But growers are experimenting with every varietal you can think of ... Sangiovese, Tempranillo, Zinfandel, you name it. I'm not always a huge fan of those from Washington. In my opinion, those grapes are best from the places of their origin. It's partly the terroir, but they also over-ripen the grapes. Americans go for ripe, fruity wines. I prefer the old-world wines myself, more balanced. Better with food."

He realized he was talking too much, then was startled when his phone rang.

"Antonio, sorry to bother you. Are you at Gabriella's?"

"Yes," he said, feeling awkward about it. Nicolo sounded out of breath.

"Good. You're about fifteen minutes from me. Someone took a shot at me," he paused and Antonio heard heavy breathing. "I was heading home from Castellina. They shot out my taillight. Might have been a hunter, shooting too close to the road. I don't think so. I think it was intentional." He paused again and his voice became calmer. "If so, they're a lousy shot. Or they just wanted to scare me. I want your help to figure out where it came from, and if they left any clues behind."

"Where are you"?

"Between Castellina and Fonterutoli. Not far from where the accident took place."

"I'll be there quick as I can."

"What happened?" Gabriella asked. "I could hear a little of what he said. Is he okay?"

"Yes," he briefly explained. "I need to go. Will you be okay?"

"I'm coming with you!"

"What? No, you shouldn't do that. You should be taking it easy."

"I'm coming," she said, with no argument in her voice. "I'm not used to lying around doing nothing. Besides, standing hurts less than sitting or lying down. And I'm damn good at this kind of investigative work."

"Okay, detective," he said in mock surrender. "Grab your crutches."

"I'm grabbing my sidearm, too."

Chapter Thirty

Thursday later afternoon

They found Nicolo's car on the shoulder, a few hundred yards beyond where Antonio and Giulia were attacked. Antonio had to wonder if it was intentional that this same spot was chosen. It felt like it.

They found Nicolo on the hillside which sloped steeply upward to the tree line. He didn't seem surprised to see Gabriella. He yelled down, "Gabriella, if you want something to do, grab the keys from the ignition and pop the trunk. See if the slug passed through and is inside. Antonio, come up and help me search the hillside."

Antonio climbed the steep hill through the brush and reached Nicolo, breathless, and in agony.

"What ground have you covered so far?"

Nicolo pointed. "I came up that way to those trees over there. Why don't you work along this tree line here and I'll be a little off to your right."

The earlier rain showers had made things muddy. Antonio was having difficulty with footing. But it would make the shooter's footprints easier to find.

Nicolo was the one who found the tracks and footprints ending behind a tree. It would have been a perfect place from which to take the shot. There was a perfect view of the road and a crook in the tree where he could have rested his rifle for stability. They followed the tracks away from the tree, lost them on some granite, but found them again and followed to a gravel road that cut a swath between the wooded hillside and a vineyard on the other side. There was a dry spot on the otherwise damp gravel where a vehicle had obviously been parked during the shower. They followed the gravel road toward the main road. A little way along they found an area where the gravel turned to muddy soil and tire tracks were visible.

The gravel road rejoined the main road, about fifty yards from Nicolo's car. When they came near, Gabriella, wearing gloves, proudly held up a mangled slug.

"In the trunk, like you thought. Lodged in the sheet metal on the inside. The angle would have been about like this," she pointed to the line between where the bullet passed through the fractured red taillight and the spot where she found the slug. "I think it might be a 7mm Remington Magnum," she said. "Probably a hunting rifle. In a newer car it would have passed clear through. These older cars are made of heavier metal. We'll need forensics to take a look at it."

"I already called Marcello," Nicolo said. "He's on his way with your forensic people."

"Great. I'm in trouble now," Gabriella said with a laugh. "He'll probably give me another hole in my rear."

"You probably deserve it," Antonio added with a wink. She punched him, again.

"We found some interesting things for them, boot prints and tire tracks which appear to belong to the shooter. These conditions today work to our advantage. Hopefully, it doesn't start pouring rain before we can get casts."

Nicolo looked up the hill. "That spot we found; it lines up perfectly. I kept driving after the shot, stopped further up the road. I waited a few minutes, then came back and got as close to the spot as I could figure."

"Risky. Thought you said you were being careful, Nicolo?" Antonio said.

Nicolo gave him a look. "Do I look like a rookie? I knew he wouldn't hang around. The shot was loud, sure to draw attention. And there was a car not far behind me when it happened. They pulled over when I did, up beyond the curve. The driver was pretty rattled, but he wanted to help."

"Sofia's not going to be happy about this, Nicolo."

"Yeah. Tell me about it. Just let me be the one to break the news."

*****

Marcello arrived with the forensic people, an eager looking young man, and a slender, middle-aged black woman who took charge.

Marcello grimaced when he saw Gabriella. "What the hell are you doing here? You're supposed to be home recovering."

"Okay, Doctor Marcello. Whatever you say."

"Smart ass."

"Yeah, well, it hurts too much to sit on. I may as well be doing something useful."

While these two were sparring, Nicolo was already working with the forensics people. He handed them the bullet and showed them where it passed through and been lodged. Then he turned to Antonio. "Can you take them up and show them where we found the boot prints and tire tracks?"

Antonio's body really didn't want to climb that steep, muddy hill again but he nodded affirmatively. He slogged up the hill and showed them everything they had found, then left them to their work and limped back to the trio of detectives. Nicolo saw him coming and frowned. "Sorry, Antonio. Forgot how much pain you're dealing with."

Antonio gave him a grimaced nod and listened in. Marcello was up to speed. They were discussing theories of who and why.

"I'm pretty sure it was just meant to scare me," Nicolo said, "or be a distraction. If they were trying to kill me, they're in the wrong business."

"But who?" Gabriella asked. "What did they have to gain?"

"Well, your forensics people have some good stuff to work with," Nicolo added. "We probably won't know the answers 'til we find who it was. I think we have enough to do that."

"Leave that to us … I mean *me*," Marcello stammered. He glared at Gabriella again, making sure she got the message. Antonio could see she wasn't intimidated in the least.

"How worried should we be, for Nicolo's safety?" she asked.

"I'm not lying low, if that's what you're suggesting," Nicolo said. "But I will be watching my back."

"Hate to tell you this, Nicolo," Marcello said, "but we're going to need your car for forensics. Hitch a ride with Antonio. I'll drop your car at the garage for repairs when forensics is done. And please drop off this troublemaker." He looked at Gabriella. "I'm going to be here a while."

Antonio turned to Gabriella. "I'm making pizza tonight, if you'd like to join us. I can take you home after. Your cannelloni can wait a day."

Now Marcello gave Antonio a look, and shook his head, hiding a half-smile. *Why does everyone do that?* Antonio thought, feeling annoyed.

Nicolo broke in, "Marcello, I need to tell you something else." His tone was serious as he dropped the bombshell. "I went to see one of my CIs this afternoon. There's talk on the street ... that it was cops who killed the drug dealers. I hope it's just a crazy rumor that someone schemed up—you know how rumors catch fire on the street—but I thought you should know."

"Is there a chance it's true?"

"I don't want to believe it. But I have to tell you that one or more of my detectives have motive." Marcello stared in stunned silence. "I may need to step back from these murder cases too," Nicolo said.

"That's a decision for the magistrate. But if I were her, I would ask you to. Tell me about these motives."

Nicolo explained the situation with Paolo, and about Riccardo Coppola walking free due to mistakes on the case by Mancini and Jordy. "Paolo is the one I trust the most, we're very close, but he has the greatest motive."

Marcello nodded grimly.

"I'll call the magistrate as soon as we get back to the house, while Antonio makes us his world-famous pizza. I suspect you'll be hearing from her."

"Can we meet up in the morning, Nicolo? Someplace other than the questura? I need all the info you can give me on these guys."

Chapter Thirty-one

Thursday evening

Three people in the tiny Lancia was a tight fit. With Gabriella's injury, Nicolo sandwiched himself into the back seat, with a bag of groceries he pulled from his car.

Nicolo told them that he'd gone to Castellina to pick up the ingredients for the pizzas. He bought a ball of medium-aged provolone and two kinds of fresh mozzarella: mozzarella fior di latte—of cow's milk, and mozzarella di bufala—made from the milk of water buffalo in Campania. He had also procured Prosciutto di Parma, some locally-made sausage, porcini mushrooms, and vegetables for antipasti.

"I was on my way home when someone took that shot at me."

A thought bounced around in Antonio's head before it landed in his frontal lobe. "Nicolo, if this was intentional, how did they know to expect you on this part of the road? It is beyond your house when coming from Siena."

"I've been wondering about that," Nicolo said. "They must have followed me. Guess I'm not being so careful after all if I didn't see them. They must have pulled off and set up, knowing I'd be coming back this way."

The sun was setting when they arrived at the house. It dipped below the rain clouds for a short but brilliant sunset. The heavy rain was almost here.

The ladies gathered around Gabriella, welcoming her warmly and asking what they could do to make her comfortable. The brothers had taken the night shift at the hospital, so it would be Antonio and Nicolo, and six ladies. A dangerous ratio. Antonio told them to go and relax, that he and Nicolo were cooking tonight.

Nicolo went into seclusion to call the magistrate. While he was away, Antonio got busy. He stepped out onto the veranda and started a fire in the wood-burning oven with well-seasoned cherry wood Nicolo kept on hand. It would take over an hour for the stone hearth to get to the temperature he wanted, above 700° F. He pulled the dough balls from the refrigerator to let them warm up to room temperature.

Nicolo returned, looking pensive. Antonio carefully phrased a question, uncertain of the response he would get. "Zio, I'm wondering, I'd like to look into your detectives as well, on the down low. But only with your blessing. Marcello has a lot on his plate."

"Seriously!" Nicolo said sternly. Antonio thought he'd crossed a line, but didn't care. Then Nicolo cracked a smile, "Relax, Antonio. I'm ahead of you. I brought copies of their files home, and trial transcripts. I want you to look at them with me and give me your thoughts before I give them to Marcello. I know I'm too close to this. And as expected, Magistrate Mariani told me hands off."

"Not surprised. I'd do the same thing. We can work on it after I take Gabriella home. Right now, you need to put on an apron. We have some cooking to do."

They gathered the tools they needed: cutting boards, knives, pizza peels and pans. Antonio went to work slicing the two types of mozzarellas. "Thanks for getting the good stuff," he told Nicolo. "We'll stick to tradition and use the fior di latte for Pizza Margherita, and Quattro Formaggio. I'll use the mozzarella di bufala for the other pies."

He asked Nicolo to slice the porcini mushrooms, and cipollini onions. Antonio began preparing the cheeses for his Quattro Formaggio pizzas. Every chef had his own recipe. He liked to experiment, using whatever he had on hand. Tonight, he started by grating the medium-aged provolone which Nicolo bought. Then he rummaged through the refrigerator and found some gorgonzola and Chiara's pecorino. He preferred a young pecorino such as this one. It was less salty and intense. He crumbled some of the gorgonzola, not too much, grated the pecorino, and tossed these together in a bowl with the fior di latte, and provolone.

With that done, Antonio moved to the range. He added olive oil to a skillet and heated it until the oil began to shimmer. He added the onions and sautéed over medium flame. He asked Nicolo to watch it for a moment. He stepped outside the kitchen door, added a log to the oven, and cut sprigs of rosemary from the herb garden. He pulled it off the stems, chopped it roughly with a chef's knife, and added it to the onions when they were almost fully caramelized.

Alessia entered the kitchen to retrieve another bottle of wine. They were drinking Soave from the Veneto. "Wow! Smells good. I know what you're making," she said. Nicolo looked up, curious, but left it alone.

"Another job for you, Nicolo," Antonio said. "On the cutting board there, I set aside the yellow squash, eggplant, leeks, and peppers for the antipasti. You know what to do with them." Nicolo went to work thinly slicing the vegetables for grilling. He cut the leeks lengthwise.

While they were busy prepping, Antonio overheard his name and laughter coming from the other room. *Great! They're having a good laugh at my expense*, he thought, smiling to himself. He didn't mind so much. He believed that laughter is a better healer for body and soul than any medicine. There hadn't been enough of it in his life the last few years, nor in this house the past week.

*****

Nicolo brushed the vegetables with olive oil and charred them on the outdoor grill. He made small plates for the two of them, then arranged the remainder artistically on a platter and sprinkled them with coarse sea salt. He brought the platter to the ladies to satisfy their appetites until the pizzas were ready. Then he disappeared. Antonio was starting to wonder where he'd gone when he returned, dripping wet, with a wood crate full of treasure. He had run to the cellar and returned with several bottles of Barbera d'Alba from Piedmont. He opened a bottle and poured two glasses.

"Salute," he said, raising his glass. "You're going to love this. I traded two cases of my wine with an old college chum, now a detective in Turin, for two cases of this. His family owns the winery." Antonio touched his glass to Nicolo's, took a sip, and grinned. A good Barbera is the perfect pizza wine; generously fruity, with lovely acidity, and low tannins because the grapes have a thin skin.

The oven was ready, creating such intense heat you couldn't stand in front of it for long. It was time to make pizzas. Antonio began to stretch the doughs. The girls made their way to the kitchen. Wanting to show off a little, he spun each dough into the air with an upward flick of his wrists. It made for great fun, and laughter, especially when he nearly dropped one. He sprinkled semolina flour on two of the wooden pizza peels, to keep the dough from sticking, and placed a stretched dough on each.

The girls asked if they could help, so he put them to work topping pizzas. He was planning to man the oven so he put Alessia in charge, telling her what he wanted on each. She had made pizzas with him on many occasions. The girls took turns topping the pies, making two each of four different kinds. The first were traditional Pizza Margheritas, with tomato sauce and fresh fior di latte mozzarella. After baking, they drizzled them with aromatic extra virgin olive oil and topped them with fresh basil leaves. Most pizzaiolo add the basil before baking. Antonio liked to put it fresh on top, so it did not turn black.

The next two pizzas were the Quattro Formaggio—four cheese pizzas—very simple—tomato pizza sauce, topped with the four cheeses he had blended together. The following two were one of Antonio's signature pies: good extra virgin olive oil, mozzarella di bufala, paper-thin prosciutto, and the caramelized rosemary-cipollini onions. The final two pizzas were topped with tomato sauce, mozzarella di bufala, local sausage, and porcini mushrooms.

It was a good thing the wood-burning oven was located under the covered area of the veranda. Otherwise, there's no way they would have been using it tonight. The heavy rains had arrived, accompanied by thunderclaps and lightning. The air was damp and cool, but the heat of the oven overcame both. *God, how I love cooking with fire,* Antonio thought.

The oven was big enough to cook two pizzas at a time, each cooking in about three minutes. Antonio tended them constantly, rotating them with a long metal peel to ensure even baking. Sweat formed on his brow as the blazing heat of the cherry-wood coals worked its magic. The cheeses bubbled and browned as the aroma wafted from the oven. Alessia rushed the finished pizzas indoors and placed them in a low oven to keep them warm.

When Antonio pulled the last two pizzas from the oven, he set aside a couple of slices of each and hid them away. Raphael and Leonardo had made him promise to save them some. The remainder were spread out on the long wooden table. They bowed their heads as Sofia made the sign of the cross and said a prayer of thanks. As they filled their plates, Nicolo made his way around the table, pouring the Barbera like a wine steward. He was rewarded with kisses on the cheek along the way.

Outside, the rain came down in torrents, lightning lit the sky, and thunder rolled. Suddenly the power went out. They gathered a couple of candelabras and ate by candlelight. It felt right somehow.

*****

An hour later there were only scattered slices of pizza remaining. They raised their glasses and toasted the chef. Antonio stood to his feet and took an exaggerated bow. His ribs screamed at him. *The price I pay for acting like a ham,* he thought.

He took his seat and looked at Gabriella, sitting on his right. Her eyes reflected the candlelight. "Tell me about this restaurant of yours, Antonio."

"Well, I call it *Antonio's Pizzeria and Italian Cafe.* It sits on the west side of a hill overlooking the Sammamish Valley, about ten minutes from my home. This house here," he swept his hand around, "was my inspiration. We took an old house and re-faced it with stone. The veranda is similar to this. We have a fountain, an herb garden, and a small greenhouse. The view is nice, but nothing compared to what you have here. We have about two acres of property, less than a hectare. Inside, we only have a dozen tables, another six outdoors. I'll never get rich from it. But

I still have my pension and disability from my days as a policeman."

"Disability? That's right, you were injured on the job."

"A serious hip injury. That's a whole other story for another day."

She nodded and picked up her wine glass. "What's your menu like?"

"Simple, really. It's easier that way. About eight pizzas, similar to what we had tonight. We built a wood-burning oven outdoors, under cover like this one. We serve about a half dozen pastas, and a couple of entrees. I've tried to keep it as authentic as possible. We change up about a third of the menu each season. We grow most of our herbs, and buy most of our other produce from local farms."

"Restaurants are such hard work. How do you manage to get away?"

"Ah, that's where I'm more fortunate than most. Alessia's son, Shane, runs it for me. The kid's got the touch. He's had some huge struggles in his past," he looked at Alessia across the table, not sure how much he could share, "but he's turned his life around."

Alessia didn't hesitate to tell the story. "Antonio has helped him so much. Shane spent a couple of years in jail. He was a wild child … hell to raise … rebellious … started using drugs. At nineteen he borrowed our sailboat to go on an overnight sail with a friend. They came back from

Mexico with drugs aboard, enough to sell, and got busted. He says he found God while he was in prison. He's been sober ever since. Antonio and Randi took him in when he got out. He lived with them for over a year."

"He's housesitting for me now," Antonio added.

Alessia went on, "While he was in prison, he started working in the kitchen. He excelled so much he was practically running it by the time he got out. Says he loved the challenge, trying to cook anything decent on a prison food budget. Apparently, it made him popular with the other inmates. They watched over him."

Antonio poured them each another half glass of wine. "He's been a Godsend for me," he said. "I really didn't know as much as I thought I did about running a restaurant. I grew up cooking with my nonna, my mom, and aunts. During college, I worked in an upscale pizzeria, did a little of everything. Sometimes they had me run the night shift. Learned a lot but not enough. Shane filled the gaps for me. He has surprisingly good organizational skills. The staff loves him. Sometimes he's too easy on them. Then I have to come in and play the tough guy."

"You have a tough side?" Gabriella said with a nudge and a wink.

"Yeah, well," he paused as the house shook from thunder. Moments later, lightning flashed nearby. It gave him a chance to change the subject. "Not surprisingly, Shane also has his mother's charm in dealing with our guests. On the flip side, he's hardheaded like her too. We argue all the time." He looked at Alessia and gave her a wink. The thunder rolled again. His mood suddenly changed. "But I couldn't have done it without him after losing Randi and Christina." He fixed his eyes on the wine in his glass. "I lost all interest in running the restaurant. I hardly showed up for months."

The conversation fell silent. Alessia looked at her brother knowingly, then picked up a bottle of Barbera and poured the last of it into their glasses.

"I thought I might like to visit sometime," Gabriella said cheerfully. "Just to see your mom and sister, of course." She was getting ready to punch him again, but he held out the palm of his hand. "Hey, give my bruised arm time to heal." All three of them laughed.

"You *should* come," Alessia said. "The best time is spring or summer. May is my favorite month."

For the next few minutes, Alessia and Gabriella carried on a conversation about Seattle. Aunt Frankie joined in. Antonio, fully sated, just sat back and watched. He looked around the table. His mother caught his eye and smiled. He thought about how much he loved these people, and how much he missed the ones who weren't here.

He looked to his right and found himself staring into Gabriella's eyes. He was fairly certain she could read his mind right then. She was radiant.

Chapter Thirty-two

Thursday later in evening

About two hours after they'd gone out, the lights came back on, as if signaling the end of the evening. Nicolo and the girls went to work cleaning up. Antonio told Gabriella he needed to take her home because he and Nicolo were planning to work late. "No problem, Antonio. I'm fading anyway. You know what it's like trying to sleep in a hospital—the pain, and nurses checking on you all the time."

Antonio got drenched running to the car. He pulled it near the door and gently assisted Gabriella into the passenger seat and put her crutches in the back. The roads of Chianti are very dark at night, especially when it's pouring rain. His headlights reflected off the heavy drops and wet pavement. As he drove, it lightened up, then stopped, then came down in torrents. They rarely got rain this hard in Seattle. Visibility was terrible. He slowed down, wishing he'd drunk a little less wine.

"Thank you for inviting me, Antonio. Your pizza was amazing. It was delightful being with your family. Your mother is a strong and beautiful woman. I hope I age so gracefully. She thinks the world of you, you know."

"I do know. I'm very blessed." He hesitated too long. She looked at him. "Can I be completely honest?" he asked.

"You never have to ask me that—not ever."

"I say 'I'm blessed'. But as soon as I say it, something inside of me says 'What the hell are you talking about?' That voice reminds me of how much I've lost. And yet…" he took his eyes off the road to steal a glance, "despite it all, so many blessings remain."

"I understand."

"Thought you would."

"I found it hard to give myself permission to be happy again," she said. "I knew where your mind went tonight. I go there often. Life gives us such sharp contrast … what is … the blessings of what we have … the people we love … but a deep yearning for those that should still be with us." Her voice almost broke. "Life can be so hard … and yet, so beautiful at the same time."

He glanced at her. "You seem to have more peace than I do. I can't seem to find it. That's one of the reasons I came here."

His eyes were glued to the road but he could tell she was looking at him. "You won't find it in a place, Antonio."

"I just thought …" his voice trailed off.

"You're angry with God, aren't you?"

"How do …?"

"I know? Because I was too. Still am sometimes. I think everyone who goes through the kinds of losses we have goes there. Some just stay longer than others."

*****

When they arrived, Antonio pulled near the front door. He stepped around the puddles to help her from the car. He retrieved her crutches and walked her to the door. They stood inside the entry, dripping on the floor, and he looked at her, thinking how beautiful she was. He wanted to stay, to be with her, find comfort in her arms. But he needed to get back. Or so he told himself. There was an awkward silence. He wanted to ask a question but didn't want to ruin whatever was going on between them.

"Can I ask you a difficult question? If it's uncomfortable, you don't have to answer."

She looked at him. "There you go, being all polite again. I told you …"

"Yeah, I know. But it's not a question I'm sure I should ask." He looked away. She didn't. "When you and Pucci were being loaded in the ambulances, he looked at you. He knew you. He told you he was sorry."

She hesitated before answering. Antonio was kicking himself.

"I knew Sandro. Before I knew he was a bad guy." Her voice was quiet. "We met at a church event, cooking and serving the homeless in Siena. What kind of bad guy does that?" It was genuine perplexity. "He told me he was new to the area, that he'd moved from Campania. I knew that from his accent. He told me he bought a small villa north of Siena. He acted like a real gentleman. He asked me out. We had dinner together, on three occasions."

She paused, unsure how to go on. "As I got to know him, I started having questions. I am not sure how much was my woman's intuition … how much was my detective instincts. He was vague whenever I asked about his business. He mentioned restaurants and other business enterprises. I had a sense he was hiding things. He also started to ask me questions. At first, they seemed innocent enough. But over time, they became more specific. Like he was using me to get information.

"I decided to stop seeing him after our third date. He invited me to his place for drinks after dinner. I went, curious to see his villa. But then I got nervous … uncomfortable. I knew I'd made a stupid decision. When he started making advances, I pushed him away. He got aggressive … started to get angry."

Her voice was trembling as he saw the scene play out in her distant eyes. "You don't have to go on."

She looked up at him. "I was afraid he was going to rape me. I wouldn't have gone down without a fight. I got angry. Enough to scare him, I think. He probably knew I could kick his ass," she laughed, but it was strained. "I had come in my car, thankfully, so I left quickly and that was the end of it. A few months later I found out who he was. I felt like such a fool."

The silence now felt uneasy. She'd taken a risk, made herself vulnerable. He wanted her to know he didn't blame her, that we all make mistakes. But he floundered like a fish out of water, unable to find the words. *What an idiot, Antonio.*

"Goodnight, Gabriella. Sleep well."

"You too." Her eyes searched his. "Don't work too late." He turned and stepped out the door.

"Antonio. Wait."

He turned around. "Thank you for being a gentleman. For not judging me. Your eyes told me everything I needed to know. You're a kind, generous man." She leaned forward and kissed him. It was brief, but not on the cheek this time. Then she pushed him away firmly, "Go, do your work."

Chapter Thirty-three

Thursday late

Antonio's mind reeled as he drove back. He didn't remember a thing about the drive. The rain mesmerized him, and his thoughts were a jumbled mess. His passions were aroused, but he felt wrong about it. Those stupid feelings of guilt and disloyalty refused to release their grip, fueled by regrets over mistakes in his past.

Arriving back, he saw a light in the garage. He stuck his head in and found Nicolo aggressively stirring the wine must.

"Almost done here. I'll meet you in the study."

Antonio entered the study and found Nicolo's gun spread out on the desk. Nicolo came in behind him, drying his head with a towel. "Cleaning and oiling," he said. "Then I remembered I promised the boys I would stir the wine."

Antonio saw his shoulders droop. His voice was forlorn.

"You okay, Nicolo?"

"Yeah. Fine." He was lying. "I finally told Sofia about what happened this afternoon, and about the shoot-out in the bottini. She hadn't noticed that we arrived in your car. She's pretty upset with me, about what happened, and that I hid it from her. She says she wants me to retire. Says she's spent enough years worrying, that she doesn't want to spend her older years alone. I know it doesn't help that Giulia is lying in the hospital."

"What did you tell her?"

"Not much, that I'd think about it. Reminded her how much I love what I do, that I'm not ready to be put out to pasture." He took his eyes off Antonio and went back to assembling his gun. "She's got me thinking though, wondering if it's time. I think I'm losing my ability to see things as they are, instead of how I want them to be."

"Thirty-seven years is a long time to be on the force, Nicolo. I only had twenty and I found it hard to adjust afterwards. Gets in our blood."

"Yes," he said pensively. "It does."

"On the flip side, some guys get really burned out, dealing with all the sordidness. My father did. I sometimes wonder if he would have adjusted to retirement." Nicolo finished assembling his gun and looked at him. Antonio continued, "He was a good detective. But he brought it home. It was hard ... hard to watch it eat away at him. And to see him take it out on my mom. I don't think any other woman could have handled him the way she did, the way she supported him. She stood up to him when he got mean. But somehow she did it in a way that preserved his dignity."

Antonio sat down across the desk from Nicolo. He rubbed his face. "I should be more forgiving. He gave his life in the line of duty." His thoughts returned to Nicolo. "Whatever decision you make, I know it will be the right one. Just don't make it in the heat of the moment."

Nicolo nodded. "Meanwhile, we have some bad guys to catch. God, I hope it's not one of my men."

*****

They spent the next two hours poring over the files. They had little to offer. Nicolo answered any questions which came up for Antonio.

Paolo had been working for the Polizia Municipale for fourteen years, nine as a detective. He was highly capable. Nicolo considered him his go-to guy, but didn't feel he was showing his best work on these murder cases. Was it because he had done the murders himself? Or maybe he was just glad that these guys were dead.

Mancini transferred from Turin as a detective six years ago. Of the three guys, Nicolo felt he knew him the least. He was single, and a lady's man. He was capable, highly intelligent, but impatient and sometimes hot-tempered, which could cause him to lose his objectivity. Nicolo thought he was too willing to take short-cuts. On the case with Riccardo Coppola, the drug dealer who sold the drugs to Paolo's nephew, he and Jordy got impatient and did an illegal search of his apartment, which led to the acquittal. Nicolo blamed it mostly on Mancini, though Jordy was involved. They both received a seven-day suspension and a reprimand in their file. Mancini still seemed to be holding a grudge.

Jordy grew up in Naples. His family moved to Siena when he was in his teens. He was the youngest of the three, and newest on the force. He'd been in the department seven years and a detective for three. Nicolo said he was more a follower than a leader, maybe too much of a people pleaser, but smart, and loyal. He hadn't been happy about his suspension either but took responsibility, and didn't appear to be harboring any hard feelings.

Antonio asked, "With his family ties to Naples, do you think there's any chance the Laganà family have gotten their hooks in him?"

"I've considered it. But he's a lousy liar. I don't think he could keep it hidden from me without being a nervous wreck."

One thing Antonio discovered in the court records was that all three murder victims had been arrested at one time or another for their drug dealings, and all three were acquitted for various reasons. They had all been represented by the same attorney, who they were now certain was on retainer with the Laganà family, their consigliere perhaps. Antonio thought about Robert Duvall's role in *The Godfather*.

The second murder victim, Federico Ricci, had also been arrested by Mancini and Jordy. The attorney argued that the confession was coerced. Nicolo strongly disagreed.

He'd seen the video and felt they did it all by the book that time.

Nicolo voice carried deep conviction, "The judge ruled against us. I seriously wondered if he'd been bribed. He came across like a zealous human rights advocate. But it didn't fit the pattern of his past rulings."

Antonio recalled that Italy does not use a jury system. Judges make final rulings, either alone or as a panel, depending on how big the case is. *More expeditious, but I don't like it,* he thought.

With the final victim, Baccio Camilleri, the GDF were the ones involved in the investigation and arrest, less than a year ago. But the case never made it to trial. The guy had been arrested three times but always managed to get off. Some of the evidence magically disappeared before the trial. What remained was insufficient. Nicolo believed the GDF had botched it.

"So, give it to me straight, Antonio. What's your opinion?"

"I think you know the answers, Nicolo. You've just been afraid to face them. Any of those guys had motive. You told me yourself, Paolo has the greatest, but you trust him the most. Not so sure I agree. After that I'd say Mancini over Jordy, but only because of what you told me about Jordy. I suppose two of them could even have done it together. Maybe even all three. But I highly doubt it."

Chapter Thirty-four

Friday morning

Antonio was dog tired but couldn't sleep. His mind was a jumble of thoughts and useless questions. He tried to argue against his feelings for Gabriella. She was beautiful. But it was more than physical attraction. She was mature, and compassionate, with the depth of character developed by the losses she had faced. Pretentiousness falls aside. She could have walked the path of hopelessness, or bitterness, but chose the noble route. She found a way to have peace again. But he kept circling back to his same stupid argument, *how do you have a relationship with someone half a world away?* He didn't believe that long distance relationships ever worked. *Besides, I haven't even known this woman for two weeks!*

He tried to take his mind off her. He did his best to focus on the murder cases, and the attack on him and Giulia. He tried and failed to make the connection with the murder cases. If one or more of Nicolo's detectives committed the murders, would they also have gone after Nicolo? He couldn't reconcile it. Unless they thought he was on to them. Even then, it would be a desperate act of betrayal. He certainly couldn't imagine Paolo doing it.

He finally fell asleep about two in the morning. Somewhere in the night the dreams returned. They were never quite the same, but certain images kept repeating themselves—the truck, its face of evil, the screams, falling, being helpless to do anything. As he lay half-awake in the morning, he could still see the slow-motion image of the face in the Alfa Romeo as his body flew past it. The bed was soaked with sweat. Sun was streaming in the window.

He looked outside. Only a few lingering clouds remained. He opened the French doors. A breeze stirred the air. It smelled sweet and fresh. Normally, a morning like this would lift his spirits. But he couldn't shake the image.

He picked up his phone to check his emails. He hadn't done so for days. Then he pulled up the composite drawing that Nicolo sent him two days before. He thought he might see those eyes. But they were not the same eyes he saw in his dream.

*****

He stripped the bed and put the sheets in the wash, took a long shower, and redressed his wounds. They were looking better. But the pain in his ribs, not so much. They screamed at him with every wrong move.

He stiffly made his way down the stairs and across the courtyard to the kitchen where he found a lively scene. Alessia and Chiara were cutting up fruit and warming a batch of croissants. They had already gone out that morning to pick them up fresh from the bakery … some plain, some almond, and some with chocolate in them.

Croissants were one of Antonio's weaknesses, *like gelato, and pizza, and ... the list could go on. All this food and no exercise makes a man fat and lazy. I wish I could get out for a ride.* Normally, if he wasn't going cycling, he at least did pushups and core body work. But with his injuries he hadn't done a thing except a few morning walks.

Starting with his mother, he made his way around and gave each of the ladies a kiss on the cheek. His sister pulled no punches, "You look like death warmed over. Here." She handed him a cup of steaming coffee.

"Thanks, sis. I can always count on you to be honest." She gave him a look of concern. He raised his cup. "Didn't sleep well. I'll be better after this."

"Can't blame it on girl problems; just look around at all these women who adore you. And I think maybe there's another that does, too." He caught her sly smile.

"You're nothing but a troublemaker." He grabbed a plate and loaded it up with sliced melons, pears, and two croissants, one plain, one almond.

Nicolo showed up, not looking too spry himself, but doing his best to hide it. "*Buon giorno*, ladies, and to you, Antonio. Who's going to the hospital today?" He too made a round of the ladies, then held Sofia in a warm, enduring embrace.

"Frankie and I are going," Sofia said. "And I got a call from Raphael." Her countenance brightened. "He told me that Giulia was stirring and mumbling something last night. He thought for a minute she was waking up. I waited to share it until you came down."

The mood in the room brightened. Antonio felt a bit of life return to his body.

All five girls decided to ride together to see Giulia, then the others were going shopping in Siena. After they left, Antonio asked Nicolo if he could accompany him to his meeting with Marcello.

"You have no choice since I don't have a car."

"Oh, yeah," Antonio said. "Forgot you had no wheels."

The girls looked up questioningly. "I'll explain later," Sofia said without a smile.

Nicolo looked at Antonio and changed the subject, "The way you look, I'm guessing you didn't sleep well. Me neither." He poured them each a second cup of coffee, "We leave in an hour."

*****

The early autumn sun glaring on the still damp road nearly blinded Antonio as they wound their way toward Siena. Two motorcyclists passed him on a curve. Antonio shook his head. *Pazzo!* he thought. They would meet Marcello at the **Provinciale Stazione Carabinieri**.

"Did the magistrate have anything else to say last night?"

"Nothing I wasn't expecting. She was shocked to hear that it could possibly be one of my detectives. She wasn't happy that I didn't bring it to her sooner. She said Marcello needs to take the lead in any investigation of them, but knows I need to be a resource to him. I'm free to follow leads on any other suspects."

"Seems levelheaded," Antonio said. "I have something I need to tell you." Nicolo looked at him. "I have a feeling Mancini may be in the middle of this."

"Your gut, or something you haven't told me?"

"This is going to sound farfetched. You know the dreams I've been having, and the part where I fly past the car window? I think the face in my dreams might be him. I think my subconscious has been trying to tell me all along. Of course, I could be totally wrong. You know how dreams can be."

"Yeah. If yours are anything like mine, I wouldn't put much stock in it. But I suppose there could be something to it, your psyche digging deep into your memory bank."

"Should I mention it to Marcello?"

"Not yet. He already thinks you're *pazzo*!"

"Well, he's got that right. Doesn't take a detective to figure that out."

"Yeah, but I'll make sure he knows that he's someone we want to look at."

"One more thing. I was looking at the composite drawing from the girl at the car rental. It doesn't look like him. So maybe I am crazy, or it's not a good drawing, or maybe the second person rented the vehicles. I think we need to get photos of the detectives down there for her to look at."

"Good idea. I'd like us to do that on our own. Then if she IDs anyone, we can let Marcello know."

Antonio stared at him with eyes wide. "You sure? You just said …"

"No, I'm kidding," he said sarcastically. "Yes. I'm sure. I'll get you the photos as soon as we're done with Marcello. You can take them down or ask Raphael and Leonardo to do it. They have her contact information." He hesitated. "Actually, forget I said that. I don't want the boys to know about this yet."

*****

When they arrived for the meeting, from a distance they were surprised to see Fiero Belluci, the GDF General, standing out front with Marcello. *"Merda,"* mumbled Nicolo. His whole body seemed to tense up. "Looks like you'll be sitting this one out."

Belluci was his usual self, about as warm as leftover pasta. He told them with a tone of arrogance that the magistrate called him and suggested the GDF provide assistance. "With Gabriella out, and the investigation shifting to the detectives of the municipale, I thought Colonel Bianchi could use my help." Standing behind Belluci, Marcello rolled his eyes. He obviously wasn't happy but had little choice other than to go along.

Belluci looked at Antonio. "That leaves you out, Americano," he said scornfully.

Antonio's fondness for this guy grew icier each time they met. He excused himself politely, choosing the high road for Nicolo and Marcello's sake.

"This won't take long," Nicolo told Antonio.

"No problem. I'll be next door at the basilica. If I'm not on the piazza, check inside."

Chapter Thirty-five

Friday mid-day

T he Basilica di San Francesco is located next door to the headquarters of the Carabinieri. Antonio had never been inside. He loved these old cathedrals, so decided to explore it. The interior was cavernous, with wide open space, and a simple design. The most unique architectural feature was the grey and white horizontal striping. Unlike most cathedrals, the ceiling was composed of huge timber beams.

He went to the Google app on his phone to see what he could find out. He learned it was originally built in the 13th century, enlarged in the following two centuries, then destroyed in the 17th century. It was rebuilt in a fake-Gothic style early in the 20th century.

There were few frescoes, but colored light filled the cathedral as the sun streamed through its many stained-glass windows. He watched a group of nuns, in navy blue habits, strolling slowly and pointing as they admired the scenes in glass. They spoke in French. He caught an occasional word he could understand. He wanted to ask what brought them here, but didn't trust the little French he knew. Then he heard a familiar voice, whose French rolled fluently off his tongue as he addressed them. He turned, and saw Nicolo, smiling and turning on the charm. He could see by their smiles and laughter that they were enjoying this interaction a great deal.

Nicolo walked over to Antonio smiling. "I needed that to lighten my mood after being around Belluci. I would have much preferred dealing with Marcello." His mood had already soured again. "I just explained the facts and left them to their own conclusions."

"What's the story with this Belluci guy?"

"I really don't know much. He arrived in Siena a couple of years ago from Roma. I heard his family is well connected. Someone told me his wife never came with him. I've made no effort to get to know the guy. You can see why."

"Yeah. His mother should have invested in charm school. So, what's next?"

"Belluci made it clear that he wants to be the one to review the CCTV footage. He could access it himself but since we've already backed up the relevant portions, he asked me to send those to him. Save him the time and trouble."

Nicolo's phone rang. Antonio overheard Marcello's voice, louder than usual, and agitated.

Nicolo answered him, "Yeah. I'll make backup copies and get those to you this afternoon." He ended his part of the conversation with, "God, I hope we're wrong about all of this."

Antonio overheard enough to know that Marcello agreed. Cops never liked to see good cops go bad, knowing the job could pull any of them in that direction.

Nicolo put his cell phone in the pocket of his suit coat. "Marcello wants a copy of the CCTV footage too. Seems he doesn't trust Belluci to get it right."

"Tug of war?"

"It is. He reminded me to keep my guys on task. Obviously, we don't want them to know they are suspects. Not yet anyway. But he said he may have to interview them soon. If that happens, things could get damned interesting at the questura."

"Nicolo," Antonio spoke, "how soon can you get me photos of the detectives to take to the Europcar attendant in Roma? I'd like to drive down there today."

"I got to thinking, it might be a lot easier to send them to the Carabinieri in Roma … ask them to do it."

"Do we really want it public knowledge that we're investigating your detectives?"

"Yeah, yeah. What was I thinking? Guess there's no harm in you doing it. If we need her to provide ID for a court case later, we can have Marcello's people re-confirm."

"Good. I'll give her a call."

"By the way, you better let Marcello know what you're up to."

*****

Antonio drove Nicolo to the questura, a circuitous route because of the pedestrian only areas in between. He parked and strolled to a small piazza, where he found a dry spot on a wall to sit in the sun. He phoned Raphael. "*Ciao*, Raphael! We have some new suspects in the road incident, and I need to contact the woman at the Europcar in Roma. I remembered you had her contact information. We want to show her some photos."

"*Si*, Antonio. I'll text that to you. Who are the new suspects?"

"I'm not at liberty to share that yet."

"Really? Must be someone we know then. You know you can trust me."

"Not my decision, Raphael."

There was a pause, "Okay. I'll send that right over. But if you change your mind, we could go later this afternoon. I'm in the middle of adding yeast for fermentation at the moment, and Leonardo is out cycling with Luca, but should be back soon."

"*Grazie*, Raphael. I appreciate the offer but this is something I have to do."

Antonio hung up. Less than a minute later he got the text. He dialed the number. After several rings, the call went to voicemail. He left a message. "*Arrivederci*, Franca. This is detective Cortese with the Polizia Municipale in Siena. I'm working on the case that involved your rental vehicles. We have some new suspects and I wanted to show you some additional photos. I'm wondering if you are available today? Please return my call. *Grazie mille.*"

When he hung up, he realized that his phone would have a U.S. prefix. *Oh well. We'll see if that's an issue.*

He sat daydreaming for a minute, enjoying the warmth of the sun. He'd felt a pang of jealousy when he heard Leonardo and Luca were out cycling. He would love to be out there on this beautiful morning. *How long until my body will be ready?* he wondered. His thoughts were interrupted when he heard a text notification and saw it was from Nicolo. It had three attachments, photos of the detectives.

While he was waiting for a call back from Franca at Europcar, he decided to call Gabriella. "*Buon giorno,* Gabriella. How is your posterior feeling today?"

"It hurts like hell. You?"

"Getting a little better. A few days ago, my leg seemed to be getting infected. It looks better."

"What are you doing? Would you like to come over?"

"I'd love to but I'm waiting on a phone call. I may need to go to Roma."

"Roma?"

He explained. Halfway through, he realized he hadn't told Marcello yet.

"How about I go with you?"

"Is that a good idea? Shouldn't you be in bed resting?"

"Yes. I should."

"But…"

"But you know me. I'm going stir crazy. I can sit on a pillow. Besides, it will legitimize this for you. Keep you out of hot water."

"And get you in more hot water. But I'm not sure yet when I'm going. I'll give you a call."

"If you're not doing anything in the meanwhile, why don't you come over? We could share those cannelloni for lunch."

He thought for a moment. If they ended up going today, he'd need to pick her up anyway. "Sure. See you in half an hour."

*****

On the way to Gabriella's he got a call from Franca, the Europcar attendant. He pulled to the side of the road. He could see Fonterutoli from where he sat.

"Why is a detective from Siena calling me on an American phone?" she asked suspiciously. He decided to come clean and explained that he was a cousin to Raphael and Leonardo. He told her she could call detective Nicolo Zaccardi if she needed confirmation. "I will also be bringing a Carabinieri detective."

"Okay. Sounds safe. But we'll meet in a public place. I'm off today. I live near Monterotondo, northeast of Roma.

There's a wonderful gelateria, Cremeria del Borgo. I'll meet you there. It's 11:00. 1:30?"

"Probably closer to 2:00. I'll call you if we hit heavy traffic."

He dialed Gabriella. "Got my call. Can you be ready to leave in fifteen minutes?"

"If you don't mind me without makeup."

"I like the natural look."

"I'll be ready."

He decided to shoot off a text to Marcello. *On my way to Roma to show photos of detectives to car rental lady. Will let you know what I find out.*

He read Marcello's reply when he arrived at Gabriella's. *Should have okayed with me first. Be careful.*

*****

Gabriella was in the bathroom when he arrived. He looked around the living room while he waited. She had a few family pictures on the mantle: one of her, her husband, and daughter when she was about two years old. There was another of her and her husband. He paused on the third one, of Gabriella, her daughter—looking about thirteen—and an older couple at the seaside on a sunny day.

He did not hear her enter the room. "That was taken about six years ago on the Adriatic in Molise where I come from. Liliana, and my parents. They are in their mid-seventies now. I haven't seen them for over a year. I

282

thought since I have some forced time off, I might take a trip home in a couple of weeks."

"That would be nice," he said, but his thoughts lingered on Liliana. There may be no worse pain than when a parent loses a child. *How was it Aeschylus said it?* "There is no pain so great as the memory of joy in our present grief."

She interrupted his thoughts, "Is your leftover pizza good at room temperature? Sofia sent the leftover slices home with me last night. Since we have no time for the cannelloni, I thought we could bring them for the drive."

"What kind of question is that?" he said, smiling.

Chapter Thirty-six

Friday early afternoon

Gabriella brought a pillow to sit on. He watched her wince when she climbed into the car. He drove south on SR222 to the SS674 which took them around Siena and to the E35, the main highway leading southeast toward Roma.

He loved driving in Italy. Italians drive fast, but are more focused on the road than Americans. They rarely get in the fast lane and drive slowly. Traffic was light this time of day so it appeared they would make it on time. He was glad they were going to Monterotondo, not Roma. Traffic was almost always horrible as you neared the Eternal City.

He glanced at Gabriella. *God, she might be even beautiful without makeup,* he thought. "Tell me about your parents and growing up in Molise." Molise, east of Roma on the Adriatic, was the smallest, most remote region in Italy.

"I grew up in Termoli, an old fishing village. Have you heard of it?"

"I have, but I've never been. Aren't there ancient fortifications surrounding the old part of town?"

"Yes. It's incredibly beautiful. Few tourists because of its remoteness. I loved growing up there. The beaches are lovely."

"Your parents still live there?"

"Yes. And my nonna, on my mother's side. She is ninety-six. Starting to have some health issues—another reason I should visit."

"You miss living there?"

"Not so much anymore. I love visiting. But Tuscany is home now. When I retire from the Carabinieri, I will probably stay."

"Tell me about your parents."

"My father was a builder. He had few guys who worked for him. They mostly did restoration work but would build an occasional house or winery. He worked hard, until just a few years ago. Now he is somewhat stooped from all those years bent over. My mother was a high school language teacher."

"Is that why your English is so good?"

"Probably. I speak French too, and fairly good Spanish."

"How'd you end up joining the Carabinieri?"

"When I was in college, in Campobasso, a recruiter came. I was young, restless, ready to get out of Molise. They had a program which would pay my tuition for my last two years, then I had to commit to six years of service. It was too good to pass up. And I think I've always had a strong sense of justice. I hate bullies." She smiled, "I once beat up a boy older than myself because he was picking on my younger cousin."

He looked at her and laughed. "Good to know. You've obviously done more than the six years in the Carabinieri?"

"I've reenlisted three times. Nineteen years now. I will probably do twenty-five."

"Did they send you to Tuscany right away?"

"No. No. I spent two years in Tarvisio, a little town in northern Friuli, foothills of the Dolomites. Quite a difference from the warm climate I grew up in. That's where I met Renato. He was a lieutenant. He'd been in the Carabinieri seven years. Swept this young, innocent girl off her feet with his looks and charm. We married six months later. About a year after that he managed to get us relocated to Siena, close to where he grew up. We were lucky. We moved in with his parents so we could save up to buy our own house. I think I got pregnant the first night we were in Tuscany. Liliana was less than a year old when he deployed to Albania, a NATO peacekeeping mission. A few months later, a bomb at a train station took him from us."

Her voice trailed off. Antonio looked intently at her, trying to see deep inside. Part of her had died, but so much life remained. "Eyes back on the road," she said, "I want to make it there in one piece."

*****

Neither spoke for a few minutes.

"Your turn, Antonio. I want to know more of your story. You didn't tell me about your retirement from the police. But first, I want to know how you became a policeman in the first place. I've heard of Newport Beach. Isn't that where John Wayne used to live? I heard he had a big, fancy yacht."

"Yeah. The Wild Goose. You know about John Wayne?"

"Of course! Every *little lady* knows about the Duke," she laughed. "My nonno used to watch his movies when I was a kid, over and over. I could probably quote you all of his famous lines."

"Well, you might have heard my father was an MP in the army. He was stationed at Camp Darby. That's how he met my mom. After they got married, they moved to California. He got a job as a cop in San Pedro, a port close to Los Angeles and Long Beach. That made him part of LAPD. Not an easy beat, lots of crime, gang violence, drugs being smuggled in from Mexico. We lived in Seal Beach, a sleepy little beach town down the coast from there. I loved growing up there. And you know my uncle Nicolo, of course. He had more influence than my father towards my becoming a cop.

"My wife, Randi, was from Newport Beach. Surprised she married me. Her family had money. We met at college, got married shortly after graduation. We lived in Costa Mesa. It sits on a plateau, just above Newport. I applied for several departments in the area. Newport

Beach was first to offer me a job. I was a street cop for about seven years. Then became a detective."

"Sounds like a nice place to be a cop."

"You'd think. Not so bad. But it had its issues like anywhere, especially in the summer when the beach strand becomes party central. And those rich people have their expectations."

"How'd you get hurt?"

"My partner and I were on a drug smuggling case. A lot of drugs come into the bay on pleasure craft, like Shane tried to do." He paused a minute. "We followed a couple of suspects to a secluded area called Little Corona del Mar."

"Crown of the Sea," she said.

"Right. Anyway, there are cliffs there. For whatever reason, these guys didn't want to bring their drugs into the bay. They were bringing them into a cove on jet skis at night. We followed them on foot to the cliffs … lost them in the dark. Then we saw the jet skis unloading … called for a helicopter and police boat. We started creeping our way down the cliff face and a guy jumped me. In the struggle, we went over the edge. It was only about twenty feet, but we landed on rocks. I broke my left hip in three places, cracked two vertebrae, did lots of muscle and soft tissue damage. The guy who jumped me came out worse. Paralyzed to this day."

"I'm surprised you can ride."

"Yeah. They had to screw my hip back together. Riding is one thing I can do without a lot of pain. Sometimes it aches on long rides."

"So, you had to retire?"

"Doctors said I might never get back in the field. I didn't want to ride a desk for months, or even years."

"Must have been hard."

"I didn't handle it well." *That's an understatement.* "They gave me opioids for pain. Had a hell of a time weaning my way off. They really messed me up for a while. I could have ended up a junkie. A few months later my dad died, he was killed in a drug bust, just months before he was going to retire. Our relationship had been rocky. I started drinking too much. A couple of months later, we found out my mom had breast cancer." He paused again, wondering how much to tell her. *She might not think too highly of me.*

"I wasn't fun to live with. Randi and I nearly got divorced. We separated for a while." He paused and took a deep breath. "I'd had an affair, been dealing with the guilt ever since, especially after she died." He looked at Gabriella. Saw no judgment.

"We all have regrets, Antonio. None of us have done it all right." She paused. "You must have worked it out."

"Thankfully. Randi was a strong woman. She gave me a second chance. She knew how sorry I was ... how much I wanted to rebuild her trust. We went to counseling.

Her parents pretty much disowned me though. Can't say I blame them."

He stared at the road in a trance. She stayed silent. Finally, he continued, "The kids were teenagers. Christina got over it quicker than Jonathan. I don't think he fully forgave me until he married Leah. She's a remarkable young woman, a redhead of Irish descent. I think she helped him get past his anger at me. Have I told you they're expecting twins?"

"No." Her eyes lit up. "Should I start calling you Nonno Antonio?"

"Soon enough. I'll carry the title proudly," he smiled.

"I bet you'll be good at it."

"I don't know about that, but the idea of new life … after the loss. It's brought me joy in the midst of my pain. So odd how those things can co-exist … joy … sorrow."

"Seems unexpected, doesn't it? Like they should be mutually exclusive."

*****

He nodded. They drove quietly for a while. Each lost in their thoughts.

"How'd you end up in Seattle with a restaurant?"

"That's a bit of a story. Alessia's first husband traded her in for a younger model. His loss. Worked out great for her though. She met a guy from Seattle and got re-married. Matthew's a great guy, and highly successful.

He sits on the board of directors with Amazon." Antonio changed lanes to pass a tractor on the shoulder.

"Alessia talked Mom into moving up so she could help take care of her. They have a gorgeous home in a wealthy community called Medina. It's on Lake Washington which is a rather large lake near Seattle. Medina is on the east side of the lake, looking back at the city. They have a guest cottage on the property. That's where my mom lives. It's perfect. She has a killer view, and her own terrazza with a grape arbor, a rose garden, and a vegetable garden. Feels like Tuscany in miniature, or maybe Lake Como."

Antonio saw a sign stating fifty kilometers to Roma. They would reach Monterotondo in about twenty minutes. "Did they tell you about the eightieth birthday party we had for her a couple of weeks ago?"

"They did. She seems in great health now. She's vibrant, beautiful. Hard to believe she's eighty. Is her cancer gone?"

"It is. Took her a few years to get her energy back. Now she's as active as I've seen her in years. Walks three or four miles every day."

"You still haven't answered my question."

"Oh yeah. Randi and I thought moving to Seattle might be a good idea, a fresh start. And we wanted to be there with my mom while she was battling her cancer. Randi and my mom were close. She got on well with all my family, both at home and here in Italy.

"So, we moved up, and I was trying to figure out what my next life would be. I thought about starting a winery but didn't know enough about it. I'd always loved to cook and entertain, learned Italian cooking from the best, my nonna, my aunts, my mother. But as I told you last night, I couldn't have done it without Shane. He had learned all the management skills. And he learned to cook from the same people I did. So, we have that in common. It's the other stuff we butt heads over. But he tends to be right as often as I am."

"Do you like it?"

"Being a restaurateur? Love it! Just glad I don't have to be married to it. So many people are, can't ever get away. Or if they do, things go to pieces. I'll probably let Shane take ownership someday. My daughter Christina worked for us until she left for Paris. And Jonathan worked for us for a while. He and Shane always got along well. Shane's a year older. When they were teens, I worried about Shane being a bad influence. But he turned his life around in prison, thanks to a man in the prison ministry. Seems like the faith he found set his feet on a solid path. Jonathan and Leah opened up a brewery a couple of years ago. They make Irish-style ales. Excellent beer! They've done well. I'm proud of them.

"God, I think I've talked enough. I'm starving. Didn't you pack some leftover pizza?"

Chapter Thirty-seven

Friday afternoon

They arrived in Monterotondo a few minutes early and found the gelateria. Franca had already arrived and figured out who they were the moment they walked in. Gabriella showed her Carabinieri badge, which appeared to set her mind at ease. Antonio didn't blame her for being nervous, knowing there were criminal elements involved.

"May I buy you a gelato, *signora*?" He saw she wore a wedding band. "We should support the establishment."

"Of course. Why do you think I met you here?" She swept her hand around. "This place belongs to my cousin. I'll have a cup of the gianduja. It's her special recipe."

"Gabriella?"

"Sounds delightful."

He ordered three of the medium size. The creamy blend of chocolate and hazelnut flavors was fabulous. He suspected she added a little coffee and Frangelico in her recipe. After savoring a couple of bites, he pulled out his cell phone.

"As I explained on the phone, *signora*, we have some new suspects. I have the photos on my phone. There are just three I want to show you."

He pulled up the photo of Jordy first. She shook her head. Next, he pulled up Mancini. She stared carefully, considering it, then slowly shook her head side to side. *Merda. I hope it's not Paolo.* He pulled up the last photo. Her eyes flickered and narrowed. "I think that's him. I'm almost certain."

He and Gabriella looked at each other. "You're sure?"

"About ninety percent. Like I told the guys before, he was wearing a hat and sunglasses. He never took them off, even inside. And I think his hair was a little longer than in this photo. *Yes, it is,* Antonio thought.

"I have one more question. If this man were arrested, and had to go to trial, would you be willing to testify? It may not be necessary. But I want you to know there would be no danger. This man is not part of a mob family."

"How can you know that for certain?" There was a tremor in her voice. "The family influences are everywhere. Even the police."

She's right about that. "We have every reason to believe he is not. And we will be investigating it further, if he is arrested."

"I cannot say for sure. Let me think about it. Speak with my husband."

"*Grazie, signora Franca,*" said Gabriella. "That's all we can ask."

Franca finished her gelato then went and bid her cousin, a slender young woman, farewell. She started heading for the door, then stopped and turned. She put her hand on Antonio's arm and asked, "Your cousin, how is she? Is she still in a coma?"

He looked up and saw her deep brown eyes locked on his. "Yes," he said. "We are hoping for the best."

"I don't need to talk to my husband. I will testify if you need me." She turned and hurried out the door.

*****

"That bastard! He put Giulia in a coma and almost killed me!" They were standing outside on the sidewalk. "And to think, Nicolo has considered him a friend all these years."

"Don't jump to conclusions, Antonio. It was probably him, but it needs to be investigated further. We need to let Marcello know right away," she said.

"I agree. Before Nicolo finds out. I'm not sure how he'll react. I want to hurt him myself." She looked him in the eyes and nodded.

"I need caffeine. Let's get an espresso before we drive back," she said. "I saw a bar near where we parked."

Antonio ordered a double latte, Gabriella a straight double espresso. They bought bottles of water for the road.

"You should be the one to call Marcello," she said. "I doubt if he knows I came with you. If he asks, tell him the truth. Otherwise, no need to make him worry."

"Or chew your rear end out again."

"Yeah. That too. It hurts enough already."

He took a sip of his latte, then dialed. Marcello answered right away. "*Ciao*, Antonio. News?"

"Yes. You're not going to like it. The girl identified Paolo. Said she's ninety percent certain."

"*Merda*! I can't believe it. He may also be involved in the murders. I could understand his motive for that, especially the first one, but to betray his friend like that, and put his daughter in a coma. I don't get it."

Antonio remembered when Paolo visited Giulia in the hospital. He doubted he had intended to hurt her. It was probably eating him alive. Served him right. "Me neither, Marcello. The only thing I can think of is that Nicolo was getting too close to finding out. But even then …"

"Yeah. God, I was hoping it was none of these guys. Have you told Nicolo?"

"Not yet. I don't want to, either. Not unless I'm there to control his reaction."

"Good. Don't tell him. Don't answer your phone if he tries to call you, which he probably will. I'm going to bring Paolo in for questioning. Once I have him in custody, I'll let you know."

"I'll be heading back. It'll probably take me over three hours this time of day. Can I come by the station and listen in on your interview?"

"If I'm not done by then. I'm not waiting. By the way, you should know he also showed up on a CCTV feed a couple of blocks from our first murder victim, about twenty minutes before it occurred. So much for his alibi. And there's something fishy going on. Later, there is a time gap in the CCTV feed, over four minutes missing. My tech guy noticed the time jump. I've got him looking for the original feed. Somebody cut it out, probably Paolo. He must have missed the earlier feed which showed him nearby. It's not looking good for this guy. We still need to figure out who else was involved in your road incident. That was a two-person operation. I'll try to bring him in quietly in case it's one of the other detectives."

"Good. Listen, I'll be driving, can you text me when you've got him in custody?"

"Sure. *Ciao.*"

He hung up. "I'll fill you in while we're driving," he told Gabriella. "I want to get going." He downed the rest of his latte and used the restroom before the long drive back.

*****

As Antonio navigated toward the autostrada, he filled her in on Marcello's reaction, and what he'd found in the CCTV footage.

"I've been thinking, Antonio. I don't think he was trying to murder Nicolo. Otherwise, the Alfa would have come straight at you. I think he was just trying to scare him. Or maybe they were trying to distract him, to buy time while they covered their tracks."

"You may be right. Or maybe they just did a bad job of it. But that lousy shot taken at Nicolo lends credence to your theory."

"What about the second person?" Gabriella asked. "Who do you think it could be?"

"Has to be someone he's close to, someone he trusts, someone with the same agenda. It could be one of the other detectives. Or it could be a family member, who also wanted revenge for his nephew's death. Or maybe …"

"Or maybe he's been compromised," she said. "Bought off, by a mob family. Maybe they promised him the revenge he desperately wanted. None of it feels right to me."

"Me neither. Seems way out of character. I'm thinking he set out for revenge, then tried to cover his tracks. Needed time to do that."

*****

Traffic thinned out, but they had another couple of hours to go. They didn't talk much for a while, both deep in thought. Then, out of nowhere, she asked him the hard question.

"Antonio, I know your wife and daughter were victims of a terror attack in France. May I ask what happened? You don't have to answer if it's too hard."

"Yeah. It's hard. Really hard." *But I relive it in my mind every day.* He stared out the driver's window at the passing landscape. Turning his eyes back to the road, he began, "Not sure if I told you, Christina was a music student. She was given the opportunity of a lifetime, to study in Paris for a year. She loved it so much. When the school year ended, she stayed on to travel Europe for a month. That July, Randi and I flew to Paris to meet up with her. Spent a few days in Paris, letting her show us the sights. From there we planned five days in southern France. Then we were flying here."

He took a deep breath, "We went to Nice for a couple of nights, the second being Bastille Day." He paused. His eyes were on the road but his mind was replaying the scene. "We went to the promenade with thousands of others to watch the fireworks. Do you remember what happened?"

She nodded. "The night the terrorist drove his big truck through the crowds. Dozens of people died."

"Yes. After the fireworks, we were walking back to the hotel. I needed to find a restroom. We saw a row of portables near the promenade. The girls waited while I went to use one. I had to wait in line. When I was inside," his voice grew raspy, "I heard the terrible sounds … screams, tires screeching, crashing noises. I knew something horrible was happening. I ran back. The truck was already beyond where the girls had been. It was pandemonium. I couldn't find them. And when I ..."

"You don't need to tell me anymore, Antonio." There was a long silence.

"My mom and Alessia were on a plane to Paris. We were going to meet them the next day and fly to Tuscany. They came to Nice instead. Nicolo, Sofia, and Giulia came too. A day later my mom's other sisters and nonna showed up. I don't think I could have done it without them. The following day we all flew to Seattle with the bodies to plan a memorial."

"I'm so sorry." Her voice was strained. He glanced at her, seeing tears in her eyes.

"They were so loved. The memorial was standing room only. I still remember ... how lonely and hopeless I felt ... surrounded by all those people. I was a wreck. Still am, sometimes. It's been over three years. I'm sick of grieving. The world has moved on, but I can't. That's why I came here, I think. This has always been such a happy place for me."

Gabriella put her hand on top of his.

He continued, "I thought about what you said last night. About anger at God. I used to scream at him when I was alone. I was angry at God, at myself, at the world ... didn't know what to do with it." He was quiet for a minute. "And then the accident with Giulia. I should have ..."

Gabriella interrupted, her voice firm. "It's not your fault, Antonio. You couldn't have stopped either of those events. Don't believe the lie. Things happen that we have no control over."

"You're not the first person to tell me that. I was finally starting to accept it." He paused, "On one level, I know you're right."

Her tone changed. "Of course I'm right. Haven't you figured out yet … that I'm always right?"

He looked at her and she laughed, breaking the tension. "I'll try to remember that."

Chapter Thirty-eight

Friday late afternoon & evening

A few minutes later, Antonio's text notification chimed. "Can you check that?" he handed her his phone.

"What if it's one of your girlfriends?" she asked. "Oh, you're safe, it's Marcello." She tapped on the message and read it aloud, "Looks like Paolo may be on the run. Not answering calls or texts. Nobody knows where he is."

"*Merda*," Antonio said.

"*Merda* is right! I'm going to Siena with you."

"Are you sure? Won't Marcello get upset with you?"

"I don't really give a damn."

"It's your butt."

"Don't I know it. Speaking of which, do you have any Tylenol or anything in the car?"

"Yeah. Open the console. You'll find a bottle. Been livin' on the stuff. I need to start weaning myself off before I ruin my liver."

*****

After receiving that message, Antonio drove as fast as he thought he could get away with. They met Marcello at the Provinciale Stazione Carabinieri. Gabriella had phoned him to warn him she was coming. After a brief argument, he relented. He knew full well how headstrong she could be. Antonio wondered if she ever lost an argument. *She must have been a handful for her parents*, he thought, with a smile.

"I've alerted all of the Carabinieri in the field and sent officers to watch his house and the questura," Marcello told them. "At this point, I haven't notified the polizia municipale. We need to do that. But not until we tell Nicolo."

"He needs to know. Let me call him and arrange to meet."

*****

Antonio phoned Nicolo.

"*Ciao*, Nicolo! You still at the questura?"

"Yes. Are you back? I was just about to leave and remembered I didn't have my car. I was getting ready to requisition one. I've been trying to get hold of Paolo. He never came back from lunch. He's not answering his phone. I want to go to his house."

"Yes. I'm back. Be there in ten minutes."

"Don't park. I'll meet you out front."

Antonio told Marcello and Gabriella that he was going to pick up Nicolo.

"All right. In twenty minutes, I'm putting out an APB," Marcello said. "You help Nicolo keep his cool. I'd prefer it if you brought him here."

"A good call. Hope he's willing."

*****

Nicolo got in the passenger seat and looked at Antonio. "What?" he said, having read Antonio like a book.

"The woman from the car rental place ID'd Paolo, at least she was fairly sure it was him. Marcello is looking for him too. He's getting ready to put out an APB."

"Damn it. What the hell, Antonio! You've known this for how long? You didn't tell me. You tell Marcello first!"

"He wanted to bring him in for questioning. He asked me not to tell you yet. He was afraid you would overreact, do something to jeopardize his case." *Or hurt Paolo,* he thought. *He's angry enough.*

"That's how much you trust me, nephew?"

"Your reaction … you're just confirming what I feared, Nicolo. You wonder why I didn't want to tell you?"

Nicolo's hands were clenched tight. He looked like a fighter who had just taken a knockdown punch.

"I'm sorry, Nicolo …" *What do I say to diffuse this?* "I know what I'd be feeling in your situation. I'm angry too. If he's the one who ran us off the road, I want to hurt him. Not sure I can even trust myself. I can only imagine how you feel. He was your friend. It looks like he betrayed you. But it's not our job to exact justice."

"Hell, it's not! My daughter might die because of him."

He looked at Nicolo. His face was beet red. *Have I caused permanent damage to our relationship ... this man I love and admire? Please God, I hope not.*

"There's more, Nicolo." Nicolo looked at him gravely. "He showed up in the video, not far from the murder location of Coppola, about twenty minutes before he was murdered."

"What?" It seemed as if this information didn't penetrate the firewall he'd thrown up.

"Plus, there was some footage which had been clipped from the video file."

"*Merda.* We're going to look for him, Antonio."

"Marcello told me to bring you back to the Carabinieri."

"Forget it. I want to find him before they do."

"Marcello has officers watching his house."

"I don't think he'd go there anyway. We're going to go check out his sister's house."

"If I help you, Nicolo, you have to promise me. Promise me you won't hurt him."

Nicolo nodded but Antonio had his doubts.

"Where does she live?"

"In Quercegrossa. About twenty minutes north of here."

"I know it."

*****

As Antonio drove, Nicolo seemed to calm down a little, but hardly spoke for most of the drive. The last of the sun's rays shining on the stone houses and hamlets gave them a golden glow, as if the light were emanating from the stones themselves. A few minutes later, the setting sun created one of those sunsets that puts you in awe of God's creation. It should have lifted his spirits.

Nicolo finally spoke, "Did you find out anything about who the second person could be?"

"No. Gabriella and I talked about it," Antonio said, turning to glance at Nicolo. "She rode to Monterotondo with me. It has to be someone he trusts. Possibly one of the other detectives?"

"I've never seen either of the others ride a motorcycle, or even talk about it. The way you described it, whoever rode the Ducati was a seasoned rider."

"We hadn't considered that."

"There's someone else he knows and trusts that rides though. I just can't imagine her being involved."

"Her?"

"His sister, Amara."

This brought silence back to the two of them. As they were driving, Antonio's text notification sounded. Nicolo saw it was Marcello and spat out, "Ignore it."

"Don't you think ..."

"No. I don't!"

*****

They arrived at Quercegrossa. Nicolo directed Antonio to Amara's house on the eastern edge of the hamlet. They parked a hundred feet beyond. Nicolo asked Antonio to cover the rear exit.

A few minutes later, Nicolo stuck his head out the back door, "Paolo's not here." He waved him inside. Amara was bent over with her head between her knees, sobbing. She looked up, wiping the tears from her eyes. Fear was etched on her face. He heard Nicolo saying, "Please, Amara, contact me right away if you see or hear from him." She nodded, but her gaze seemed a million miles away.

Antonio looked at Amara closely, wondering if she could have been the one riding the Ducati. She was too short, too curvy. *Surely, I would have noticed,* he thought. Then he remembered the lady at the pizzeria, saying the rider had a mustache. He breathed a sigh of relief.

As they climbed back into the little Lancia, Nicolo said, "Head back towards Siena. I'll tell you where to go."

Chapter Thirty-nine

Friday evening

They took SR 222 south to SS 674, looping the west side of Siena. Nicolo directed him to turn north toward the city on Strada di San Carlo, to Strada Comunale Giuggiolo.

Being in **Amara's** presence had changed Nicolo's disposition. The dark shadow of his anger had lightened. Antonio felt like he could speak. "There's no way that Amara was the Ducati rider."

Nicolo stared out the window and nodded. "I know."

As they approached their destination, Antonio realized where they were going. The road only led to one place, a place he knew. Cimitero Laterino was one of the early cemeteries in Siena, the place where his great-grandparents were laid to rest.

"What are we doing here, Nicolo?"

"Just a hunch. A long shot. This is where Paolo's nephew, Stephan, is interred. Whatever Paolo did, he did to take revenge for his death."

Antonio stared at him. Was he in, or out of, control?

Nicolo continued, "Taking the life of Coppola, I can almost understand, even forgive. But he went too far."

Antonio felt the same, but his concern right now was keeping Nicolo from doing something he'd regret.

"Cut the lights, Antonio. Park in that lot there." He pointed. "We'll walk the rest of the way. If he's here, I don't want him to see us coming."

Antonio did as told. He grabbed his phone from the console and got out of the car. They had just started toward the gate when his text notification sounded again.

"Ignore it!" Nicolo growled in a whispering voice. "Put your damned phone on silent."

As Antonio was doing so, he saw the text was from Gabriella. *Where are you? Worried.* He wished he could answer.

*****

The cimitero was deserted this time of night. There was little light. Antonio's eyes gradually adjusted. The place was large and foreboding. Built in the late eighteenth century, it reminded Antonio of Roman ruins that had weathered the ages. The entrance took them under an arch with a cupola on top. There was a chapel on their right.

Nicolo paused, leaned in to Antonio, and whispered, "His ashes are in that columbarium," he pointed, "the north side." Antonio nodded, but his thoughts were on how creepy this place was in the dark of night. The pale light from the city above cast long shadows from the

Italian Cypresses and tall tombstones. During the day, he found these cemeteries fascinating. At night, not so much. He shivered involuntarily.

Nicolo resorted to hand signals now. He slowly circled into the shadows and moved quietly. Antonio stayed near, thankful that Nicolo did not have his weapon drawn.

Without warning he heard Nicolo call out "Paolo!" in a loud, stern voice. He saw a shadow move in the darkness. It ducked around the corner of the columbarium. After a few seconds, the shadow took off in a sprint toward the north end of the cimitero. "Stop, Paolo! We need to talk!" Nicolo yelled. But the shadow did not pause. Nicolo took off in pursuit. Antonio followed. His body screamed at him, not taking kindly to the pounding. *Should I keep running or stop ... call Marcello for help?* He kept running. *I can't stop or I'll lose them.* It would take Marcello and his officers a long time to get there, and they'd be somewhere else by then.

Paolo ran north, disappearing through the trees, up a rise, and out of the cemetery, toward the heart of old Siena. They followed and found themselves on Via Laterino which took them under the Porta Laterino arch into the old city. Nicolo was about fifty yards behind Paolo. Antonio another twenty-something yards behind Nicolo. *Looks like we'll lose him in the labyrinth,* Antonio thought.

There were people on the street now. Paolo slowed to a fast walk—maybe exhausted—maybe not wanting to draw attention to himself. Nicolo did the same. Antonio finally caught up—breathing hard, and sweating—and found Nicolo doing the same. It had turned into a surprisingly warm autumn evening. Paolo continued past Hotel Athena onto Via Paolo Mascagni. *More irony*, Antonio thought. He continued straight, past a convent. The street curved right, and they lost sight of him. Nicolo started to run. Coming around the curve, they caught sight of him turning right at Trattoria Nonna Gina, which sat on the corner. Nicolo called his name again. When they rounded the corner, he was nowhere to be seen. There were two main ways he could have gone, south on the broader street, or a quick left under an arch onto a narrow back street. Nicolo chose that way, with Antonio in tow. Antonio saw a tile on the wall, Via Stalloreggio. Near the tile were the flags of the contrada district, Pantera, the Panther.

The street curved gradually to the left, following the contour of the cliffside. The buildings on their left sat upon the edge of the bluff. There was no sign of Paolo. It appeared they had lost him.

*****

Nicolo made a decision to split up. "Antonio, go north here toward the Piazza del Campo. He might be trying to get lost in the crowd. I'm going left, towards the Duomo. Pay attention to your phone. Call me if you catch sight of him."

Antonio went a half block. He stopped and looked behind him, then pulled out his phone. He called Gabriella, walking onward as it rang. She answered on the second ring. "Antonio! Are you …?"

"Wait. Listen. Nicolo and I followed Paolo into the old city. We lost him just south of the Piazza del Campo. Nicolo split us up in two directions. He's headed toward the Duomo. I'm headed toward the piazza."

"We'll put out word to our officers and the polizia to be on the look-out. Marcello and I will head your way. Let's meet at the Fontana Gaia. We can be there in ten minutes. And, Antonio, we don't think Paolo is our murderer. We found other suspects on the CCTV. I'll explain when we get there." She was gone before he could reply.

A couple of minutes later, Antonio reached the Piazza del Campo. He made a circle of the rim, searching for Paolo among the crowds. *Like trying to find a needle in a haystack.* The restaurants on the piazza open earlier than other parts of the city to accommodate the tourists. With the warm evening, they were packed with people, especially the outside tables which spilled out under the sienna-colored awnings.

He did a three-sixty, scanning the crowd for any sign of him. From one of the streets a parade of elegantly dressed Senese, people of all ages, emerged into the piazza. They carried the red and white checkered flags of contrada Leocorno—the Unicorn—singing proudly as they marched. These parades were regular occurrences. He wondered who decided which contrada marched when.

He searched among the marchers to see if Paolo had slipped in among them.

Seeing no sign of him, he made his way to the center of the piazza, to the Fontana Gaia, to look for Gabriella and Marcello. It came to mind that the fountain is fed by the bottini, the same underground aqueduct that the drug dealers used to escape, like so many rats, a few nights previous. He wondered if Paolo could have used it as an escape route. He probably knew all the secret entrances.

Moments later, he saw Marcello and Gabriella coming across the piazza. She was not using her crutches and walked with a limp which looked painful. "I can't get this damn woman to take care of herself," Marcello muttered. But Antonio sensed a begrudging admiration in his voice.

"What happened?" asked Marcello. "You were supposed to bring Nicolo to me."

"He had his own ideas. We went to the house of Paolo's sister. Nicolo thought he might have gone there, but no sign of him. Then we went to the Cimitero Laterino."

"What the ...?"

"That's where the ashes of Stephan, Paolo's nephew, are interred. Nicolo had a hunch. Turned out to be a good one. But Paolo got away and headed into the heart of the old city. We lost him when he turned the corner by Trattoria Nonna Gina. Nicolo had us split up. That's when I called Gabriella. Nicolo told me to search the Campo while he headed toward the Duomo. I figure we've lost him. The question is, where will he go on foot? I think you should have someone go to the cimitero. He may double back."

"Good idea." He looked at Gabriella. She nodded and stepped a few feet away to make the call. "But I'm more worried that Nicolo might find him," Marcello said. "I don't think Paolo is our murderer. On the CCTV we ..."

"Hold on," Antonio said, "a text." He pulled out his phone and read it aloud, *"Come to Duomo."*

Gabriella was back already. "Let's go," she said as she turned to head that direction. The Duomo was not far, but if you didn't know your way through the maze of streets you could easily get lost, especially at night.

Their pace was brisk but not a run, for Gabriella's sake. They crossed the south end of the Campo, then climbed the stairs under the arch to the next street level, which took them into the Aquila, *the Eagle,* contrada. They turned left, then right a couple of times as they wound their way through the narrow, poorly lit pedestrian streets. They emerged in the piazza which lies in front of the Duomo di Siena. The Duomo is dedicated to the Virgin Mary, thus known as the Cathedral of Santa Maria Assunta. Antonio had never seen its ornate façade at night. The light of the floodlights gave it a spectral feel, made more so by the scattered clouds, backlit by a nearly full moon.

Chapter Forty

Friday night

The duomo was closed this time of night so Antonio assumed they would find Nicolo, and possibly Paolo, outside. There was no sign of them, either in the piazza or on the grand steps leading up to the duomo entrance. They circled around the south side, past the horizontally striped tower, and through the grand arch that connects the cathedral to the Duomo Museum. On their left they spotted a few steps, and a door, slightly ajar. Pale golden light spilled its way down the steps.

Antonio motioned. The three of them entered the door and found themselves in the vast empty nave, near the banks of candelabra holders. Dozens of candles were still burning, though there was not a visible soul in the place. Behind the candles was the rear of the cathedral with its pulpit and wooden choir loft. High above, in the stone wall, a large, round stained-glass window loomed.

Though he had been here many times, Antonio was awed by the feel of the majestic gothic design at night. The floor plan, laid out like a cross, had dozens of striped columns running the length of the cathedral, rising high to support ornately sculpted capitals, statues, and arches.

Surrounding the base of the central dome were busts of every pope from the time of Peter until the sixteenth century. Their faces peered down sternly, disapproving of the unwelcome intruders. The floor consisted of dozens of mosaics by various Renaissance artists. Along the exterior walls of the nave were numerous frescos of extraordinary craftsmanship, and statues by the likes of Donatello and Michelangelo. By the light of the candles, it felt mysterious, otherworldly.

There was no sign of Nicolo, or Paolo, or any other living creature; only the dead, cast in cold marble. They split up to do a more thorough search, each side chapel, the sacristy, the baptistry located under the choir, and the Piccolomini Library, connected to the nave. Antonio was just finishing his search of the baptistry when he heard something. It sounded like urgent voices from somewhere below.

He glanced around and saw neither Gabriella nor Marcello. But he did see a dark stairwell, spiraling downward, closed off by an iron gate which stood ajar. He pulled out his cell phone and turned on its flashlight. Slowly and quietly, he descended the stone steps into what he realized was the crypt. He had never been down there but had heard the story. This ancient room below the pulpit had been unknown for centuries. In the late thirteenth century, it was filled in to create the foundation of the cathedral above during its construction. It was rediscovered unexpectedly in 1999, and work begun to excavate it. Despite all the years hidden away, it contained stunning frescos covering the four walls.

The muffled voices grew louder as he descended. Nearing the bottom, he saw a pale light. He extinguished his phone. The voices were clearer now. He could make out the rising anger in Nicolo's voice. He peered around the corner and found a breathless and red-faced Nicolo, handgun at his side, standing over Paolo, slumped against the wall in the corner.

*****

"Don't lie to me, Paolo! I know you rented the car and motorcycle. We have a witness."

"Yes. But … please, please … I can explain. I did not drive those. I didn't kn …"

"You betrayed me! I thought you were my friend!" he bellowed like a bull elephant, then paused to catch his breath. "My daughter's in a coma! And for what? Why? To cover up a murder? I should kill you here and now. You think running … hiding in the church is gonna save you?"

"Nicolo!" Antonio called out. He had never seen his uncle so full of rage.

Nicolo turned, stared hard at Antonio with dark, angry eyes. He remained silent for several seconds. "Don't worry, I'm not going to kill him," Nicolo said in a low growl. "Though I should." He put his gun in the holster under his suit. Antonio saw a second gun tucked in his belt, probably Paolo's.

Moments later Marcello descended the stairs into the crypt, followed by Gabriella. Her face was creased with pain.

"Nicolo," Marcello said firmly, "Let's hear what he has to say. I have reason to believe he didn't commit those murders. We found other evidence on the CCTV footage. Footage that had been cut out of the files you sent me."

Nicolo turned and looked at Marcello, his face a complex mosaic—disbelief—shock—anger—regret.

"Please, Nicolo, let me explain," Paolo pleaded, his voice on the edge of breaking.

Nicolo turned back slowly toward Paolo, leaning aggressively over him. "What about the rentals? Did you attack Giulia and Antonio? Did you think it was me? Don't lie to me, Paolo!" The rage was still there but he was questioning it.

"No, no, I swear! Yes, I rented the vehicles. But not for myself. I didn't know what they were going to use them for."

"They? Who? Tell me!"

"I'm afraid, Nicolo. Afraid for my family. If I tell you, you have to protect them. They threatened to harm them if I didn't go along!"

Antonio watched Nicolo soften. His shoulders fell. He was a protector of the innocent. It was deeply ingrained in his nature, the reason he did what he did.

"Gemma, Bettina?" Nicolo asked. Paolo nodded. "Are they at home?" Nicolo asked.

"No. I sent them to stay with Gemma's sister and husband … near Radda in Chianti."

Nicolo turned to Marcello. "Can we send Carabinieri there to watch them? Paolo is going to tell us who is behind all this." He spoke the words with certainty.

Marcello nodded, and spoke, "Call them, Paolo. Tell them to expect the Carabinieri. Then give me their names, address, and phone numbers."

Paolo gave him the information. They tried to make their calls but there was no cell reception in the crypt. They ascended the stairs into the candlelit nave, where they came upon an aging janitor staring at them dumbfounded, his eyes wide with fear. Gabriella showed him her badge and said they were leaving. She gave no further explanation.

On his way out, Antonio picked up a lighter and lit one more candle.

Chapter Forty-one

Friday night

Outside, they huddled on the rear steps. They could have gone to the questura, just a few blocks away, but they wanted to stay away from prying ears and eyes. Paolo called Gemma. He hung up quickly before she could ask questions. Marcello called for a team to go and keep watch on their house. Then the interrogation began.

"Hit the high points quickly, Paolo," Nicolo said, "We need to know who we're looking for."

"Mancini … and Fiero Belluci."

Nicolo, looking stunned, turned to Marcello who nodded. "It fits," he said.

"Did they drive the Alfa and the Ducati?"

"Yes. Mancini drove the Alfa. Belluci rode the Ducati."

Marcello asked Gabriella to call and put together two armed teams to aid in the manhunt. She walked off, phone in hand.

"And the murders?" Nicolo asked.

"Mancini did the first two. Belluci shot Baccio Camilleri. Mancini was with him."

Nicolo paused and looked at Marcello. "You better call Magistrate Mariani. We probably shouldn't arrest Belluci without her knowledge."

"You're right." He dialed and walked away.

"Why didn't you come to me? We could have arrested them and kept your family safe."

"It's not just the two of them. Belluci's been working with the Laganàs, the local clan of the 'Ndrangheta. He dragged Mancini in."

"Yeah. I know who they are. How the hell did this all go down?"

"Mancini killed Coppola on his own. I was on my way to do it. I was beside myself—blinded with sorrow and rage—a desire for revenge for Stephan. I had a syringe with a triple dose of heroine. But when I saw him, I couldn't go through with it. I couldn't become the animal he was." He paused and looked up at Nicolo. "Mancini suspected what I was doing. He followed me. When I changed my mind, I was only a half block away. He found me in tears. He took the syringe from me. I thought he was taking it so I wouldn't do something I'd regret. I didn't know he was going to finish what I couldn't do."

"And Federico Ricci?"

"Mancini was on a roll, angry about the verdict, angry at himself for screwing up, angry at you for disciplining him. He couldn't deal with the guy still being on the street peddling drugs. More kids dying. The lack of justice was eating him alive. And there was something else ..."

"What?" Nicolo asked.

"He also lost someone to drugs—a cousin—two years ago. They grew up together. He's very private, you know ... never talked about it. Didn't help that he never felt like he fit in here ... never felt respected."

Nicolo stared at him, his face a complex jumble of emotions. He opened his mouth, as if to say something, but didn't.

Paolo took a deep breath. "He killed Ricci the same way. Somehow Belluci found out. He blackmailed him. Offered him money if he cooperated, threatened prison, or worse, if he didn't. They even sent some flowers—black roses—to his family in Turin. A not-so-subtle message ... 'go along or else.' Apparently Belluci has been on the take from the 'Ndrangheta family for some time."

"Baccio Camilleri?"

"I confronted Mancini. He confided in me. He was scared. We both were. Told me it was an opportunistic killing. The timing was right. Camilleri had been skimming money and drugs. They figured if they took him out, that it would all look like the same killer. But Camilleri fought back, wouldn't take the needle, lunged at Belluci. So, he shot him. He wasn't using a silencer. So, they found the slugs and left in a hurry. I'm surprised no one reported the shots."

"So why the attack on Antonio and Giulia?"

"You had that partly right. It was supposed to be you. Belluci cooked it up. But it was supposed to be more than a distraction. He wanted to take you out. He thought you'd be onto him if given enough time. But Mancini couldn't go through with it. He came to me a few hours later ... told me he swerved away at the last moment. Otherwise, Antonio would have been hit head on. He figured out at the last second that it was Antonio. Then he saw Giulia go off the road. He was sick about it, knowing she was in a coma, knowing it was his fault. That was never supposed to happen. He's the one who called the polizia to report the accident."

So those were his eyes I saw, thought Antonio. *I knew it in my dreams. No wonder he looked surprised.*

Nicolo's mind was reeling. Antonio entered the interrogation. "Why did you rent the car and motorcycle, Paolo?"

"They threatened me on two fronts, blackmailing me on the murder charges, but I think they knew that wouldn't be enough, so they threatened my family. I say *they* but it was really Belluci and whoever is pulling his strings. They had CCTV clips showing me near the site of the first murder minutes before it happened. I was afraid to bring it to light ... the blackmail. Didn't know who I could trust in the Carabinieri, knowing they had turned someone as high up as Belluci. And they lied about why they needed the vehicles. Belluci said it was for an undercover operation. I didn't know something so sinister was afoot. I should have. I'm sorry, Nicolo, I'm so sorry." He buried his face in his hands. It took a couple of minutes before he could continue.

Marcello returned from his call with the magistrate. He nodded. "We're good. She wasn't even shocked. Apparently, she's had her own suspicions."

"That bastard!" Nicolo said. "Make sure you find him before I do." He turned back to Paolo.

"Why did you hide, Paolo? Why did you run from me?" His tone had changed to that of a disappointed father, speaking to his son.

Paolo hung his head. "It was stupid. I panicked. Knew I looked guilty, and that I could endanger my family. I wanted to get them farther away, to a safe place, before I turned myself in. I was heading to Gemma's sister as soon as I left the cimitero."

"Alright. We'll hash out the rest later. We need to get after these guys."

Marcello had answered his phone again as they were talking. "Our people are almost here, Nicolo. We have two cars with three officers each. I suggest we divide into two teams. One to look for Mancini, one to go after Belluci. Gabriella and I can lead one team. You and Antonio go with the other. Keep Paolo with you. But neither he nor Antonio can be armed." Paolo nodded in surrender.

"We should look for Mancini," Nicolo said. "I know where he lives and his haunts."

Marcello stared at Nicolo, sizing up his emotional state. "Do you really think I would send you after Belluci? Can I trust you with Mancini? Do you have yourself under control?"

Nicolo looked at him but didn't answer. He just nodded. "We'll start by checking the questura. He often works late. He might still be there." He looked at Paolo, then Marcello. "Either of you aware of anything that might have tipped him off, sent him on the run?"

"I don't think so," Paolo said, "unless Belluci knows. I left while he and Jordy were out. Told the desk I'd be in the field working on the investigation."

"Nor anything on our end," Marcello said. "I never contacted anyone at the questura when I went looking for Paolo. When I put out an APB on Paolo, I also put one out on Mancini, but only with the Polizia di Stato and Carabinieri. I excluded the Polizia Municipale. I didn't want to alert your people. Thought there could be another accomplice. And I sure as hell didn't tell Belluci what I'd found out. I didn't trust him even before I found out he was dirty."

As they were answering, Antonio saw the Carabinieri Jeeps coming around the corner of the duomo towards them. No lights were flashing. Good call.

*****

It was nearing 8:30 PM now. They made quick introductions. Antonio remembered four of the six Carabinieri from the osteria op. They conferred and

325

decided that Marcello and his team would check the GDF offices first, then Belluci's home. Marcello placed a call to track down Belluci's home address.

Nicolo, Antonio, and Paolo would go to the questura on foot, with the Carabinieri team in the shadows in case of trouble.

Marcello gave last-minute instructions. "Everyone put their phones on silent but with the vibration on. Gabriella, Antonio, I want the two of you to be the primary communicators between the teams. Text updates as your search goes on. Call immediately if backup is needed. If you get no answer from that person, contact me or Nicolo."

"We also need the numbers for the Carabinieri team leaders," Nicolo said. "In case we get separated."

They exchanged numbers. The leader of their trio was Sergeant Moretti, accompanied by officers d'Allesi, and Messina, a tan, blonde woman as tall as he was.

"Let's go," Marcello said.

Chapter Forty-two

Later Friday night

Nicolo, Antonio and Paolo walked together, with the Carabinieri a half block behind in their Jeep. They entered the questura as if nothing in particular were going on, not wanting to alert the front desk that anything was awry. Nicolo asked the sergeant casually, "Are Jordy or Mancini still around?"

"No sir. Jordy left about 6:00. You didn't miss Mancini by much, left maybe fifteen minutes ago."

"*Grazie*, Gino."

Gino looked at Paolo. "*Ciao*, Paolo. Marcello Bianchi from the Carabinieri tried to get hold of you earlier."

"Thanks, Gino. I've spoken with him," Paolo said casually. A good acting job, considering his frame of mind.

Back outside, Nicolo asked, "Paolo, would Mancini go straight home, or stop along the way?"

"Could be either. My guess, he'd head to his apartment to change and shower before dinner. He usually eats out. I know his favorite haunts."

*****

The six of them piled into the Jeep designed to seat five. Nicolo instructed the driver to head toward the Fontebranda and park there. Mancini's apartment was about a block east of there. Antonio, sardined in the back with three others, managed to find just enough arm space to text Gabriella ... *No Mancini at questura. Heading to his apartment near Fontebranda.*

The drive was short ... thankfully. The tight squeeze was killing Antonio's ribs. And someone needed a shower. They parked near the ancient gothic fountain of Fontebranda, and piled out. They made their way east on Via Fontebranda. When they reached Mancini's apartment building, Nicolo kept the Carabinieri with him. He instructed Antonio and Paolo to watch on the street below as they made their way through the dimly lit foyer and ascended the worn terra cotta steps to the second-floor apartment.

As Antonio and Paolo watched outside, one watching left, the other right, Mancini rounded the street corner and saw them. He stopped in his tracks, a look of cold fear in his eyes. He pivoted, and took off in a sprint, leaving Antonio with another dilemma. *Crap! If I wait for Nicolo he'll get a huge head start.* He made a quick decision, "Paolo, grab the team. I'm going after Mancini." He took off running before Paolo could argue.

The pounding of the pavement was even more painful than before. *Damn, damn, damn,* he thought with every footfall. His nerves were taut. *What am I doing? I've got no weapon. He's probably armed.* He rounded the corner and caught sight of Mancini about fifty yards ahead. He tried desperately to make up ground, but Mancini was faster. He disappeared around another corner. When Antonio made the turn, there was no sign of him. He moved ahead cautiously, clutching his ribs, trying to catch his breath. His heart pounded wildly in his chest. Then he heard the tinkling sound of breaking glass, followed by a duller smashing noise. He moved quietly but quickly toward the sound. He found a door ajar, with broken glass. The hand-painted sign on the shop window said *La Dolce Vino*. He remembered the name from Nicolo's story. This is the wine shop where they made the drug bust. The windows and doors were boarded up. Mancini had broken the glass and kicked in the plywood to reach the door handle.

He stepped into a shadow and phoned Nicolo, who answered immediately. "Lost you. Where are you?"

"La Dolce Vino. He broke in."

"Be there in one minute. Do *not* go in!"

Antonio assured him he wouldn't, then shot off a quick text to Gabriella, *Mancini on run. Broke into La Dolce Vino wine shop. Probably trying to escape into bottini.*

His phone rang almost immediately. "Are you going in after him?" she asked.

"Probably. Nicolo and the team will be here any moment. I'll explain later."

"I'll see if we can round up any more officers to watch other bottini exits. Odds are in his favor though. Keep me posted."

"Any sign of Belluci?"

"We're on the way to his house. He lives near Monteriggioni."

"Okay. Gotta go."

*****

He hung up just as Nicolo, Paolo and the Carabinieri were arriving. They flanked the door. The Carabinieri, wearing body armor, entered first. The place was vacant, except for shelves and shelves of wine. The shop had been closed and boarded up after the bust. Antonio couldn't help but wonder what they were going to do with all the wine. And now the entryway was unsecured. *If someone figures this out, they'll have a field day in here.*

The Carabinieri, guns drawn, led the way down the brick stairs to the cellar. Again, no sign of Mancini. They found the heavy wood door which led to the bottini. The clasp which held the lock was pried off.

Nicolo huddled with the team. "We need to be quick. The bottini goes two directions from here before branching off. Nearest exit is the Fontebranda. He might be circling back for his car. Moretti, we're going to divide into two groups. I want Paolo to go with you and d'Allesi; Messina with Antonio and me." Moretti nodded his approval.

"I'll take my group toward the Fontebranda." He turned to Paolo. "Call Gino and tell him we need Municipale officers at as many of the bottini exits as possible, on the lookout for Mancini. Priority one is the Fontebranda, then any other exits near this location. Tell them that if they spot him to follow but not engage. He's probably armed."

"Gino's going to want an explanation."

"Tell him whatever you want but keep it brief. Time is critical!"

Sergeant Moretti nodded. "You guys go. We'll come as soon as Paolo makes his call. Once we go in there, he won't have reception."

Nicolo, Messina, and Antonio crept down the carved stone steps, and stepped into the cool, ankle-deep water of the aqueduct. Messina had a powerful flashlight. She cast its beam ahead of them, illuminating the walls of carved stone, which looked like limestone. Nicolo had his Beretta drawn. Antonio hoped like hell he didn't use it. Treading through the water made their shoes sodden and heavy. After about a hundred yards, the bottini widened. The walls here were brick, with arched ceilings like those of a wine cellar. Here the water funneled into a channel down the middle, and they were able to walk on dry stone on the sides. A few minutes later, they reached the stairs going up to the Fontebranda.

*****

They climbed the uneven steps, carved into the stone. Exiting through a wrought iron gate, again with a broken lock, they entered the dark, shadowy portico behind the three gothic arches where the fountain was located. The famous Fontebranda was built in the 13th century. It felt mysterious, as a cloud passed over the moon, deepening the darkness.

They stepped through an archway to the outside of the fountain and were greeted by the unexpected. There was Mancini, sitting on the ground, his back against the base of an arch. His knees were pulled to his chest, his eyes cast downward. Jordy was crouched down in front of him.

"You can put your gun away, boss. He's ready to turn himself in," Jordy said.

"How did you get here and find him?" Nicolo asked.

"I heard the call Gino put out. My apartment is just over that way," he pointed to the west, "a kilometer or so from Mancini's. I was here when he came out from the bottini. I didn't need to threaten him. He's done. Giving himself up of his own free will. Here's his gun. I pulled the magazine an' checked the chamber." He handed it to Nicolo, grip first, with the barrel pointed at the ground.

Nicolo passed the gun off to Messina. He turned back, and in the blink of an eye his rage rose to a ten. He grabbed Mancini and pulled him to his feet, his face just inches away. "You bastard!" he spat, shoving him hard against the column. Mancini knew better than to say a word. He couldn't look Nicolo in the eyes.

Nicolo's voice was hoarse, "Call Gino for me, Jordy. I'm not sure what Paolo told him but tell him we found Mancini, and everyone is okay."

Nicolo released his grip on Mancini, who slumped back to the ground. Nicolo turned to Messina. "Radio Sergeant Moretti. Tell him we have Mancini and to meet us back at the Cherokee."

As he was speaking, a pair of Polizia Municipale pulled up in their Fiat Panda patrol car, offering assistance. They knew the detectives.

"Good timing, officers. I want you to take Mancini to the questura for questioning. Our Jeep is overcrowded. Take Jordy, and Antonio too. Put Mancini between those two. No need to cuff him. We'll meet you there after the rest of our team arrives back here."

"You got it, Commissario Zaccardi."

*****

The Fiat Panda is like a small SUV, but at least there were only three of them in the back seat. Antonio shot off a text to Gabriella. *Mancini in custody. On way to questura. What's happening with Belluci?*

About thirty seconds later she called. "Belluci's on the run! He's on foot. When we arrived, he bolted out the back. Must've known something was up. I'm with the Jeep. I heard … wait! I just heard two shots fired … three more."

Antonio could hear them. "I'll call Nicolo. We'll send help."

"Please. I'm worried."

"What's that sound?"

"*Dio santo!* A motorcycle. Came from the barn, just blew past me to the road. Has to be Belluci."

"Which way is he headed?"

"Looks like he turned toward Siena. But he could go many different directions from there. Here comes the team. Thank God, looks like they are all okay. Call Nicolo. Then call me back. We'll be in pursuit."

Chapter Forty-three

Still later Friday night

He hung up and called Nicolo.

"Moretti and his guys are coming up the road now," Nicolo said. "We'll join the pursuit. Switch communication to the car radios. Drop Mancini at the questura. Tell Gino I said to lock him in an interview room. Then you, Jordy and the Municipale officers join us. Get on the radio for directions when you're heading out. We're on channel six-point-three. Got it? Six-point-three. I'm hanging up to call Marcello. I'm hoping he called for air support. We could use a chopper or two." He was gone.

Antonio hung up just as they were pulling up in front of the questura. Mancini turned to him. "I might be able to help, Antonio. I think I know where he's headed. I swear I won't try to escape."

"I need to talk to Nicolo."

He tried to call Nicolo back. The line was busy. Antonio leaned forward to the officer in the passenger seat, "I didn't catch your name."

"Marzano, sir. Tony Marzano—*piacere*. This is Officer Gharbi." Officer Gharbi, the driver, was a woman of about thirty, with short black hair. She looked like she might be Tunisian. She nodded her head and smiled.

"Okay, Marzano, call me Antonio. Will the cable for your radio mic reach this far?"

"Yes, sir. Prob'ly makes more sense than you trying to use me as a middleman." He handed the mic to Antonio.

"Set the channel to six-point-three, *per favore*."

"That's not our normal channel, sir."

"Nicolo changed it up. Probably so Belluci can't monitor it."

"Okay." He rotated the dial. "You're all set."

Antonio pushed the transmit button. "Nicolo." No answer. After a second attempt, he figured Nicolo was still on his call.

He looked at Jordy, who read his mind. They'd have to make their own decision.

Jordy nodded, "I believe we can trust him. I'll take responsibility."

"Alright, we're putting our butts on the line." Antonio handed the mic back to Officer Marzano and asked him to continue trying to reach Nicolo. He turned to Mancini, "Tell us where we're going."

"One night, after I met Belluci, I followed him out of the city. I didn't like that I was being blackmailed. I wanted to know where he went. Thought it might be useful one day."

"Looks like you were right," said Antonio.

"He went to a villa, a small castle really, located in a wooded area near Carpineta, almost due west of here. From SP101 you take Strada di Santa Colomba. Do you know it?" he asked toward Officer Gharbi.

"Yes," she answered. She executed a quick three-point turn and headed west.

A moment later, Antonio heard Nicolo's voice on the radio. Marzano handed him the mic. "Nicolo," Antonio spoke.

"Yes. Antonio?"

"Listen. We still have Mancini with us. He knows a place Belluci may be headed. A villa in the woods near Carpineta. I think we should check it out. Probably shouldn't go it alone."

"You guys are taking a gamble. What makes him think he might be going there?"

"He trailed him there once."

"Put him on."

Antonio handed the mic to Mancini.

"Tell me about this place, Vincenzo." Antonio had never heard him call Mancini by his first name.

"The night after the road incident, Belluci came to see me. He was really angry that I hadn't taken you out.

We got in a big argument. He threatened to turn me in for the murders. I was so worked up, I didn't care about my own safety anymore. When he left, I tailed him. It was tricky on the country roads. He passed through Santa Colomba and Carpineta. I knew the road didn't go much further, so I parked and went on foot. There's a narrow road into the woods. I hiked through the trees and spotted him. It's quite a place, a mob house I think, more like a small castle. I saw him talking to two men by the swimming pool. There were other guys that looked like bodyguards. Their dogs started to bark, so I got out of there."

"Alright. We've got all the highways being watched, but otherwise this is all we've got. We'll meet you in Carpineta. Don't go in without us. And don't pull any stunts, Mancini."

Mancini pushed the talk button. His voice cracked, "Don't worry, boss. I know how badly I've screwed up." He paused. "I'm only hope I can redeem myself a little before I face my judge."

Once out of the city, there was little traffic. Officer Gharbi pushed the little Fiat Panda to its limits, driving like she was trying out for team Ferrari. Antonio turned and stared hard at Mancini. He wasn't the man he remembered. His heart had abandoned him, leaving behind a broken man. He knew he should be angry with him, but felt sorrow instead. His rage was now entirely directed at Belluci, the guy behind all this. His anger rose in his throat, and his adrenaline with it.

From SP101 they turned west onto Strada di Santa Colomba. The road had no lights. The clouds with silver edges came and went over the moon, first brightening, then darkening the landscape.

They arrived in Carpineta five minutes later and found Nicolo and his team already there. They huddled up.

*****

"Okay. Marcello has a helicopter on its way," Nicolo told them, "A Carabinieri chopper coming from Firenze with four armed responders aboard. Marcello's group is meeting us here. They're just a few minutes out. When they arrive, I'll turn the operation over to him. This place probably belongs to the Laganà family. Even if Belluci isn't here, we'll at least detain them for questioning. So, this will probably get dangerous."

The other Jeep Cherokee pulled to a quick stop and Marcello's team tumbled out. He and Nicolo stepped aside to discuss their plans. When they returned, Marcello did the talking. "Our chopper is just a few minutes out. I checked this place out on Google Earth. There's only the one long driveway in with a gate at the end. Can you confirm that, Mancini?"

"Yes. The gate is only across the entrance road. On either side there is no fencing. But I'd bet they have some kind of electronic alarm sensors."

"Did you see any guards when you were there?"

"Yeah. I saw two but there may be more. They also have dogs. I was only there a minute when the dogs began to bark, so I hightailed it out of there."

"Alright. Nicolo, we have extra Beretta assault rifles, helmets, and Kevlar vests in the Cherokees. I want you and your people wearing them. I assume your two officers here," he looked at the names on their uniforms, "Marzano and Gharbi, have little experience with this sort of operation? Have you been trained with these weapons?"

"Yes sir." Marzano answered, a little too eagerly. Antonio figured he'd never seen action like this. He hoped he didn't feel compelled to prove his manhood.

Marcello continued, "Paolo, you're going in with us. I need the manpower." Paolo nodded, his face showing no emotion. "We're going to keep our same two teams. Marzano, Gharbi—I'm splitting you up, one with each team. You'll be in a support role. Jordy, I'm adding you to Nicolo's group. Gabriella, you're staying here with Mancini. I don't want you slowing us down." She nodded reluctantly. Marcello looked at her, "But be ready in case anyone gets past us. Stay with the radio.

"Antonio, I have a job for you. I want you to do blocking and surveillance for us. When I give you the command, you'll drive our Jeep in slowly, staying behind the advance of the teams. Park in front of the gate, blocking the road, headlights pointed at the villa but off until your cue. The Cherokees are armored but I want you in a helmet and vest anyway. Our hand radios—each team will have two—will be on the same frequency as the ones in the vehicles. The two teams are going to hike in, looks like about two hundred meters. Stay just off the road in the trees. Nicolo, I want your group to circle about fifty meters east of the gate and spread out. We'll do the same to the west. On my order, the chopper will come in and light up the grounds. They'll use LRAD to instruct everyone to exit the villa, unarmed, hands in the air." He pointed at Antonio. "That's when your headlights go on, and the floodlights on the roof. Moretti, give him the keys. Show him how to turn on the floodlights."

He paused while Moretti did so. He turned to Nicolo. "When I give you the word, Nicolo, you and I will move in with two of our men each. Keep the others in the edge of the woods to provide cover fire if things get ugly. I'm hoping they come out as ordered. If not, we may have to go in. If that's the case, we'll have the chopper unload the armed responders to lead the way. They have stun grenades. Might become a necessity. Okay, is everyone on channel six-point-three on your radios?"

Heads nodded.

"Questions?" Marcello looked around. "Okay, let's move."

The groups headed out. Antonio got in the Cherokee and started the engine. He let the group get about thirty meters ahead, then moved at their pace. He paused while they circled into position, then slowly edged close to the gate. He glanced at his watch. The time was 10:27 PM.

Chapter Forty-four

Still later Friday night

A ntonio was in awe of what he saw in front of him. The castle, though small by castle standards, was imposing and beautiful. It looked like an elegant hotel. He figured it to be about seventeenth century. Like most historic architecture in Tuscany, you could see the variety of stonework used where additions or repairs had occurred over the centuries. The walls were illuminated by floodlights hidden at ground level. Others lit up the trees. An aura of misty light emanated from what he assumed to be the swimming pool. There were two towers visible from this side. Ivy stoically climbed the walls and towers, clinging by tiny tendrils.

From the edge of the woods to the house appeared to be about fifty meters. Beyond the illuminated areas, the manicured lawns were shrouded in darkness. He knew that would change momentarily.

Through the thick bulletproof glass, he could hear the muffled sound as the dogs began to bark. He caught sight of one as it prowled the perimeter. The large hound, with droopy jowls, smelled trouble. He lifted his head, sniffed the air, and let loose a menacing howl. A second hound moved alongside and joined him.

The radio crackled. Marcello gave the order for the chopper to move in. About a minute later—seemed like a forever minute—he heard the rotors, growing louder by the moment. Soon they were overhead. Antonio craned his neck toward the windshield. It was a menacing machine, black, with "Carabinieri" in bold white letters on the side. Machine guns and cannons were visible on its front. He remembered that the Carabinieri were a military body. *Damn, these guys don't mess around.*

Suddenly, the chopper's floodlights lit up the grounds like a soccer stadium. He turned on his headlights and the bank of floodlights. Then he heard their loudspeaker. The instructions sounded garbled because of the deafening, rhythmic sound of the rotors, and the thick bulletproof glass. Adding to the cacophony of noise, he could just make out the sound of the baying hounds.

Nothing happened for a time. The helicopter continued to warn the occupants to exit the villa with their hands up. Finally, three men appeared, hands held high. All three looked young, in their twenties or thirties, lean, and muscular.

Antonio knew right away that these guys were guards, probably sent to divert their attention. He suspected it was their job to slow things down while the others escaped some other way, or hid themselves in some secret chamber within. He grabbed the radio mic. "I don't think these guys are the ones we're looking for. Be on the lookout. I suspect the others are exiting elsewhere or hiding out."

His radio crackled. "Good call, Antonio. My exact thoughts," Marcello replied.

Marcello gave his orders. He and Nicolo moved in, each accompanied by a member of their team. The helicopter was instructed to send two of its armed responders down to assist, then go high enough to have a full view of the grounds. The two men rappelled down, unhitched, and the helicopter rose like a giant black wasp.

*****

Antonio heard a new sound, higher pitched than the receding thump-thump-thump of the chopper. He recognized the sound of a motorcycle. *That's gotta be Belluci*, he thought. *The guy never gives up!*

His peripheral vision caught movement to his left. The motorcycle came from behind the castle, screaming down the driveway, headlight extinguished. He was headed right toward Antonio's Jeep. Someone fired a burst of shots which missed him and ricocheted off the castle wall. Antonio saw there was just enough room for the bike to pass between the trees and the stone column of the gates, and to get past his Cherokee on the driver side. *Merda. No time to move the vehicle.* With no conscious thought, his instincts took charge. Moments before Belluci arrived, he threw the driver's door open and dove away from it. He knew it was coming back hard.

It did. Belluci clipped the door, slamming it violently. It was just enough. Belluci lost control. He tried to correct but his opposite handlebar caught a tree branch, launching him off the bike. Paolo and Marzano were on him in moments. Marzano stood proudly with a Beretta assault rifle pointed at him from a few feet away. Antonio jumped out of the Jeep and saw that Belluci appeared to be knocked out, or worse. Paolo put his hand on his neck artery. He must have found a pulse because he rolled him over, cuffed him, and began to pat him down. He found what looked like a Beretta APX Compact, the same gun Nicolo carried.

Things continued to happen quickly. Antonio heard another sound … a car engine. He turned and saw a vehicle flash by the far end of the entry road and turn toward the tiny hamlet of Carpineta where Gabriella and Mancini were waiting. Again, with no conscious thought that he would later recall, his instincts took over. He lifted the motorcycle upright, another Ducati. It was still running. He jumped on and took off in pursuit. *What the hell am I doing?* The thought raced through his brain. *No weapon. No radio.* He was about 200 yards behind the car. *Damn! Looks like an Alfa Romeo Stelvio, over 500 horsepower.* He wondered how he knew this, but knew he loved Italian cars and motorbikes and read a lot about them.

His mind registered the sound of gunshots ahead. *Who's shooting at who?* Moments later he found out. Gabriella was lying across the hood of her Cherokee, firing her sidearm … four, five, six, seven shots he counted. He heard a windshield shatter. She swiveled as they passed and got off three more rounds. *She has five more rounds in the magazine*, he thought.

Gabriella whirled, ready to fire. *Oh God*, he thought, as he ducked. But somehow she must have recognized that it was not Belluci wearing a Carabinieri helmet and Kevlar vest. He slowed momentarily, lifted a hand at her, then accelerated again. In his peripheral vision, he saw her jump into the Cherokee. *No way she can catch them, they're too fast. But I probably can. But what can I do then? Why am I risking my life?*

But old habits die hard. Bad guys need to be caught, and these guys pulled the strings that put Giulia in a coma. He decided his smartest move was to trail them, keeping enough distance to be a difficult target. They came to a straight section of road and were now doing about 130 kph. He knew they'd be going a whole lot faster after they passed through the curve at Santa Colomba He knew this bike could do twice that, but couldn't imagine it. Not while wearing a Carabinieri helmet. Its shorter visor was not designed for this, and his eyeglasses offered little protection. Air rushed in, stinging his eyes, causing them to water and blur his vision. He assumed their driver would be dealing with the same problem since his windshield was shot out. The car slowed to take the curve in the road, then accelerated like a rocket. He knew if they reached SP101, not far ahead, they might be able to outrun him.

So, he was extremely grateful when he heard the chopper approaching from behind. It was hard to tell how near above the roar of the Ducati, but soon he caught sight of its stealthy black form moving ahead of the Alfa, appearing to be at about 300 to 400 feet elevation. It continued to distance itself. Then, suddenly, it executed a quick turn, hovered, and descended menacingly. Antonio guessed they were going to try to block their advance. *A risky move*, he thought. Then he saw quick flashes of light as the chopper laid down a volley of machine gun fire in front of the Alfa. *A warning shot.*

Antonio had begun to back off but found himself closing fast when the Alfa swerved and skidded to a stop. He hit his brakes. A man jumped out of the back seat on the driver's side and aimed a machine gun at the chopper. *Crap! He's going to try to bring that thing down!* His instincts took over again. He accelerated quickly, catching the attention of the gunman. He began to swivel his direction, but not soon enough. Antonio clipped him with his right handlebar, throwing his body against the car door. A burst of gunfire rattled wildly into the air.

The collision sent the Ducati out of control. He swerved right, then left in an overcorrection, as he tried to regain control. It was too late. He lay the bike down in a slide. By the time it stopped, he was beneath the hovering chopper. He could feel the stiff wind of the rotors washing over him.

His helmet had hit the pavement. He was stunned, but his mind was well aware of the searing pain in his leg as he struggled to remain conscious. He heard shots— more shots—a scream of agony—then another. He couldn't make sense of it. His vision was blurred, then misty grey. He sensed a lapse of time but didn't know how long. He had a vague awareness of someone lifting the bike and pulling him out from under. He heard voices he knew, Gabriella among them, and Paolo he thought ... nearby ... fuzzy. "Are you okay? Antonio? Can you hear me?" *Is that Nicolo's voice?* He nodded and tried to focus on his face. Then everything went black.

Chapter Forty-five
Early Saturday morning

For the second time in eleven days, Antonio awoke in the university hospital, Santa Maria alle Scotte, in Siena. Through blurry eyes he could see the coming light of dawn beginning to show pink in the east window. Once again, his body hurt all over. His first conscious thought was, *this is not what I had planned when I came to Italy.*

No one had yet noticed his eyes open. Nicolo, Marcello, and Gabriella were in the room, all three slouched in chairs, looking exhausted and worried. Nicolo looked like he might be asleep. Antonio moved his arm to try to get their attention. Gabriella caught it. He tried to smile and say, *"Buon giorno,"* but wasn't sure if it came out clearly, if at all. Now they were all looking at him.

He tried to speak again but his mouth was a desert. Gabriella lifted a plastic cup with a flexible pink straw to his lips. It was a cool oasis.

He managed to croak out a few words, "Tell me what happened."

"We will, we will," said Nicolo. "But hold on. First someone wants to see you." He left the room in haste.

Gabriella moved to the edge of his bed. She brushed his hair back from his forehead. "Are you ever going to stop hurting yourself?" she asked, wearing a smug grin.

"How bad am I?"

"Pretty bad. But nothing that won't heal. Second degree burns on the inside of your left leg. You totally tore the scabs off the outside. You damaged some ligaments and tendons on that ankle. I might have to lend you my crutches for a while."

He wiggled his toes and moved his fingers. Everything seemed to be working. But he had another huge headache to go along with the other pains.

"You also have a concussion. They don't think it's too serious. You didn't do your bruised ribs any favors either. No more detective work for you for a while. It's going to take a while for you to mend."

"I've had such a great role model at being a good patient," he rasped. He tried to wink but couldn't tell if his eye muscle responded.

"Yeah, well …" she looked him in the eyes. "Maybe we can both take some time to recover. These cases are a wrap for now, except for the mopping up. Not our job."

She smiled at him but there was something else, some hint of sadness lay behind her eyes. *Somethings not right. Am I hurt worse than she's telling me?*

"So, tell me …" He stopped cold. His peripheral vision caught movement, a beautiful sight, as into the room Giulia arrived, walking unsteadily with a brother on each arm. She was followed by a radiant Sofia and smiling Nicolo. His heart soared.

"*Buon giorno*, Zio Tonio," she said weakly. She looked like an angel, though she was pale, and clearly unsteady.

Gabriella made way. The brothers helped Giulia to the edge of the bed, where she sat gently. She slid closer to Antonio, leaned in, and embraced him. It was painful, but he didn't care. Her embrace brought healing to his soul, where he needed it the most. He felt warm tears run down his cheek. He wasn't embarrassed in the least. Then, through the window behind her, he saw the sun beginning to show itself over the hills in the east, and the room was illuminated by clear morning light.

*****

Giulia had woken at 10:27 the previous evening. During the chaos, Nicolo missed Sofia's call, which of course caused her great worry and alarm. When he finally returned her call near midnight, he was riding in the ambulance with Gabriella and Antonio. She didn't tell him about Giulia on the phone, but insisted he come to her room the moment he arrived. He later told Antonio his mind was a jumble of tension—physical and emotional exhaustion—and worry when he arrived. Then he saw Giulia sitting up with her eyes open, and his stress fell away like leaves in an autumn windstorm.

*****

Doctor Giordano strode into the room, smiling more than Antonio had ever seen him. He informed them that he wanted to keep Antonio for another day, and Giulia for two, for tests and observation. No one objected. They sat Giulia in a wheelchair and wheeled her back to her room to eat a recovery breakfast and rest.

Sofia took her place on the edge of the bed. She took Antonio's hand. "Your poor, poor body," she said. Her eyes glistened as she looked for the words she wanted to say. "Thank you, Antonio. Thank you for helping find the men who hurt Giulia and you, and tried to kill Nicolo. I knew Giulia would make it. I believed. God gave me faith. But when I saw you last night, my heart faltered. I feared that the price had been too high. But now he has given me both of you." She leaned over and kissed his forehead. Then she was gone.

*****

Nicolo reentered the room and came to his bedside. Antonio wondered why his smile had evaporated. His face deeply serious. "Mancini is dead."

"What! No. Oh God. No!"

"He died two hours ago on the operating table. They knew there was little chance they could save him. I didn't have the heart to tell you before you saw Giulia."

Antonio was stunned, possibly in shock. He tried to sit up. Nicolo put his hand on his shoulder and pushed him down. "Take it easy. You're in pretty bad shape."

"But …"

"I'll give you the details in a while, Antonio. Nurse Isabella is kicking us out for a while. But there's something I want you to know. He saved your life."

*****

Before he could get more of the story, little nurse Isabella marched into the room. She was almost pleasant and even smiled when she said, "You again! Mother Mary of Jesus! Every time I think I'm done with you, you come back like a bad stomachache. Can't get enough of this place, huh?"

"Missed you too," he said. He wanted to enjoy this banter, but his mind was reeling.

"Wish I could say the same."

About the time he was thinking he could learn to like this woman, she transformed back into a drill sergeant and kicked everyone out of the room so she could attend to his needs. She removed bandages, cleaned his wounds, applied burn and antibiotic creams, and gently redressed the wounds.

"Do you need any more pain meds?" she asked.

"More? You guys didn't ..."

"No, Mr. Antonio. Don't worry. We gave you ibuprofen intravenously. But it's probably wearing off. You must be in great pain. If you'd like something stronger ..."

He shook his head no, breathing a sigh of relief. "Can I talk you out of three Tylenol?"

She relented. He set them on the tray. "I think I should have something in my stomach first." He realized he hadn't eaten since yesterday's gelato in Monterotondo.

"What would you like? I'd go soft if I were you. Scrambled eggs?"

"Sure. Any chance of warm croissants to go with them?" he asked jokingly, thinking Michelangelo would rise from the grave before that happened.

"Always the demanding one, huh? Let me see what I can do."

What? Is she going soft on me?

It didn't take her long to return with eggs, cut up melons, and orange juice, *"Tu mangi!"* she commanded. His momentary hopes fell to the floor as she turned and marched out.

The eggs tasted surprisingly good, clearly fresh, not powdered. He devoured them, along with every morsel of fruit. He took his Tylenol with the juice, and laid his throbbing head back on the pillow, thinking that he was still hungry.

But nothing ... not the screaming pain in his leg, the roaring headache, nor the hunger ... could take away the emotions which resettled on him; the shock and sorrow of hearing the news of Mancini, a dramatic contrast with the overwhelming joy of Giulia's return. He whispered aloud, "Thank you, God. Thank you for bringing Giulia back. May Mancini's soul find rest in your bosom."

He only had a few minutes alone to dwell on his thoughts, then Gabriella waltzed in with a sly smile, carrying a bag of warm croissants. "Nurse Isabella sent me on a mission. She really didn't give me a choice. You must have really charmed her."

"Yeah. Must be my boyish good looks," he said, knowing he probably looked even worse than he felt.

"I'm sure that's it," she said with a laugh.

Chapter Forty-six

Saturday late morning

The croissants didn't help his pain, but they improved his outlook. He began to feel slightly human again. Nicolo and Marcello returned, followed shortly by Leonardo and Raphael. He was surprised that nurse Isabella was allowing so many in his room. She'd probably thrown her hands up in surrender.

Leonardo was back to his old, cheerful self. Even Raphael looked less serious than usual as he bantered with his brother.

"I'm sure you want to know the rest of the story," Nicolo said. "You up for it?"

"If someone will bring me coffee." *Geez, I'm getting demanding*, he thought, not really caring.

Leonardo nodded and left to find some.

"I'll wait 'til he's back," Nicolo said, "The boys know part of the story. They want to hear the details. If you get tired, let me know. There's no hurry.

"Meanwhile, I'll tell you Belluci's in custody, in the hospital here, under guard. Also, one of the bodyguards who was shot at the scene. The bodyguard is in ICU, in critical condition, may or may not make it."

"Is Belluci cooperating?" Antonio asked. "Or continuing to be a pompous ass?"

"I've heard he's cooperating." Leonardo returned with the coffee. It was lousy, bitter and burnt. He drank it anyway. "*Grazie*, Leonardo."

Nicolo continued with the story. "We have six of the family in custody. Two of them were bosses, a bodyguard who was in the car in ICU, and the three bodyguards from the villa. Those three tried to escape in the chaos but we managed to corral them before Marzano blew their heads off."

Antonio smiled at the comment, but wasn't in a laughing mood. Not after hearing about Mancini.

"So, were those guys all part of the Laganà family like you thought?" Raphael asked.

"Yeah," Nicolo replied. "The two capos are brothers, the younger one was in charge here in Siena, lived in the fancy villa. His older brother runs things in Firenze, a more established operation. We're hoping to bring down their entire operation in Tuscany."

Antonio was perplexed. "Wait. Go back. I thought there were four guys in the Alfa."

"There were." Nicolo held up the palm of his hand. "You're getting ahead of me. The other bodyguard was killed at the scene. Not the one you ran into, the other one. He was riding shotgun in the front passenger seat.

Gabriella and Mancini arrived just as he was jumping out. He also had a machine gun. Mancini emptied the last of the clip into him just as he swung around and took aim toward you."

"Five shots," Antonio said.

Gabriella looked at him in surprise. "Yeah, how …?"

"You fired ten shots. Your clip holds fifteen." He looked at her and grinned. "Old habit. It was a guess that he used your gun. How did he get his hands on it?"

"You don't miss a thing," Gabriella said. "When we were in pursuit, I thought he should be armed, for both our safety. I radioed Marcello. He gave the okay. A risky decision, but he felt Mancini had proven himself." Antonio looked at Marcello. He just shrugged his shoulders. But there was sadness in his eyes. "I gave him my handgun," she continued. "There was an assault rifle in the Cherokee which I had access to. Turned out to be good fortune for you," her voice cracked, "but not Mancini."

Antonio was still processing this when Nicolo moved on.

"The bodyguard that you struck with the motorcycle recovered enough to find his handgun. He got three shots off on Mancini. One caught him in the neck. Gabriella took out the bodyguard. He took six bullets. Amazing he didn't die on the scene. He was in surgery most of the night."

Antonio looked at Gabriella. She looked somber, neither proud nor ashamed of what she had done.

"Sounds like I'm lucky to be alive," Antonio said in gratitude.

"You are," Nicolo said. "At that point, the two capos, the Laganà brothers, exited the Alfa with their hands up. Gabriella had them from behind, the chopper in front, and our jeep, with Paolo, me, and two Carabinieri, pulling up. The younger Laganà brother, Dante, had been driving the Alfa. He got part of an ear lobe shot off by one of Gabriella's earlier shots. He'll live."

Gabriella added her two cents, "Officer Gharbi and Jordy immediately tended to Mancini. They loaded him on the chopper and brought him here. He was in surgery for hours. Paolo helped Nicolo lift the bike off you. He held it while Nicolo pulled you out from under it."

Marcello spoke for the first time, his tone one of authority, "Nicolo and I have come to a mutual decision about something. We want to keep what Mancini did—the murders and betrayal—under wraps. There's no need to disgrace his name and put his family through shame. He paid the ultimate price to redeem himself. He died a hero. May God have mercy on his soul." He paused. "I called Magistrate Mariani. She agrees. Can everyone here agree on this? I would like a solemn oath."

He looked each person in the eye, one by one. Each one nodded. "Good. This never leaves this room. We're going to leave the first two murders on the books unsolved. We'll need to convince Belluci to keep his mouth shut but we have plenty of leverage."

"What will happen to Paolo?" Leonardo asked.

"Remains to be seen," Nicolo said. "We'll consult the magistrate on that one, and my commander. I'll push for leniency. I doubt he'll get jail time." He paused, looking sad again. "Not likely he'll remain on the force. At least, not as a detective."

Marcello began filling in some other details. "You were obviously right, Antonio, about them having an escape plan. There was a tunnel under the grounds. It came out in the woods, near what looked like an old woodshed covered in vegetation. You'd have had to be looking for it. They apparently kept the car there for just such an occasion."

"Expensive escape vehicle."

"Yeah. Obviously, these guys love their Alfa Romeos."

"Can't say as I blame them," Antonio mused. "Damn fine cars. You can give me that Stelvio, if you want." Marcello chuckled. "Sorry, I've got first dibs."

Nicolo spoke up, "They didn't count on some *pazzo Americano* on a Ducati chasing them. What the hell were you thinking?"

"I wasn't, not rationally anyway. I just knew I didn't want the guys who put Giulia in a coma, and tried to kill my favorite uncle …"

"Your only uncle," Nicolo interrupted.

"Yeah, well," Antonio smiled, "I didn't want them to get away with it. Old habits die hard." He didn't tell them the rest of the story, what he held inside … *How many times have I felt helpless in the face of evil? I'd rather die than feel that way again.*

"Where'd you learn to ride like that?" Marcello asked.

"Spent my first two years on the force as a motorcycle cop. Of course, we didn't ride Ducatis. My older brother loves to ride too. We've taken a few road trips together."

"Not too sure I'll let you be involved with any cases in the future," Marcello said. "You're a menace to yourself." He tried to come across like a stern father, but Antonio knew what he really felt.

"I hope this will help you take down their mob operations here in Tuscany," Antonio said. "That would make all this pain worth something."

"I imagine it would," Marcello nodded, and continued, "Marco is helping us piece it all together. He was here last night with the GDF investigators to grill Belluci and they had magistrate Mariani in. The GDF are really unhappy that one of their generals was working for the mob. Worried there might be others. Indications are he's cooperating. He's probably hoping for some plea bargaining, and most likely witness protection. We're expecting there to be some good intel. They'll also be working on the other bodyguard … if he survives.

"By the way," Marcello added, "I nearly forgot to tell you. You know those cigarette butts? The one you found near Nicolo's house. Guess who it belonged to?"

"Belluci?"

"You got it. And we found out why the other one had no DNA. Paolo passed it off to Mancini. It was his. Belluci had loaned him one. So, he swapped it."

"I suspected something like that. That reminds me. Who took the shot at Nicolo on the road the other day?"

"Apparently Mancini," Marcello said. "Belluci was pressuring him to finish the job."

"But he intentionally missed, as we suspected, at least according to Paolo," interrupted Nicolo. "He's a…", he hesitated, "was a much better shot than that."

"It would seem so," Gabriella added, looking at Antonio. "I saw him in action."

"Curious about Jordy," Antonio asked. "Did he have a hand in any of this?"

"Doesn't look like it," Nicolo said. "Told me he'd had suspicions, nothing to back it up. Couldn't believe his partner would do the things he did. Blames himself for being too naïve."

"Hard lesson to learn," Antonio added. "When we care about a person, we always want to believe the best about them."

"I hope he learns fast," Nicolo added sullenly. "I'm going to need his help to train new detectives."

Antonio nodded. He looked at Nicolo. His gaze was a million miles away. Antonio saw a battle raging within. *We need to talk ... alone,* he thought, *after we get some rest.*

"I have one other question before I kick you guys out. What about that wine shop? It was unsecured when we left."

"Hoping to stock your cellar?" Raphael, the serious one, asked jokingly.

"Sure. Why not?"

"The good news, I suppose," Marcello mused, "is we secured it before anyone got after it. Gabriella had the presence of mind to call it in. They're moving the wine to a secure location. It will be auctioned off."

"You know, with a little inside information we could hijack the truck," Leonardo said.

Nicolo rapped him on the head. "Shhhh. Don't tell our plans to the Carabinieri." In the blink of an eye he was serious again. "We better let you rest now, Antonio. I'm going to take Sofia home so we can get some sleep. We'll be back this afternoon."

"Don't hurry back for my sake, Nicolo. You look exhausted."

"Anything you need before we go, Zio Tonio?" asked Raphael.

"No. Just tell Commander Isabella to leave me alone for a few hours." He laughed. It hurt like hell.

Gabriella came to his side as the others filed out. She locked eyes with him, kissed him on the cheek, and said, "Get some rest. Marcello is going to drop me at home so I can do the same." She squeezed his hand and was gone.

He was glad to be alone. He was exhausted, yet so many thoughts to process. He lay, staring out the window. His mind was numb. The last thing he remembered was saying, "Okay, God. I'm done wrestling with you. I give up." Then he was asleep.

*****

When Antonio awoke, he felt a presence in the room.

"Thank God," Alessia said. "I thought you were dead. I was afraid I was going to have to eat a second gelato myself. Can't let this stuff go to waste." She handed him a cup of slightly melted frutta di bosco and flashed her big-sisterly smile.

He heard a laugh, then saw his mother standing by the door. "We're getting really tired of visiting you in the hospital," she said. "Can you be a good son for a while, and stay out of trouble?" Humorous sarcasm, one thing his family was good at.

"How are you feeling?" asked his sister. He found her nurturing tone comforting.

"Groggy. My headache is getting better. Not so sure about the rest of my body."

His mom came close and touched his arm. "We were so worried about you. Nicolo called us last night from the ambulance. We were up the rest of the night, praying and waiting for updates. Then Sofia called to tell us about Giulia. What a night!"

Alessia chimed back in. "Then this morning we heard about Mancini." She squeezed his hand. "So sad. We stopped at the duomo and each lit a candle for him."

They remained quiet for a minute, each lost in their own thoughts. Then Alessia spoke again, "We're starting to think about when we want to head home. Probably late in the week. We may go to Venice for a few days. Mom's never been. Shocking, huh? Do you have any idea when you'll be heading home? You could join us if you want."

"Hadn't really thought about it yet."

"I talked to Shane this morning. He says everything's fine at the restaurant. Said to stay as long as you want. He knows you wouldn't be much help anyway in your condition."

He nodded, and finally took a bite of his melting gelato.

"Doctor Giordano thinks he can release you in the morning," his mom added. "Sofia wants to know if you'll come to late mass with us."

"Tell her I would love to."

Chapter Forty-seven

Tuesday afternoon & evening

Marco arrived and joined Nicolo and Antonio on the terrazza in the warm afternoon sun. Antonio understood why Nicolo had such high regard for the man. He was sure he must have some flaws. He just hadn't discovered them yet.

On the table was an open bottle of Chiara and Sylvio's Vino Nobile di Montepulciano Riserva, 2011, just coming into its prime. Antonio took a sip. It was a richly beautiful expression of Sangiovese, flavors of dark cherries and plum, a luscious mouthfeel, perfect tannic structure, and a long finish. Chiara said they only made a Riserva in the best years. Vino Nobile was one of Antonio's favorite wines. Wine historians believe it was named by the cellar master of an early pope who declared it to be a wine fit for nobles.

He heard laughter coming from the kitchen. In addition to working on tonight's dinner, the women were beginning preparations for the big family dinner to be held on Thursday. They had proclaimed it "A Feast of Life", to celebrate Giulia's return. It would also be a going away dinner for Elena, Alessia, and Antonio. Antonio's cousins would be arriving tomorrow, with all of their children.

Tonight's dinner would have its own significance. Nicolo and Sofia had invited Paolo, Gemma, little Bettina, Paolo's sister **Amara,** and her daughter Caterina. *No wonder I love being part of this family,* Antonio thought, when he heard.

Marco had a lot to share with them. "Belluci turned out to be quite the source of information. I'm surprised the Laganàs let him in on as much as they did. He must have had a lot of leverage, a lot of trading of information, using whatever he knew to find out even more. A form of self-preservation. The magistrate has offered him immunity from prosecution and witness protection, a new life." He paused for a sip of wine, which brought a smile to his lips. "Necessary, I suppose, but a damn shame after he betrayed everything he stood for," he turned to Antonio, "and nearly killed you and Giulia."

"I suspect he'll be entering protection alone," Nicolo said. "His wife has already distanced herself. I doubt she wants to give up her life in Roma."

"You have to wonder if he was always like that," Antonio pondered. "Or if something happened, some event, some wrong choice which made him cross over to the dark side."

"Sometimes, when a person crosses that line, they can't find their way back," Marco said. "So, they plunge headlong into the darkness. The trick will be to keep him alive until the trial. The 'Ndrangheta family is extremely powerful. They won't take this lying down. But as far as their operations here in Tuscany, most of it is being dismantled as we speak."

This made Antonio smile. First, the Pucci clan of the Camorra family, losing their foothold. And now the Laganà clan of the 'Ndrangheta. He wanted to think that Tuscany might regain some of the innocence of his youth, at least for a time. But he knew evil men, driven by power and greed, would always be looking for an opportunity to return.

Marco continued, "The biggest intel he gave us was another drug shipment, arriving in Livorno harbor last night. The GDF and Carabinieri boarded the ship and seized heroin, cocaine, and ecstasy. It was crated up as Colombian coffee. Looks like a value of about three hundred and fifty million euros. I don't know how these guys keep taking such big hits."

"If they can absorb losses like that, it tells you just how much they're profiting," Nicolo said.

"I wonder how much got by undetected over the years because of Belluci?" Antonio pondered. Nicolo and Marco nodded.

Marco changed the subject, "Don't know if you've heard yet but they're considering a promotion for Marcello. If he takes it, they'll be moving him to Firenze. The families will try to reestablish their base there first. He's impressed a lot of people."

"Well deserved," Nicolo said. "Speaking of Firenze, I had an unexpected conversation with Raphael this morning." Antonio leaned in and raised his eyebrows. "He plans to apply for the Polizia Municipale there. Says he's been considering it for a few years. News to me. He knows it would make no sense to work in Siena, where I am."

"How does Sofia feel about that?" Antonio asked.

"Haven't told her. He wants to tell her himself. He wants to wait a couple of days, let her enjoy these happy times with Giulia home." He smiled. "He talked to me because he wanted my blessing."

"What did you tell him?"

"That he's a grown man. He gets to make his own decisions." He paused, "And that I thought he'd make a damn fine policeman, if that is what he wants to do." He paused a moment. "I believe that."

"I do too." Antonio looked at Nicolo. "He has his father's character, stubbornness, sense of justice, and his mother's brains."

"You just better hope you're not around when he tells Sofia!" Nicolo chuckled nervously. He turned and looked at Marco. "You're staying for dinner, by the way. No argument. We've got more than enough food, and plenty more good wine where this came from. I want you to try the Sangiovese blend we made in 2015. I think it is our best."

"I was hoping you'd ask."

Antonio sat back and took a sip of Vino Nobile. He closed his eyes and let the sun warm his face and penetrate his soul. It occurred to him that despite his injuries, he was happier than he had been for a long time. He asked himself if he should really leave. He knew the answer.

*****

It was late when Antonio found Nicolo alone by the fire. The guests had gone home, and the girls had wandered off to bed. Nicolo had just added a fresh log to the fire. The warm afternoon sun had given way to a chill much too quickly. Soon, Tuscany would fall prey to autumn. He thought how wonderful the ribollita soup and bread had been with dinner. He'd have been content with that, but the girls followed it up with Cappellacci di Zucca, a pumpkin-filled pasta, similar to large tortellini, drizzled with sage-butter, and simple pan-fried chicken with lemon-rosemary oil, served over tender broccoli raab, known as rapini to the Italians.

Antonio had been quiet at the table. It was enough to sit and take in the scene. He watched Paolo's uneasiness ebb away in the warm hospitality shown by Nicolo and Sofia. He found himself moved to the edge of tears, as he watched Giulia and Amara's daughter, Caterina, talk and laugh. Both had come so near to death ... to not being here tonight. But here they were, happy and safe. His mother Elena, seeing his emotion, gave him an understanding look, and they smiled at one another. He wondered how many more times she would sit at this table.

The one person he missed was Gabriella. She'd been dealing with a lot of pain since overdoing things on that eventful night. But she had also withdrawn into some inner sanctum since the two of them had talked about the future.

Antonio leaned against the tall stone hearth. He was tired of sitting. Nicolo sat staring into the fire.

"Want company?"

"Why not."

"What an evening, Nicolo. Paolo seems to be handling things well."

Nicolo nodded. "Feels like a heavy burden has been lifted."

"What's going to happen to him?"

"Still undetermined. He has a hearing with the magistrate next week. Then our commander a few days after that."

They made small talk for a time… the weather, Elena and Alessia's trip to Venice, and how the wine fermentation was coming. Antonio finally decided to take a shot at the elephant in the room.

"Something's weighing heavy on your mind, Nicolo. Feel like talking about it?"

"No … maybe." He stared at Antonio, weighing things in the scales of his mind. "You're probably the only one who would understand."

Antonio nodded. It's a sacred trust when a man thinks enough of you to speak from his heart.

"I'm thinking of retiring." He stared transfixed into the fire. "Don't know if I'm cut out for the job anymore." He stood up and picked up the fireplace poker. "I saw things inside me this past week ... hatred, rage, desire for revenge ... it scared me." He used the poker to move the fresh log. "I kept telling myself, 'Stay cool, be objective,' but I couldn't. When I found Paolo in the crypt, before you arrived, I was so angry. I had already tried and convicted him in my mind. There was a voice telling me to pull the trigger. Then I remembered seeing his sister. I remembered how much she's lost already, and of Gemma and Bettina."

"Nicolo. Don't be so hard on ..."

"Stop, Antonio!" He jabbed at the log assertively. "We're supposed to be the good guys. Revenge is not something we can afford ourselves!"

Antonio nodded, wondering how badly Nicolo was broken.

"I was blind to what was right in front of me. Two guys I thought I knew ... thought I trusted. I wasn't willing to see their betrayal until I had no choice."

There was so much Antonio wanted to say, but he bit his tongue.

"I blame myself for Mancini too. He was a good detective. I never showed him enough respect ... never made him feel part of the team."

"Nicolo, you can't..."

Nicolo ignored him. "It would be a really bad time for me to step down. The department is in shambles, thanks to me. I should get it back on its feet. And if I give it a few more years, I'll maximize my retirement, make things easier for us in our later years."

"I know someone who'd like to work for you."

Nicolo pried his eyes away from the fire and stared blankly at Antonio.

"Gabriella told me Marcello's going to accept that promotion to Firenze. She thinks it may be time to leave the Carabinieri before they relocate her. She considers Tuscany her home now. She thought you might consider her for a detective position."

Nicolo was caught off-guard, "Couldn't think of anyone I'd rather have."

"I agree."

Nicolo found that impish smile that seemed to show up every time her name was mentioned. "What about you and her, Antonio? It's obvious you care deeply for one another. She's a remarkable woman. You're falling in love with her, aren't you? What do you plan to do about that?"

"Damned if I know." It was Antonio's turn to stare into the fire, let the flames carry him somewhere far away. "Go home to Seattle. Back to my life, my restaurant, my son, my grandkids that are coming soon." Nicolo kept silent. "Our lives are worlds apart." He turned back to his uncle. "I'm not sure I can do it yet, Nicolo. Love a woman the way she deserves. I'm stuck. I've never stopped loving Randi. Don't think I ever will. Is that fair to another woman?"

He searched Nicolo's face but found no help. He turned back to their earlier conversation.

"Have you talked to Sofia anymore about it? Does she still want you to quit?"

"We talked last night. I was nearly as honest with her as I am with you."

"And?"

"She threw me a curve ball. She doesn't think I should quit right now. She thinks I'd go out feeling like a failure." He turned from the fire and plopped down in his favorite leather chair. Antonio took a seat on the couch. "She might be right. She knows that what I do is because of who I am."

"A wise woman, Nicolo. Sounds like you have convinced yourself to stay on." *God, I hope he listens to her.*

"I don't know yet. I'm going to take a couple of weeks off, be with the family, think about my future. Marcello told me the Carabinieri can assist the department as needed, fill our shoes so-to-speak."

The two men sat quietly for a while, lost in their thoughts. Nicolo stood and poked the fire again, then returned the screen in front of it. He turned to Antonio. "You know I don't meddle, Antonio. I rarely give advice. And I don't have the strong faith that Sofia has. But I feel like God has something more for you than living in the past. It may be time to find out what that is."

Chapter Forty-eight

Wednesday

Antonio awoke slowly the next morning. He peeled himself out of bed and opened the French doors to the tiny veranda attached to Leonardo's bedroom, bringing the outside world in. He thought it was brilliant of Nicolo and the boys to add these onto the rooms when they built the apartment.

He leaned on the rail and took in the sights, sounds, and smells of the countryside. The late morning fog still sat in the low areas, waiting for the sun to burn it away. He could smell wood smoke, and the aroma of freshly cut hay. He heard a distant tractor, birds bickering, a dog barking, ladies' laughter coming from the house. The air still had a chill, but the morning sun felt warm. It began to warm his bones. He was surprised that he felt rested despite having lain awake for hours when he went to bed, wrestling with himself, and the unseen force that he thought might be God.

He knew Nicolo was right.

It took him another half hour to get his body moving. He was in no hurry. He had no cases to solve, nowhere he had to be. It was time to take life slow for a while until his body began to mend. When he finally moved, stiff as a board, as they say, he showered and shaved and redressed his wounds. He put on the most comfortable clothes he could find and headed down to find some coffee.

*****

Bella joined him eagerly as he headed out for a walk, awkwardly on crutches. He knew tomorrow would be a full day and wasn't sure he would have time to get out. This might be his last opportunity. He took it slow. Crutches aren't really designed for uneven terrain. But once again, movement helped with the pain as his stiff joints began to loosen up.

He nearly lost his balance climbing the hill beyond the vineyard. Arriving, he sat on a rock and looked back toward the house, glistening in the morning sun with its red tile roof. Bella meandered, following her nose wherever it led, but never wandering far. Finally, she came and sat down beside him, as if she too wanted to take in the beauty. She mirrored his melancholy. He scratched her behind her ear.

He thought about this trip, so different than he'd imagined it. *I'll never forget this trip*, he thought. He knew he was not the same man who arrived here two weeks ago.

He asked himself again if he should move here. He'd thought about it a lot recently. But it didn't feel right. Not yet anyway. But he made the decision to return next year, and probably every year, for as many as he had. This place was as much home to him as Seattle was. In some ways, more so.

He also made another decision.

*****

When he arrived back, the ladies were laying out lunch, a serve-yourself buffet of cheeses, prosciutto, thick pan focaccia, grapes, and slices of fresh pears. Perfect timing! He had gone off without breakfast and was famished. The French doors stood wide open to the terrazza. He made a plate and carried it outside, no easy task with the crutches, but he insisted on doing it himself. As he sat down, he looked up and noticed there were two easels set up. Giulia came and sat beside him. He could see her color and strength returning more each day.

She locked arms with him, looked at him and returned his smile. "I was hoping you would do me the honor of painting with me, Zio Tonio?"

He looked at her and his melancholy evaporated with the morning fog. "Can't think of anything I'd rather do." He felt a little more healing take place. "As long as you don't expect mine to be nearly as good as yours."

"Oh, it won't be," she laughed. "But if I remember, you have a real eye for capturing light."

"You know I love light, its nuances, the way it constantly changes, and the way the world changes with it. But I haven't painted for a long time, not since…"

"That's what I figured," she said. "Call it therapy. It will be for me. Besides, I need to stay in practice. I'm going to take the rest of the semester off. I'll go back after the holidays. I thought we could paint the view from here. It will give us something to remember it by when we're away."

Chapter Forty-nine

Saturday

Antonio leaned on the railing that bordered the promenade and looked out over the Baie des Anges, the Bay of Angels. An appropriate name he thought. The evening sun was getting low and the billowing clouds to the west were beginning to turn multiple shades of pink, coral, purple, and grey. Everything the sun still touched was golden. Soon, that light would turn from gold to shades of blue. He recalled his conversation with Giulia about light. He could paint this scene every few minutes, and it would be different every time. She'd been right. The afternoon they'd spent painting was therapy, restorative for his soul, and possibly his faith.

There was a patch of clear sky above him. It had been one of those crazy-weather days … rain squalls, sun, wind, calm. Much like his life. Everything looked clean and the sea air filled his nostrils. He turned his head and saw the rain was still hanging out to the east.

He didn't know if he had accomplished what he came to Nice for. He stood not a hundred feet from where Randi and Christina had been run down on the promenade, along with so many others. He tried to block out the memory of the screams as he thought about how many lives had suddenly changed on that sad July night. Eighty-six people died. He wondered if others had moved on any better than he had. But that was the reason he had come, one more step in his attempt to move on. It was a symbolic act for him, to throw roses into the ocean and say goodbye. Something he'd been unable to do until now. He stared at them as they floated away upon the water.

*****

He thought back over his last couple of days in Tuscany. They had been everything he hoped they would be. Being on crutches had gotten him out of much of the cooking. He had savored his time sitting in the middle of the kitchen on a stool, being harassed by his aunts and cousins for being in the way. He did manage to get his fingers in the bread dough.

Nicolo had prepared three legs of lamb, stuffed with rosemary, garlic, spinach, lemon zest, and pine nuts. There was so much food they could have fed a Roman legion for battle, but then there had been twenty-five mouths to feed. They were given the gift of a rare warm October night, so they moved the large wooden dining room table outside and put it end-to-end with the outdoor tables. They ate under the stars and strings of lights. It was a feast he would never forget.

His thoughts settled on Gabriella. He had tried to fight it, but he knew he was falling in love with her. He thought about how radiant she had been, right in the middle of the kitchen preparations, despite the pain he knew she was dealing with. They sat together at the table for hours, drinking too much wine. The animated conversation around them grew louder and livelier, then eventually ebbed away as the evening finally turned cool. He thought about how much everyone loved her. He knew his family was hoping something would come of their relationship. Maybe it would.

He had given up Leonardo's bed when Cousin Angelica and Umberto arrived. Knowing he'd had too much wine to drive Gabriella home, they crashed on the couch in front of a fire. There, before the last glowing embers, he told her about his plans to come to Nice. She asked if he wanted her to come with him. But he explained why he needed to do it alone. She said she understood, then lapsed into a long silence.

He had considered inviting her to meet in Paris afterwards. But he knew if he did, he'd never make it home. He had things in his life he still needed to figure out. Whatever happened between them, it would need to happen slowly. He hoped he wouldn't lose her in the process. He told her as much. The next morning, she told him she was going to take the train home to Molise the following day, and apologized that she would not be there to see him off. As he watched her board the train he was hit with another sense of loss.

*****

Antonio felt a chill in the air as the sun dipped behind the clouds. A group of raucous seagulls caught his attention. He saw them having dogfights above the sailing yachts that bobbed in the harbor. It made him smile and think of Nicolo's announcements at the dinner table.

All eyes had turned to Nicolo when he stood and tapped his wine glass. He began with a toast to the family. There was a tremor in his voice as he gave thanks to all those who had been so much help to him and Sofia during their most difficult days. The tears escaped then. They ran down his cheek as he thanked God for bringing Giulia back to them, alive, and whole. As he spoke, Antonio took in the faces around the table, illuminated by candlelight, and the strings of light overhead. He couldn't recall ever having seen more joy and thankfulness.

Nicolo wasn't finished, however. He explained how he'd considered retirement, but with Sofia's support, he'd decided to stay on the force a few more years. He'd be working hard to rebuild the department and have it running like a well-oiled machine by next summer, because he and Sofia had a plan they hoped to fulfill. He had a sabbatical and vacation coming, twelve weeks in all. For years they'd dreamed and saved to rent a sailing yacht. They planned to sail from the Italian Riviera to Corsica, Sardinia, Cinque Terre, south to the Isle of Capri, and then to Positano on the Amalfi Coast to visit Frankie and Pasquale.

Nicolo had even more news, "My friend, Marcello Bianchi, has accepted a promotion to brigade general. He will be moving to Firenze. Knowing this, Gabriella considered leaving the Carabinieri, to join my detective team. But I am happy to announce to you that Divisional General Peluso has offered her a promotion to colonel, and to take over for Marcello as the lead detective in Siena. She has accepted with the understanding that she will have the option to retire if they ever want to relocate her."

The news had surprised Antonio. He looked at her, wondering why she hadn't told him. She just squeezed his hand, smiled, and gave him a kiss.

When Nicolo finally took his seat, Raphael rose to take his place. He looked at his mother and smiled, then told everyone he had happy news. "I've been accepted into the training academy for the Polizia Municipale in Firenze. I start my training in two weeks."

Bravo! was the response. Antonio watched Sofia. She had not been caught off-guard.

But Giulia, fortified by wine, rose from her chair with something to say about it. "Congratulations, Raphe. I am very happy for you. But we need to make one thing perfectly clear. I will *only* allow this under one condition. You must promise me ... cross your heart, that you will not be the overprotective big brother when I return to school!" Everyone laughed and chanted "here, here." Raphael, left with little choice, smiled and crossed his heart.

The following morning, Nicolo talked to Antonio over coffee. "Listen, Antonio. Sofia and I hope you will return late next summer. We want you to sail with us. Giulia and Leonardo, and possibly even Raphe will join us over the first week or two. Some of the sisters might join us after that. But there will be plenty of room. The boat we're looking at sleeps ten and has a full galley. We'll need a chef, you know," he winked. "I thought you might like to go to Corsica where your grandfather came from. Maybe dig up some old family history and relatives." His face turned mischievous. "If you'd like, you can invite a friend … or a lover to join us."

Antonio's mouth fell open. It sounded like an amazing adventure. He was deeply honored. He would have a lot of work to do to get Shane set up for his absence, but would make every effort to make it happen. They hoped to sail in late August.

*****

A breeze kicked up, blowing sea air in his face and dragging his mind back to the present. In the west, the setting sun dipped beneath the clouds and shone brilliantly upon the water. He marveled at the beauty of it. Then he cast his gaze to the east where rain was still falling. The breath escaped his lungs as the brilliant light of the setting sun upon the rain created a full arc of color. He watched in awe, mesmerized. Then little by little, a second arc appeared above it, growing brighter. A double rainbow—the most brilliant he'd ever seen—illuminated the sky.

Every person on the promenade stopped to point and look. But he felt like it was just for him, a gift … one arc for Randi … one for Christina. All he could think to do was whisper a 'thank you' to God.

*****

A few minutes later, the sun gave its last flash of light, and the lights of the city slowly showed themselves. The sky over the Baie des Anges slowly darkened as the last vestiges of the sunset disappeared. The ring of city lights surrounding the bay seemed brighter now, forming their own arc of light. The breeze kicked up again, causing him to shiver. *Time to move on,* he told himself reluctantly. He had one last place to go, the little French café with the view of the bay where he, Randi and Christina had eaten their final meal together. He smiled and turned that way.

About the Story

All of the characters within the story are fictional. However, there are elements within the story which are based on fact, and others based on my own life experiences.

In a few respects, Antonio's character is based upon my own life. My family and I owned and operated an Italian restaurant, Frankie's Pizza and Pasta, in Redmond, Washington, for twenty-four years. I used that experience as a restaurateur and chef to bring rich detail to the cooking and meal scenes. During my years as a restaurateur I also gained a great deal of knowledge about wine, especially Italian wines, which allowed me to approach that subject with authenticity.

I am also a cyclist. I believe that allowed me to present those scenes with realism.

My wife and I have also made multiple trips to Italy and Tuscany. Thus, we have first-hand knowledge of most of the places described in the book.

Sadly, like Antonio, we have also had first-hand experience with extremely painful losses. Ours was the loss of our two youngest children through circumstances too personal to share here.

While writing this book, I carefully researched the law enforcement agencies of Italy and have tried to portray them as accurately as possible. This also includes Europol.

The towns and cities described in the book are real places. My wife and I have spent time in nearly all of them on our journeys to Italy. More specific place references such as cathedrals, the Duomo in Siena, the contrada districts of Siena, the streets, city gates, and cimitero are also real. However, the restaurants, wine shops, homes, villas, and other businesses referenced are fictional.

One business accurately portrayed is the Mazzei Family winery in Fonterutoli. It is a real winery and the centuries-old family history within the book is accurate to the best of my understanding. We stayed in Fonterutoli on our last visit. It is a delightful little hamlet, and the Mazzei Family make exceptional wines.

The historic bottini under the city of Siena is real. I have never been inside it, so had to rely on information I was able to find through careful research. I have portrayed this as accurately as I could, based upon that research. There is an organization which offers tours.

The names of the Pucci and Laganà mob family clans operating in Tuscany are fictional. However, the major mob families, to which they are linked within the story, are true Mafia families. The 'Ndrangheta family of Calabria and the Camorra family of Campania have emerged as two of the most powerful families in Italy, eclipsing Sicily's Cosa Nostra according to my research.

Their power extends far beyond Italy's borders. The Nigerian Mafia, referenced in the story, has also gained a significant foothold in Italy, with territory reportedly ranging from Turin in the north to Palermo in Sicily. Their main focus is smuggling drugs, weapons, and trafficking women, preying primarily on migrant women. This has brought about a great political polarization and debate regarding emigration. All of this makes me very sad. I had naively thought that the Mafia was slowly becoming a thing of the past. It appears, based on my research, that I was quite wrong.

In the story, I have written about two significant drug busts. Both are based on true events—Operation Pollina in '98, or the Genoa bust in '99. The first involved the 'Ndrangheta family. Scores were arrested in Italy and throughout Europe and four tons of cocaine were seized, along with large amounts of ecstasy. The second bust, associated with a Colombian drug cartel known as the Gulf Clan, took place in Genoa in 2019. In that raid, Italian police seized over two tons of cocaine bound for Barcelona, Spain. The reported street value was around 500 million euros.

There are various terrorist events referenced in the story, the primary one being the attack which took place in Nice that took the lives of Antonio's wife and daughter. Though their characters are fictional, sadly, the terror attack was a real event. On the evening of July 14, 2016, a 19-tonne cargo truck was deliberately driven into crowds of people celebrating Bastille Day on the Promenade des Anglais in Nice, France, resulting in the deaths of 86 people and the injury of 458 others. The driver was Mohamed Lahouaiej-Bouhlel, a Tunisian living in France. The attack ended following an exchange of gunfire, during which Lahouaiej-Bouhlel was shot and killed by police. The Islamic State claimed responsibility for the attack, saying Lahouaiej-Bouhlel answered its "calls to target citizens of coalition nations that fight the Islamic State".

I also made reference to a series of prior terror attacks in Paris which caused great concern and worry for Antonio and his wife Randi, because their daughter was studying and residing in Paris at the time. These, too, were based upon real events. The Paris attacks were a series of coordinated terrorist attacks that took place on November 13, 2015, in Paris, and the city's northern suburb, Saint-Denis. Beginning at 21:16 CET, three suicide bombers struck outside the Stade de France in Saint-Denis, during a football match. This was followed by several mass shootings and a suicide bombing, at cafés and restaurants. Gunmen carried out another mass shooting and took hostages at an Eagles of Death Metal concert in the Bataclan theatre.

The attackers killed 130 people, including 90 at the Bataclan theatre. Another 413 people were injured. Seven perpetrators died at the scenes of their attacks. The other two were killed five days later during the Saint-Denis police raid. ISIL claimed responsibility for the attacks. Then-president, François Hollande, said ISIL organized the attacks with help from inside France.

I hope you enjoyed this book. Look for more of Antonio Cortese in future books.

Frank Curtiss

About the Author

Author Frank Curtiss is a retired Italian restaurant owner. *Deception in Siena*, book one of the *Antonio Cortese Mystery series*, was his debut novel. Novel two, *Death in Florence*, is expected to be released in late 2021.

Frank also authored and published a cookbook, *Frankie at Home in the Kitchen*, published by Wild River Press. Hard copies are sold out, but it is available as an eBook on Amazon.

Frank and his wife Rhonda owned a popular Italian restaurant, Frankie's Pizza & Pasta, in Redmond, Washington, for 24 years. When the property owners sold to a developer, they chose to retire from the restaurant business. It was at that time that Frank decided to pursue his dream of becoming a writer.

Frank has a passion for all things Italian: the food, wine, people, and place. During their restaurant years they were able to travel to Italy on several occasions. It was natural for him to use Italy as the primary setting for his novels.

Speaking of his writing, Frank says, "As an author, I've drawn upon my lifetime of experiences as a restaurateur, chef, wine connoisseur, cyclist, gardener, traveler, photographer, and artist. My wife and I have also experienced some very difficult losses in our lives. I believe this has enabled me to develop believable characters of great depth and complexity. I hope you enjoy my books."

Frank and Rhonda grew up in southern California. They moved to Washington State in 1979, and currently reside in Redmond, Washington. They have two adult sons, both married. They currently have the joy of raising a teenage granddaughter.

Lightning Source UK Ltd.
Milton Keynes UK
UKHW010403231222
414357UK00013B/342/J